No one was going to give him money, even to save his life—especially some woman in a suit behind a big desk in an air-conditioned office. It didn't matter that she didn't have a clue how desperate he really was. All she'd seen when she'd looked at him was a loser. To think that he'd bought a new pair of jeans with the last of his cash and borrowed a too-large button-up shirt from a former coworker for this meeting.

After climbing into his truck, he sat for a moment, too scared and sick at heart to start the engine. The worst part was the thought of going home and telling Jesse. The way his luck was going, she would walk out on him. Not that he could blame her, since his gambling had gotten him into this mess.

He thought about blowing off work, since his new job was only temporary anyway, and going straight to the bar. Then he reminded himself that he'd spent the last of his money on the jeans. He couldn't even afford a beer. His own fault, he reminded himself. He'd only made things worse when he'd gone to a loan shark for cash and then stupidly gambled the money, thinking he could make back what he owed and then some when he won. He'd been so sure his luck had changed for the better when he'd met Jesse.

Last time the two thugs had come to collect the interest on the loan, they'd left him bleeding in the dirt outside his rented house. They would be back any day.

With a curse, he started the pickup. A cloud of exhaust blew out the back as he headed home to face Jesse with the bad news. Asking for a loan had been a long shot, but still he couldn't help thinking about the disappointment he'd see in her eyes when he told her. They'd planned to go out tonight for an expensive dinner with the loan money to celebrate.

As he drove home, his humiliation began to fester like a sore that just wouldn't heal. Had he known even then how this was going to end? Or was he still telling himself he was just a nice guy who'd made some mistakes, had some bad luck and gotten involved with the wrong people?

Don't miss
Christmas Ransom *by B.J. Daniels,*
available December 2022 wherever
Harlequin books and ebooks are sold.

Harlequin.com

"Rena, I need your help."

"My help?" Marena laughed harshly. "Seriously? If you came all this way for that, you can save yourself the trouble and get out now."

"Please, let me explain," Colt said.

"Uh-uh. What could you possibly say that I'd want to hear?"

"For starters, I'm sorry."

"Sorry? Sorry doesn't begin to cover the hell you put me through. Do you even grasp what you did to me? What you did to *us*?"

"I know I deserve your anger."

"What you deserve is to be strung up by your—"

"I know I have no right, but, Rena, I'm asking you to hear me out. After that, if you want me to leave, I will. I promise." Before she could reply, he slid down the wall and collapsed in a heap.

Marena observed Coulter lying prostrate at her feet. "This isn't very funny. Now get up." After a few more seconds, Marena rolled her eyes. "I mean it, Colt. The joke's over."

When he didn't stir, Marena crouched in front of him. She touched his face, then yanked her hand away. His skin was burning up.

"Coulter?"

Dear Reader,

I had such a great time writing about Marena, Coulter, and their friends and family in *Six Days to Live*. It was important to me that my heroine and hero rediscover the intense love that drew them together in the first place, despite the sense of urgency, impending tragedy and trust issues. The theme throughout this novel is second chances—both with Marena and Coulter and with his relatives. Family is essential, and I wanted there to be forgiveness and healing for Coulter, his grandfather and his mother. I also loved the nonstop suspense in this story. To get that, I interviewed several medical and military professionals and did a ton of research on combat, self-defense, weapons and biotoxins (to name a few). While I used fictitious names for the poison and some of the chemicals Marena used for the antidote, I wanted the danger to be authentic for the readers and the scenarios realistic for the characters. I love to travel, so I also had a blast creating the backdrop for Marena's life in Beaufort, North Carolina, and the biosafety level three biocontainment lab they used in Sedona, Arizona. Thanks so much for reading! I hope my characters resonate with you and that you enjoy this story as much as I do.

Lisa Dodson

Lisa Dodson is a nationally bestselling author and an Amazon #1 bestselling author of over eighteen novels in the multicultural, contemporary, romantic suspense, sweet romance and clean read genres. Published by Harlequin and Kensington publishing houses and indie published, Lisa writes positive, realistic characters that she hopes readers can connect with while enjoying her novels. Lisa has functioned as a publicist and radio talk show host in the literary community. She also works with aspiring and published authors in marketing and content editing. In addition, Lisa works as a business development manager at a technology consulting firm, is the mother of two young adults and a Maltipoo, Brinkley, and lives in Raleigh, North Carolina.

Books by Lisa Dodson

Six Days to Live

Visit the Author Profile page at Harlequin.com for more titles.

For Sinatra and Colin. Without you both, Coulter wouldn't be nearly as interesting. For the courageous men and women who are fighting in our armed forces. This one's for you.

Acknowledgments

Thanks to fellow authors Denise Jeffries and Cheryl Bonner for their medical and chemical expertise. You were both invaluable! To Lisa Lanier, you are a fantastic critique buddy, and I love plotting with you! Finally, to my technical adviser, Damon Lanier, your insight has been valuable to this series. Thank you.

Chapter 1

"Dude, do you ever sleep?"

Colonel Coulter "Colt" McKendrick, USA, Retired, didn't bother to look up. He would know one of his best friend's voices anywhere. "On occasion," he replied, grateful for the interruption. "Between meditation and caffeine, I get the job done. I can show you the technique I use. It comes close to the benefits of sleep and shouldn't take long to learn."

"Thanks, but no thanks," Major Neil "Tex-Mex" Wagner, USA, Retired, countered as he plopped down on his bunk. "I like my sleep the old-fashioned way," he drawled. His Texan accent was purposefully thicker than usual.

"Suit yourself."

"Hey, is that the Op order for Thursday?"

The operational order Coulter was working on laid out every detail for his team's mission: What time they would move out, how many weapons they would take, vehicles needed, tactical and additional gear necessary to get the job done.

"Yep," Coulter said. "Sources confirmed that the meeting is Saturday."

That would give his team all the time they needed to arrive at their target destination and get set up. Coulter and his men were all retired Special Forces and worked as free-

lance security contractors and consultants. His team's mission was to go to Medellín, Colombia, and surveil Javier Palacios, a wealthy businessman who dabbled in legitimate and illegal business deals, depending on the profit level.

Coulter's sources had confirmed that Palacios would meet with a contact to arrange to purchase stolen US weapons and ammunition. Because of its sensitive nature, this would be a low-visibility mission. They were all fluent in several languages, and between the clothes and other mannerisms, they could blend in and adapt to their surroundings, becoming practically invisible. Coulter even wore contact lenses when necessary to change his vivid green eyes to brown to ensure that nothing about him stood out.

"Usual bells and whistles?" Neil asked with excitement.

"More or less."

His friend grinned. "That's what I like to hear."

"Easy, Tex-Mex," Coulter called over his shoulder. "This is simple surveillance."

"Yeah? That's how they all start. Then we find ourselves in the middle of a hailstorm with no umbrella, and it ain't ever simple."

Coulter's head went up. "Don't worry. We'll have the usual complement in case we need to bring the pain."

A wide grin plastered itself on his friend's face. "Nobody brings it like we do, Colt."

Coulter shook his head and returned to his task. "Don't you have something else you could be doing?"

"Yeah, I do, like getting some shut-eye, so keep it down," Neil replied with a yawn before he doused the light, plunging his side of the room into total darkness.

Five minutes later, Coulter could barely make out Neil's even breathing. He had to smile at that. They even slept stealthily.

There would be two six-man teams. Highly trained, each team had weapons, communications, medical, and an en-

gineering expert in addition to the team lead. Whatever the situation, when they arrived in Colombia, they would be ready.

The meeting took place in a rural country estate on the outskirts of Medellín. They were dropped off about five miles from the compound and went the rest of the way on foot. When they arrived, Coulter led his team to the left side while Neil's team took the right. With night-vision goggles in place, they advanced toward a large outbuilding at the back of the property where the meeting would take place. Not encountering any resistance, they slipped inside. Then, each group fanned out in a different direction.

The building was a two-story warehouse with tables set up along the walls and stacked with crates. There were also large metal containers placed on the floor. Coulter signaled one of his men. He nodded and went to investigate. He held up his rifle and then pointed toward one of the crates. Coulter understood. He gave a hand signal, and his man got to work taking pictures and documenting the weapons.

They were almost done when they heard movement at the other end of the building and voices coming toward them. Coulter's team put everything back, then concealed themselves by hiding behind the stacked crates. Coulter took a position on an upper level with a clear view of the main floor.

"Is everything set?" Javier Palacios asked in Spanish.

"Of course," another man replied, smoothly. "You can take possession of our shipment today if the price is agreeable."

Recognizing the voice, Coulter controlled his anger and focused on the conversation. His gaze traveled to the burly man across from Palacios. Coulter noted a telltale bulge underneath his suit jacket when he leaned in to speak to the man beside him.

"Falconi," Coulter whispered.

Derek Falconi worked for Joseph Brinkley at Ghost Town Security. Years ago, Coulter had been a consultant for them on several projects and had clashed with Falconi from day one. Coulter found him an arrogant and reckless bully. He turned his attention back to the men below.

"We shall see." Javier motioned for the man behind him to step forward. He carefully inspected the weapons. While he did, Javier turned his attention back to Falconi.

"You are certain we won't have any unforeseen interference?"

Derek laughed. "None whatsoever. My contact is well placed."

"Yes, but can he be trusted?"

"I assure you, his love for money extends past his patriotic duty. He's guaranteed there will be no entanglements—military or otherwise."

Derek retrieved a card. He handed it to Javier's assistant. "If Señor Palacios is satisfied, the money should be transferred to this account number."

Coulter's men were already on standby to fall back if necessary.

"In a moment," Javier replied, not catching Derek's frown. "And the Platinum Invitation?"

Coulter eyed one of his men. He shook his head and shrugged.

"Your offer was accepted," Derek replied. "You have a seat at the table. Bidding will take place in two weeks."

"I want to see it."

"I'm afraid that we don't have it here."

Javier Palacios was a tall, well-built man with stylish gray hair tousled back from his face and a goatee. He had a commanding presence that signaled he was used to getting what he wanted.

Coulter observed a subtle shift in him at hearing Derek's

news, but Falconi was either oblivious or too focused on his own needs to notice the businessman's growing annoyance.

Javier placed his arms behind his back and rocked on his heels. "That's displeasing. You tell us about a new weapon that is undetected, untraceable and kills the person in a matter of days, yet we can't see it in person?"

"We never agreed to provide samples before the big event," Derek countered. "Besides, it's not that simple. From what I understand, Silent Night has a fail-safe in place. So, you can understand how that prohibits us from doing a dry run, so to speak."

Javier was silent for a few moments before he nodded.

"But we have brought something to show," Derek said quickly. He turned to his men. One retrieved a laptop from a briefcase along with a small box. Around his neck were a chain and key. Unlocking the box, he retrieved a thumb drive and plugged it into the USB port on the computer. After logging in, the first man tilted the computer in Javier's direction.

Coulter used binoculars to view the screen.

"Silent Night is completely secure. It requires a ciphertext code to start the activation sequence. The symmetric algorithm key encrypts and decrypts the code," the scientist explained. "It can't be activated without the codes, and once activated, the security sequence can't be stopped. So, the vial selected would need to be used or destroyed."

"Then how will my lab test the sample?"

"Each attendee will receive the necessary documentation before bidding. The winner will receive the case of Silent Night, the cipher codes, the decryption key, and the formula."

Returning his attention to Derek, Javier nodded. "I'm satisfied." Turning to his employee, he said, "You can release the funds."

A clenched jaw was the only display of Coulter's emo-

tions. Then, after making eye contact with Neil, he signaled his team to pull out.

By the time Palacios's group moved down the hall, Coulter and his men had left the building and were headed back to their extraction point.

"I want that laptop and thumb drive," Coulter told two members of his team. "We can't let a bioweapon be sold to the highest bidder on the black market. We have to stop that sale—whatever it takes."

"Roger that," they agreed before taking off in the opposite direction.

Turning to his weapons specialist, he said, "Captain Perry, light 'em up."

"Yes, sir," Perry said before retrieving detonators from his bag and disappearing down the walkway.

Coulter gave the sign for the remaining team to move out. They retraced their steps and got clear of the building when a loud boom followed by shattering glass shook the area.

Men were yelling and running for cover as smoke billowed out of the warehouse entrances, followed by repeated mini explosions as the ammo detonated. The panic was visible on their faces as they sought safety. A man rushed from the back side of the building with his shirt on fire. He was screaming as he ran until one of his colleagues tackled him to the ground. Ripping off his shirt, the helper began beating the man on his back to extinguish the flames.

After ensuring they weren't followed, the team rushed to meet their convoy.

"What are you going to do, Colt?" Neil asked as they carefully picked their way back through the jungle.

Coulter ran an agitated hand over his beard while he walked. At times like this, the hair on his face was annoying.

"What do you think? Nail Ghost Town Security to the wall, but first, we have to stop the sale of that bioweapon. Though Joseph Brinkley wasn't here, we've got plenty on

Falconi, and it's doubtful that his boss wasn't aware of what was going on right under his nose. I knew Brinkley was pompous, overambitious, and would make a deal with the devil if there was a profit to be made, but this time he's gone too far. Now we've got enough proof to make him pay for his greed and bring men like him and Falconi to justice."

"What about that invitation they talked about?"

"The bidding on Silent Night? I saw it on the laptop," Coulter noted. "The minimum buy-in to even receive a Platinum Invitation was twenty million."

Neil stopped in his tracks. "What? That's insane. I mean, we've read about it, but I didn't know it was actually in production."

"Neither did I. The United States doesn't deal in bioweapons, but an international branch of Beecham Pharmaceuticals engineered it. So clearly, it was outside of any oversight committees."

His friend's eyebrows rocketed toward his hairline. "Beecham? As in—"

"Yes."

A few moments of uncomfortable silence ensued. Coulter felt his friend's intense gaze, but he ignored it. "Don't give me that look. I know Marena didn't have anything to do with creating this thing. She worked tirelessly to save lives, not end them."

"Of course not," his friend agreed. "I was thinking that she's a scientist and worked at Beecham. Maybe she can provide some insight to—"

"Forget it," Coulter interrupted. "I'm not bringing her into this mess. Besides, I'm the last person in the world she wants to see."

"Can you blame her?"

"No," Coulter sighed before turning his attention back to work.

"I didn't see the names of the other attendees, but this

has global ramifications, Neil. They're planning on selling it to the highest bidder—along with the formula. If that happens, no one is safe."

"Colonel McKendrick, we have the scientist," his man said over the radio. "He said he'd rather die than give up the laptop and thumb drive, sir."

"Acknowledged—see if he means it."

"Roger that, Colonel."

Coulter secured his radio and continued moving.

"This doesn't make sense, Colt. Ghost Town is jeopardizing national security and endangering lives for what? Money? Power?" His friend sneered.

"I don't know much about the CEO, Cole Everett, except on paper. It's almost like he's a ghost, but there's plenty of Brinkley everywhere. I severed connections with him because of his questionable business practices, but not once did I ever think him capable of betraying his own country or setting up black market deals to sell deadly toxins."

"Well, it's useless without the cipher codes and code key, which we'll have shortly," Neil responded.

"And we need to keep them out of enemy hands at all costs. No one can be allowed to acquire the activation sequence to use this thing, understood?"

"Affirmative. No matter the cost, we'll keep it safe."

When they made it back to their extraction point, the three men from their team were already there. One came over and handed the thumb drive and laptop to Coulter.

"Thanks," he replied before handing both to their technology expert. "Once you're in, I want all the files copied and uploaded to my server. Then corrupt those drives."

"Roger that, Colonel."

They had been walking single file for several minutes. The darkness would have been a hindrance had it not been for their night-vision goggles.

Without warning, one of their men hit the ground. He was writhing in pain.

Coulter's team sprang into action. Two men grabbed the injured soldier and dragged him behind a berm, while the others ran for cover behind a clump of underbrush or downed trees.

"I got one man at seventy-five meters to my two o'clock," another shouted.

"Cover fire," Coulter yelled before turning back to his tech guy. "Get to it, and don't stop till you're done." He turned to the rest of his team. "Give him a shield," he ordered.

Instantly, two men covered the one working on the computer while the others set up a defensive line.

They cut the chatter to short, concise orders while they returned fire. The only thing seen in the darkness they were enveloped in was the muzzle flash coming from their high-powered rifles.

"Come on, guys, I need you," Neil yelled, after taking heavy fire on his position.

Dropping down low, three men worked their way over to his position.

"Target," Neil barked.

"Eyes on, twelve hundred meters north," someone yelled. Neil adjusted his position and fired. "Flank left."

The gunfire was deafening as their enemies returned fire.

"Moving," two men confirmed Neil's order and left to get behind their assailants. They ran as fast as they could, dipping behind the tree line to remain concealed.

"Lay down suppressive fire!" Coulter ordered and then crouched down to reload his rifle. The sweat poured down his face from the exertion. His breathing was labored and he struggled with loading the ammunition. "It's jammed."

"Where is our transport?" Neil ground out, returning fire. He crawled over to Coulter's position to give him another rifle.

Seconds later, the comms guy replied. "ETA five minutes."

"Colonel, it's done," his tech expert yelled out.

"Destroy it," Coulter ordered before turning to the medic working on the wounded soldier. "West?"

"It's not fatal," West confirmed before he asked. "He'll make it to the vehicle when it gets here."

Their men arrived behind enemy lines and a firefight ensued. Coulter's team continued shooting until the frontal attack stopped. They remained in their position, guns trained, until the two men that left returned.

When the Jeeps finally arrived, Neil yelled, "Move out!"

The men moved two at a time while the others covered them. Before reaching the vehicles, a truck roared into the clearing from the opposite side. Guys jumped out and trained their rifles on the group.

A split second later, Neil and Coulter took out three men while another shot the driver.

The demolition expert jumped into the truck. Moments later, he returned with a laptop in his hand. "There are two more and several weapons inside."

Neil took one of the laptops from his man and handed it to the comms expert.

"See what you can do with this."

Suddenly, Coulter felt a searing pain shoot through the side of his neck. He reached up and grasped at his skin. He pulled a dart out of his neck and peered at it. "What the—" he rasped before he dropped to his knees.

"Colt," Neil yelled, rushing to his position. He was stopped by more trucks advancing on their position.

Coulter watched as more chaos ensued around him, but he was powerless to help. Though he was losing consciousness, he tried fighting against the effects. Minutes later, everything was eerily still. "Neil?" he called out. "Tanner?"

He tried to get up, but a man was standing over him. He

pushed the butt of his rifle into Coulter's chest, effectively keeping him on the ground.

"Wh-who? Who—" Coulter struggled to continue. His voice sounded distorted, and he barely registered being thrown into the back of a truck.

"Move out," the man called out.

Before he slipped into unconsciousness, the last thing he heard was "Silent Night, Colonel McKendrick."

Chapter 2

"You do know you're not performing surgery, don't you?"

Dr. Marena Dash placed the last of her sea glass jewelry into the clear display case with extreme precision. Each of them shimmered on the satin backdrops in the lit enclosure.

"Shhh," she whispered as she gingerly set the last pendant into place. "There, all done."

"It's jewelry, not the *Mona Lisa*," the grizzled old man teased. "There's more where that came from right outside my back door."

She turned around to face one of her dearest friends.

"Burt, don't act like creating these treasures isn't one of the most rewarding things you've ever done. Heaven knows you tell me often enough."

Burt stepped cautiously toward the display case, using the wooden cane carved from a piece of driftwood he'd discovered on the beach. As his eyes reverently scanned his work, Marena noticed his chest puffed out with pride.

"Couldn't if I wanted to, darlin'," he admitted. "It was special to my dearest bride, and that makes it important to me."

Marena smiled. As the story went, Burt Templeton had been calling his dearly departed wife his "bride" for the last forty years. But unfortunately, Crystal had died three years before from kidney disease.

Marena understood that kind of pain because it mirrored her own. Losing her mother in a horrible accident three years ago had upended her life.

Heartbroken, Burt had thrown his energies into doing what his wife loved best: collecting and creating sea glass jewelry while Marena focused on learning the business from him. Then, seeing her love for his jewelry, they struck an arrangement where Burt would be her supplier for the custom-made pieces. Their friendship had blossomed from there by the shared need to desperately cling to a symbolic piece of timber, keeping them afloat on the restless sea of life.

"You know, when I found out you were buying the Sea Lily, I just knew you'd be closing up shop within six months."

Marena's head popped up over the display case. "What?"

"A few of us did," he admitted. "When Trudy told us she'd decided it was time to retire and move closer to her daughter and grandkids in Florida, we were shocked. But then, when she told me she'd sold the gift shop to you, that shock turned into flat-out worry."

Marena stood up and leaned against the wood counter, staring at him in surprise.

"Why, Burt?"

"Because Trudy said you were some fancy scientist working for some big pharmaceutical company, but things went south for you, so you left. That doesn't exactly scream new owner of a home accessories and gift store on Front Street."

"True," she conceded with a smile. "But I needed to bury the past—and have a fresh start." Marena glanced around the store. "When I got here, I had no idea I'd become a store owner. I just knew that I needed to do something different. My old career—well, let's say that it didn't hold the same passion that it once did."

"I hear what you're saying, Marigold. But your eyes tell me something different. You may have left your job behind,

but I bet that desire to discover, create, and make a difference in people's lives is still there."

Marena was thoughtful for a moment before she leaned over and squeezed his arm. "I'm still helping people, being creative, and making a difference." She smiled before moving off to greet a customer.

With picturesque views of Taylor's Creek and sunsets over Carrot Island each evening, Marena felt Beaufort brought a calmness to her life that had been missing for years. So, when Trudy announced that she was selling, Marena purchased the property, changed the name, and never looked back.

Long hours, backbreaking work, and a crash course in local entrepreneurship followed, but Marena had prospered. Burt's sea glass line, her locally made driftwood knickknacks, and one-of-a-kind pottery kept tourists and locals frequenting the store. She'd even discovered a love for creating homemade soaps and scents. It wasn't the lab environment she was used to, nor the working with cutting-edge technology with teams of scientists at her disposal, but Marena was pleased with her new life. It had permitted her a chance to find some peace.

It was only at night when it was quiet that Marena thought about what she'd lost. In those moments, she missed her old life. Before death, grief, and heartache had taken up residence and refused to leave.

Unable to help it, she thought about Coulter. She missed him with an intensity that made her forget to breathe—and how much he'd broken her heart. He had been entwined into her life for so many years that Marena couldn't imagine what it was like before Coulter McKendrick had befriended her brother, Lucas. They had been best friends since college and joined the army together.

In many ways, he'd been a constant in her life and that

of her family. Not having Coulter there had been as unbearable as her mother's tragic death.

"Marena? Hey, when are you coming back to earth?"

"Right now," Marena said, snapping out of her daydream and surprised to find her customer and Burt staring at her with concern.

"Sorry about that."

"No problem, Marigold."

She smiled every time Burt called her that. Since it was Crystal's favorite flower, Marena took it as the highest form of compliment.

"You have any plans for tonight?" he inquired.

"Not really," she replied after ringing up her customer and bagging their purchase. "Why?"

"How 'bout you accompany this old codger over to the Front Street Grill for dinner?"

Her eyebrow shot up. "Wait a minute, aren't you supposed to be dining with Delores this evening?"

Burt's sheepish expression made her grin.

"It's not a date if my second-favorite gal comes with me."

"Uh-uh. Not on your life, old man," she teased. "You've put Delores off for a week now. You promised you'd take her out, and I'm here to make sure you keep your word." Marena walked around the store, turning out the lights as she went. "Besides, she's a lovely lady, and you have loads in common."

"What's the big deal? It's not like she's going anywhere," he grumbled, looking like a stubborn seven-year-old as opposed to a man of sixty. "I can take her out another time."

Marena grabbed her purse from under the counter. Slinging it over her shoulder, she helped him up. "Not happening. You're going home to change and make an effort," she added. "Once you two are seated at the table, I'll skip out. Deal?"

Burt made a show of protest, but his eyes twinkled, and he said, "Suit yourself. Do you want a ride?"

"No, thanks. I'll meet you there."

"I don't know why you're going through all this trouble." He stopped walking and wagged his finger at Marena. "And you're wrong. Delores and I don't have a thing in common."

She didn't bother refuting that statement. Delores Michaels had been friends with Crystal since they were children. A widow herself, neither she nor Burt had left his wife's side when she grew seriously ill. Over the years, the two discovered they did share similar interests like art, playing cards, and gardening. There was no way Marena would let Burt talk himself out of a second chance at happiness. He deserved it.

Ushering her friend out of the store, Marena locked the door behind them. "You're going to have a great time. Now get going. A man isn't supposed to keep a lady waiting."

Burt snorted loudly. "That depends on the lady."

True to her word, Marena met up with Burt at the restaurant. She was locking up her bicycle when she spotted him escorting Delores through the front door. She caught Burt's eye as she walked in a few moments later. He grinned at her and waved her over.

"How are you?" Marena greeted them both with a hug.

"Doing great, Marigold." Burt grinned.

"Why don't you join us for dinner?" Delores turned to Burt. "You don't mind, do you?"

"Oh no, I can't," Marena said quickly. "I've already ordered carryout. You two enjoy your evening."

"We will," Burt said quickly. He placed a hand at the small of Delores's back as they followed the hostess to their seats.

Marena chuckled at Burt's enthusiasm. She was glad

to see that he looked relaxed and happy to be on his dinner date. While she waited for her meal, she watched them laughing and conversing while glancing over their menus.

Satisfied that all would be well, Marena slipped out of the restaurant with her carryout bag in tow.

Another piece of good fortune for Marena was finding her beloved three-bedroom bungalow on Ann Street just minutes from the Sea Lily. She'd fallen in love with the white cottage with the black shutters and crimson door when the Realtor pulled up to the house. The well-manicured lawn, inviting porch and red rocking chairs were just a bonus.

"Are you married? You know this is a great house to raise a family in," the energetic woman gushed as they walked through the house.

"Well, I don't have either, so this house will just have to make do with me."

Her Realtor had apologized instantly, but there was no point in being upset by the truth. She didn't have a husband, kids, or even a prospective date.

She leaned her bike up against the house while she unlocked the door. Juggling her food, mail, and purse, Marena opened the front door and maneuvered her way into the living room.

"I'm home," she said aloud and then paused as if listening for an answer.

Nope, no drop-dead gorgeous man suddenly appearing out of thin air to welcome me. But when she thought about her best friend, Vivica, Marena knew precisely what she'd say. "Girl, three cats will never take the place of one man."

Then she'd launch into her warning about the perils of growing accustomed to being alone. Marena found all Vivica's warnings humorous, considering Marena didn't own a pet and wasn't remotely interested in dating.

"Thank you, but no. One man breaking my heart in a lifetime is plenty for me," she said aloud.

Dropping her purse on the table by the stairs, Marena headed into the kitchen. After setting the food and mail onto the granite counter, she returned to the porch to retrieve her bike and secure it in the backyard. She turned on some music and began humming one of her favorite tunes while washing her hands, after which, Marena transferred her meal from the take-home carton to a plate, with practiced precision.

She peeked out the kitchen window while pouring a glass of lemonade. It was the perfect night to dine alfresco.

After gathering a napkin, utensils, dinner, and drink on a serving tray, Marena went onto the patio. Once seated, she retrieved a book of matches from a bright blue clay jar and lit the three candles sitting on a decorative driftwood candleholder. The sun hung low in the sky, and the evening was shaping up to be another gorgeous one.

She thought about both Burt and Vivica pushing her to go on dates. The idea of sitting across from someone she didn't know playing twenty questions in the middle of a crowded restaurant wasn't even remotely appealing.

"This is perfect. Just beautiful scenery, peaceful quiet, and a lovely meal." With a contented sigh, Marena picked up her utensils and dug into her meal with gusto.

After dinner, Marena cleaned the kitchen and locked up downstairs. She eyed the clock when she strolled into her bedroom. It wasn't even ten o'clock.

"I'm not sleepy yet, so now what?" she muttered. "Stargazing? Catching up on recorded TV shows? Making soaps?"

None of those appealed to her, so she opted for a bubble bath. When she finished, Marena slipped into bed and read for a while. Five pages later, she tossed the *Southern Living* magazine aside. She was about to douse the light when she stared at the bottom of her bed.

"Maybe a cat wouldn't be so bad." Instantly, she pictured her friend's I-told-you-so smile and cringed. "Uh-uh. Bad idea," she chuckled before dousing the light and plunging the room into darkness.

Chapter 3

Two things occurred to Coulter as he clawed his way back from unconsciousness. The first was he wasn't dead. The second and more formidable was he wished he were.

His body felt like it was on fire, scorching him from the inside out with no relief in sight. Aching muscles screamed in protest, and his mouth was devoid of any moisture. Yeah, death would be preferable.

Coulter opened his eyes to pitch black. Blinking to clear his vision didn't help. Years of training allowed him to remain calm and assess his surroundings before moving. That allowed him precious minutes to get control of the pain.

He was in a vehicle, and it was moving. From the constricted feel, he was in some type of bag. *This can't be good.*

Thankful his arms weren't bound, Coulter rubbed a hand over his heavily bearded face and tried to focus on the last thing he remembered. They'd been ambushed.

"Tomás, will you watch what you're doing?" A man griped. "You practically landed us in that last pothole."

"Hey, if you're not driving, keep your comments to yourself," came the curt reply.

Coulter focused on his captors.

"All I'm saying is that we're not getting paid to replace a flat tire. So, if we have to, it's coming out of your check, not mine."

The other man scoffed. "What does my sister see in you?"

"Whatever it is, Tomás, it's more than your wife sees in you. Oh wait, you don't have a wife."

"Hilarious, Eduardo," his brother-in-law snapped before turning his focus back to the road. His grip on the wheel was so tight his knuckles were white. "You're a regular comedian."

While his captors were bickering, Coulter tried to recall more details.

Joseph Brinkley's right hand, Derek Falconi, had arrived to meet with Palacios to purchase American weapons and artillery. Brinkley was using Ghost Town Security to cover his illegal activities, and he had uploaded the proof to his secure site.

"Silent Night, Colonel McKendrick."

He remembered that Falconi was brokering a deal to sell it to the highest bidder—and that he was injected with something. Was it the deadly biotoxin?

As the grip of unconsciousness edged closer, Coulter did his best to resist, but it was futile. Euphoria made him feel like he was floating. Unable to help it, before he passed out, his thoughts drifted to her—to Marena.

It surprised him that he'd used the last few coherent moments to think about his ex-fiancée, Dr. Marena Dash, instead of the million questions running through his head. Why wasn't he pondering who had compromised the mission? Who had shot him, and what was rushing through his bloodstream? Were the files and activation key safe on his server? Marena had worked at Beecham Pharmaceuticals. Had she known about Silent Night? Had she created it? He instantly dismissed that thought. Marena would never intentionally work on a bioweapon or contribute to anything that killed people.

Coulter thought about Neil and the rest of his team. Had

they made it out alive? *Probably not,* he told himself, *or you wouldn't be in this jacked up position.*

Grief bolted to the surface and was about to overtake him, but Coulter forced himself to compartmentalize those thoughts for later. He had to think about something else besides the possibility that they could be dead, or it would render him useless.

While he was struggling to tamp down those emotions Marena's face appeared before him. Her luminous brown eyes lit up when she was happy or flashed fire when she was angry. Then, with perfect clarity, he recalled her petal-soft skin and tall, shapely body. The two of them had been like fire and air from the moment they'd met, but he'd broken her heart, and now she was gone. The only woman he'd ever loved and the only one he'd ever lost. Then it was lights out.

A jolt brought Coulter back to the present.

"So, where are we taking him?"

"Why are you asking me?" Tomás snapped. "You're the one with the map."

"Yeah, but you're the one driving."

"Where you tell me to go, Eduardo."

"Okay, keep your shirt on."

"A *GPS* would've been nice, but no."

"Will you pipe down and give me a second? Not like it matters anyway," Eduardo reasoned. "He's dead. It's not like he's in a rush."

Tomás glanced around. "We're surrounded by nothing but a jungle. So, why are we still driving? Any place will do."

"Look, I don't like being in the car with a dead body any more than you. So I say we get the shovel, dig a big enough hole, and boom. We're done, we get paid, and we get out of here."

The vehicle lurched sharply to the right.

Eduardo's shoulder slammed into the door. "Watch it. I'd like to get there in one piece."

While the men were arguing, Coulter ran his hands along the inside of the canvas, searching for an opening. Thankfully, the sack wasn't airtight. As if to prove the point, Coulter took a few deep breaths to clear his mind. It took a conscious effort, but he focused on the surroundings and not his pounding head. The constant barrage of the engine and road noise kept him from making out any additional voices. For now, he assumed he was safe.

Though he was in one heck of a predicament, and his team was unaccounted for, Coulter managed a tiny smile, but he grimaced when the skin across his chapped lips cracked. If only two men were sent to dispose of him, someone *did* think he was dead.

Between his captives' bickering and metal clattering when they went over a bump, it was unlikely they'd hear any noise. Still, he was not about to take any chances. His gut told him time was running out.

Easing a hand into his front pants pocket, Coulter felt around and came up empty. He repeated the movement on the other side and rolled over slightly to check the back side. Empty.

Unzipping his pants, Coulter searched a hidden inside pocket until his fingers connected with a small utility knife. The cramped environment caused his body to protest, but he ignored the pain and focused on the mission. Escaping would require immobilizing his captives before they figured out he wasn't a corpse and tried to kill him.

It's now or never.

Coulter slid the knife slowly through the material with a firm motion, careful not to draw attention to himself. He stopped after making a three-inch gap in the material and gulped in the fresh air. It didn't take long before his

head cleared. Next, he cut an opening wide enough to slip his hand out.

The duo in front was gleefully discussing how much money they would make and what to spend it on. Coulter's fingers roamed over the outside of the bag until he felt a zipper. Slowly, he eased the fastener down just enough for him to crawl out. He rolled onto his side, bending and stretching a few times to loosen up. Some areas felt bruised and stiff, but at least nothing was broken. Next, he shifted onto his stomach and quickly surveyed the closed-in space. He was alone.

Coulter shut his eyes and allowed himself a moment to say a prayer for his missing team before he shoved the feelings of dread aside. Silently, he crawled along the van's cold metal floor. Adrenaline coursed through his veins. The element of surprise was imperative. He would get only one shot. Crouched on his knees, Coulter sprang into action. He had the man in the passenger seat disarmed and in a chokehold before the driver reacted. But when he saw that Coulter was alive, the driver let out a shocked gasp.

"You're supposed to be dead," he said in Spanish.

"Keep driving, and don't do anything stupid." He placed the knife back in his pocket and kept the gun. "If you so much as blink wrong, you're both dead."

Coulter knocked out the man in his grasp, unbuckled his seat belt, and then dragged him into the back of the van before taking his place. He trained the gun on the driver.

"Who hired you?"

"I don't know," the man replied in his native tongue before gripping the wheel tighter.

Coulter switched to Spanish. "You should know I'm good at what I do. I also know when someone is lying. You don't look like the type of guy who could survive extended torture—your brother-in-law either, so I'm going to ask again. It's Tomás, right?"

"How did you know my—"

"We don't have much time, Tomás. I suggest you think it over before you answer. Who hired you?"

The man's eyes widened in fear. Fresh sweat glistened on his brow. He remained tight-lipped until Coulter's left fist connected with his face.

His face contorted in pain. "I swear to you that I don't know. We got paid to get rid of a body—y-you. I'm not a killer. I just—we needed the money." He cut a sharp glance at Coulter. "They said the man we were transporting was dead. We didn't know you were alive. I swear on *Abuela*'s grave."

Coulter released the safety. "A name."

Shaking, the man held up one hand in surrender while keeping the other on the wheel.

"Okay, okay. I heard someone call the man Falcon. We got half the money upfront, and we get the rest when the job is complete. That's it. That's all I know, I swear."

"What's this Falcon look like?"

Coulter's question elicited an expression of surprise on the driver's face. "He's American. He's at least six-four with white hair and blue eyes."

"That could be a lot of people. Anything unusual about this man? A limp, scars, an accent?"

"Wait," the man cried. "He was missing a piece of his right ear."

"His ear?" Coulter repeated.

The man nodded. "It's not something I'd forget."

Coulter tensed in anger. *Falconi.* From the moment they had met, Coulter had disliked him. That he was the point of contact at the weapons exchange was proof enough, but his assignment was to discover if Brinkley was involved. Falconi didn't move without him, so he was likely pulling Derek's strings, but his employer required concrete proof.

Ghost Town may not have anything to do with manufac-

turing the toxin, but they were knee-deep in brokering its sale on the black market. Realizing Falconi could've been behind the ambush, trying to kill him...and now his abduction made him livid. He would return the favor the first chance he got, but there were more immediate matters.

If it was Silent Night they'd injected him with, time was running out. The intel reports and lab results he'd spotted on the laptop screen revealed that it would render its host dead in six days. By the time a person got infected with it, they could be miles away from the place of injection. Coulter had also read that there was no known antidote. It was the perfect killing machine. It was untraceable to most medical professionals unless you knew what to look for, and the effects of the poison were similar to a virus. The preliminary results indicated that the drug was still in the testing phase but would be ready for delivery in a few weeks.

He was living proof that the intel was false and that Silent Night was ready now.

The irony was that the United States didn't condone the use of biological agents in war. So now, he was a walking bioweapon. Luckily, his man was able to upload the ciphertext and key code to his secure server, effectively rendering Silent Night useless.

When he could, he would log in and verify that the transfer was successful. They wouldn't find out the location of the codes without him. Now, his immediate job was to find out how much time had elapsed since his ambush.

"What day is it?"

"What?"

"The date," Coulter roared, then grimaced at the pain it caused his head.

"August first."

Less than twenty-four hours had passed. "What was the plan?"

"Plan?" the man repeated.

This time, Coulter didn't yell. He merely hit the man in the jaw.

"Alright," Tomás said before rubbing his face. "We were ordered to bury you in the jungle where nobody would find you."

"You weren't planning to bury me alive in broad daylight—or were you?"

Chapter 4

Tomás stiffened at Coulter's accusation. "No, no. Of course not. We were waiting until nightfall. We're not stupid—but as I said, we didn't know you were alive."

Coulter didn't argue the point. "Pull over."

The van slowed and eventually stopped on the side of a deserted road. "What are you planning to do to us?" he asked anxiously.

Coulter trained the gun on him. "Get out."

Opening the door, the driver jumped down and backed away from the van. Coulter was there in an instant.

"On your knees."

"Wait. There's no need to kill me—us. I won't try to stop you. We didn't know you were alive, I swear it."

Even in Spanish, Tomás was tripping over his words.

"We were just supposed to bury a dead guy. We wouldn't have taken the job if we knew you were alive. We aren't killers. Please, don't harm us. I don't want my sister to become a widow," he pleaded. "I promise we'll tell him we buried you. Nobody will know otherwise. I swear on my *abuela*'s grave."

"Again?" Coulter said dryly.

He eyed him for a moment before going to the truck and opening the back door. He grabbed the shovel and tossed it to Tomás. "Follow me."

Walking several kilometers away from the road, he

didn't bother to see if the man was following. Instead, he pointed to a spot and said, "Dig."

Tomás didn't hesitate. He began digging and didn't stop until Coulter spoke up.

"Take a picture."

Whipping his cell phone out of his pocket, he waited for Coulter to get into the shallow hole. Lying down, Coulter closed his eyes while Tomás dumped a few shovels of dirt on him and then snapped two photos.

Coulter pulled Eduardo's bulky frame from the truck and onto the ground when they returned to the van.

"When you and your brother-in-law meet up with Falconi again, you show him the picture and tell him that everything went as planned. I don't want him knowing I'm alive. You got that?"

"Yes," he agreed. "I understand."

"Good. Now there's just one more thing," Coulter told him.

His captor looked worried. His gaze darted to his brother-in-law and back. "What?"

"This is going to hurt," Coulter replied before punching him. He watched as Tomás crumpled over and fell face-down in the dirt.

Returning to the van, he rifled through the backpack sitting on the floor. He kept the cell phone, but finding nothing else of use, he tossed it out the door and sped off.

While driving, Coulter worked out various scenarios in his head that didn't include him dying. If a subsidiary of Beecham Pharmaceuticals was responsible for Silent Night, had the US company sanctioned the product, or was a version of it stolen and then reengineered? He didn't have a clue where to get help or who to trust. The man hovering over him hours ago rushed back into his mind. Who was he, and why did he inject him instead of just killing him?

It wasn't clear what the plan concerning him was, but he wasn't about to walk into a trap. He was presumed dead

and needed to stay that way. The sooner he got off the grid, the longer he'd stay alive.

Eyeing the cell phone, Coulter was thoughtful. Should he call her? Was it only going to make things worse? Decision made, he picked up the phone and dialed a number. When it was answered, he switched to speakerphone.

"Hi, Mom."

"Coulter? Hey, honey. How are you? It's been two weeks since you've called. You'd better have a good reason for neglecting me," she teased.

He smiled. "I'm sorry I haven't checked in, but I'm in the field."

"You haven't had two minutes to spare to call your mom?" Sonia chastised.

"You know, if I could've called, I would have."

There was a long pause before his mother said, "Are you alright?"

In his line of work, he was no stranger to being selective with the truth when necessary. Coulter did his best to keep his tone light and even. "Of course."

"You're a terrible liar—always have been."

"Where's Dad?"

"In his garden, where else? I tell you, we've got more vegetables than the law allows. All the neighbors will have veggies this entire summer, and there's enough to donate to the local food bank. All I know is that at least one of these acres needs to go to an in-ground pool and a cabana while I'm still able to enjoy them. But enough about life on the Eastern Shore and you trying to be evasive. Tell me, what's going on?"

Despite his circumstances, he had to smile. Unfortunately, Coulter could never get away with not telling the whole truth when it came to his mother. But this was one of those times when he had to try.

"I'm fine, Mom. Just really tired. We ran into some un-

foreseen problems on this assignment, but it's nothing I can't handle."

"You sound tired, honey. When are you coming home for a visit? It's been too long, and your dad and I would love to see you."

His hands gripped the wheel. "That's true. I'll see what I can do, okay? I have to run, but I just wanted to call and say hi—and that I love you."

"I love you too, sweetheart," Sonia gushed. "See you soon. No excuses."

"Understood. Tell Dad I asked about him," he said after clearing his throat. "Bye, Mom."

Coulter ended the call. He flexed his fingers, unaware that he had been holding the wheel so tightly that the skin across his knuckles was taut. He hated lying to his mother, but there was nothing that she could do to help. The clock was ticking and couldn't be stopped. If he wanted to survive, there was only one person that could save his life in time. And it was a long shot at best.

Dread settled into the pit of his stomach. The last time he'd seen Marena, she'd told him that she never wanted to see him again.

The pain and hurt in her expression made him want to rip his heart out of his chest, but he had to do it. He had to keep her safe. He deserved every bit of her anger, but she deserved an explanation about why he'd left, and since there was no antidote for Silent Night, even if she couldn't save him, he had to find her and make things right between them. And, if he didn't accomplish his mission within five days, it would be a moot point because he'd be dead.

Unable to sleep, Marena decided to go for a run. Changing into a pair of cropped athletic leggings and a T-shirt, she slipped on a pair of socks and running shoes before heading downstairs.

She retrieved her house keys from the table and headed outside. On the porch, Marena used the steps to stretch while inhaling deeply. The smell of dew-drenched grass flooded her nostrils.

After sliding her earbuds on, she cued up a favorite play-list on her phone and began walking down her street. Min-utes later, she increased the pace to a jog and eventually settled her body in for a run. It was the middle of the night, but nothing mattered except the blank headspace she re-ceived from doing strenuous exercise.

For each house she passed, Marena listed one good rea-son why mooning over a lost love was pointless and a waste of time. On and on, she ran until her body began to tire. By the time her foot hit the first step of her porch again, she was physically and mentally exhausted. *Mission accomplished.*

Though she'd just exercised, Marena ignored the rea-sons why she shouldn't resist the sudden urge for choco-late. Going inside, she dropped her keys in the glass bowl by the door and headed straight for the kitchen. Taking a second, she grabbed a few paper towels to wipe the sweat from her face and wash her hands before opening the plas-tic container of bite-size brownies.

By the time she reached her bedroom, she'd eaten three. Setting the dessert on the nightstand, Marena went to take a shower and then fell into a blissful slumber.

Two hours later, her eyes flew open. She had heard a noise. Her gaze traveled to the small clock on her bedside table and noted it was four-thirty in the morning. She lay there wondering if she was dreaming.

That's when another sound broke the silence, and this one was louder than the last.

This isn't a dream. Someone is in my house. It was then that she recalled not setting the security alarm again after returning home. *Viv was right. I should've gotten a dog.*

Marena eased out of bed. Her feet landed silently on the

wooden floor. With sure movements, she tiptoed over to the dresser. A tiny creak broke the silence as she slid the top drawer open. Her fingers moved with surety through the pile of stacked undergarments until they connected with cold steel.

Easing the nine-millimeter SIG Sauer P226 pistol from its hiding place under her lingerie, Marena inched the slide back to drop a bullet into the chamber. Her thumb cocked the hammer. She was ready.

Holding the gun firmly, she tiptoed down the hallway to the staircase. Careful to avoid the creaking steps, Marena slowly descended. By now, her eyes were accustomed to the darkness. She scanned the space as she went.

Clicking at the front door drew her attention. The hair on the back of her neck shot up. Marena summoned her courage, flew down the stairs, backed herself against the wall behind the door and waited. The handle turned again before the large wooden door slowly opened. Taking a deep, calming breath, Marena's fingers tightened around the pistol.

When a dark form came into view, she raised the gun, wrapping her right hand around her left wrist to steady her aim. She let the intruder clear the door. Her eyes had grown more accustomed to the lack of light, so she could see that the burglar was tall and muscular. Marena readied herself. She was a Dash. She knew how to protect herself. Her father had seen to that.

"Hold it right there," she said calmly. "Show me your hands."

Arms rose slowly in the air.

"Okay. I'm unarmed."

Hearing a man's raspy voice, she raised the gun higher.

"Turn around…slowly."

He complied, but it was with lightning speed. Before Marena could blink, the intruder had reached for her pistol and thrown it across the room.

The man reached for her, but she avoided his grasp. She wasn't about to make it easy for him.

Marena got her bearings and raised the palm of her hand to slam it into his face, hoping to reach his nose, but he blocked her, so she punched him in the gut instead.

He grunted, but that was the only indication the strike had connected. He was still on his feet.

He moved forward. "Wait, I'm not going to—"

She crouched down to sweep his legs out from under him. He avoided the maneuver, landing off to her right. Marena was on her feet in an instant. The light from the front door made it easier to see her target. She set up to deliver another blow when the man grabbed her arm, halting her motion. He pulled her arm behind and firmly held her in place. "Rena, stop."

The moment he croaked out her name, she froze. Her heart raced. *It can't be.*

When he released her, she moved away. Feeling around for the lamp on the table, she finally found it on its side. Marena set it upright and flicked it on. Then wished she hadn't.

Marena shrieked and staggered backward, bumping into the same table. Her expression was incredulous. "Coulter?"

He moved toward her, but she stepped back.

Winded, he bent over and placed his hands on his knees while he caught his breath.

"Hi, Rena."

Marena bristled. "Why are you here?" she whispered.

"It's a long story."

Struggling to maintain her composure, she took in his disheveled appearance. Coulter sported a full-grown beard, and the once black hair looked brown. His clothes were crumpled, and he reeked like he hadn't bathed in days. She wrinkled her nose.

"You look awful and smell even worse."

"Apologies. There was no time." He swayed slightly. "Rena, I need your help."

"My help?" She laughed harshly, backing up. "Seriously? If you came all this way for that, you can save yourself the trouble and get out now."

"Please, let me explain."

Marena put a hand up. "Uh-uh. What could you possibly say that I'd want to hear?" she demanded. Her chest rose and fell with each choppy breath.

Annoyed, she thought the anger had left her system, but seeing him was like ripping the Band-Aid off all over again. Coulter's betrayal of ending their engagement without a reasonable explanation came rocketing back to the surface. Marena's expression darkened.

Warily, Coulter moved forward with his hands outstretched. "For starters, I'm sorry."

"Sorry? Are you kidding me right now?" Her expression went from hurt to furious in seconds. "I'm not accepting a sorry, Coulter McKendrick. Sorry doesn't begin to cover the hell you put me through. Sorry would be a walk in the park compared to what I suffered. Do you even grasp what you did to me? What you did to *us*?"

Coulter nodded. "I know I deserve your anger."

"What you deserve," she said icily, "is to be strung up by your—"

Coulter leaned back against the wall. He closed his eyes for a moment. "I don't disagree," he replied, opening them again, his gaze locking with hers. "I know I have no right, but Rena, I'm asking you to hear me out. After that, if you want me to leave, I will. I promise." He blinked a few times, and before she could reply, he slid down the wall and collapsed in a heap.

Marena observed Coulter lying prostrate at her feet. "This isn't very funny. Now get up," she told him. After

a few more seconds, Marena rolled her eyes. "I mean it, Colt. The joke's over."

When he didn't stir, Marena crouched in front of him. She touched his face, then yanked her hand away. His skin was burning up.

"Coulter?"

Marena sprang into action. She laid him flat on the floor and felt for his pulse. It was sporadic. "Coulter? Can you hear me?" She lightly shook him before leaning closer. Then, gently prying an eyelid open, she checked his pupils.

"Colt. Wake up."

After a few seconds, she stepped over him and sprinted up the stairs. Moments later, Marena returned with her cell phone, a bottle of Tylenol and a thermometer. Placing the small gadget on Coulter's temple, Marena pressed the button, and, in seconds, his temperature displayed. "It's 104.2."

She called his name a few more times, but he only groaned and mumbled something incoherent.

Running to the kitchen, Marena grabbed a bottled water from the refrigerator. On her way back, she dialed a number on the cell phone.

A man's groggy voice answered after two rings. "Dr. Meadows."

"Hi, John. I'm so sorry to call you this late," she began.

"Don't you mean early?" He chuckled. "It's okay. What's up? You didn't call me at this hour to tell me you've reconsidered my offer to work more than one weekend a month, did you?"

She scanned Coulter's face. "No. I have an unconscious patient with a high fever and erratic pulse." Marena relayed Coulter's vital signs to her friend.

"Dehydration?"

"It's likely."

"You'd better bring him in," Dr. Meadows replied in a firm and now alert voice.

"I'll have to call an ambulance. He's out cold."

"No—no hospitals," Coulter croaked out in a hoarse whisper. His glassy gaze bored into hers. "Classified."

Marena rocked back on her heels. She hadn't known Coulter was even conscious. Now he was trying to get up off the floor. She placed a hand on his chest. "Don't move."

"Marena? Is everything okay? What's going on? If this man is—"

"He's a friend, and he can't travel. I'll have to stop into the clinic and pick up what I'll need to treat him." She paused. "If that's okay with you."

"Why can't you call the EMT? I'm sure they can get to you—"

"I can't, John. It's… He doesn't like hospitals. He's got a serious phobia about ERs, blood, and—"

A few seconds ticked past before Dr. Meadows said, "Get whatever you need. We'll sort out the rest later. If it gets more serious—"

"We'll meet you at the hospital," she promised.

"Call me if there's anything I can do."

"I will, and thanks again, John." Marena hung up.

She set the phone aside and tried to get Coulter to drink water and swallow the medicine. He took it, but he was still trying to get up.

"Who's John? What does he know about me?"

Her eyes widened. "Really? You're almost unconscious, and you're grilling me about who's on the phone?"

Coulter stared at her.

She sighed loudly. "John Meadows is a physician at a local clinic where I volunteer. He doesn't know anything about you. Now lie still and stop asking questions. And don't think for a second that I'm letting you up to leave. You're in no condition to go anywhere, Colt. Do you hear me?" she said in a voice that was the perfect blend of worry and annoyance.

He closed his eyes. "Affirmative."

Satisfied, Marena helped him to his feet. Coulter swayed but caught himself. His lips were a thin line, and his brow furrowed in concentration. Marena noted that his flushed skin had an odd gray pallor underneath his light brown complexion. Cautiously, she helped him up the stairs.

Chapter 5

"Where are we going?" he asked tiredly.

"The bathroom. It'll help getting the grime off and your body cooled down. Trust me, you'll feel better."

With a flick of her wrist, Marena had the shower on and adjusted the temperature to as cold as she thought he could stand it.

"Are you able to shower without help?"

He nodded and slowly started discarding his clothes.

Marena handed him an oversize towel and washcloth from the linen closet and set them on the closed toilet lid.

"I'll be right outside the door. Call if you need my help."

"Don't worry, Rena," he said in a low, measured tone. "I can handle a shower."

She turned and headed for the door. "It's cold. I'm sorry for that, but it'll help get that temperature down."

When he didn't reply, she stopped walking and spun around. "Coulter?"

"Reduce fever. Got it."

His voice wasn't that loud, but the timbre was deep enough for her to hear over the spray.

Once out into the hallway, Marena left the door cracked to hear Coulter if he called out. Closing her eyes, she leaned against the wall and struggled to get herself together. This was the most bizarre morning she'd had in years. Her emo-

tions were a jumble of memories and fear. Something was seriously wrong with Coulter, and all she knew was that it was classified, but if that were true, why had he shown up on *her* doorstep?

She hurried back to her room and straight for the closet. She grabbed the handles of the French door but then stopped. Her hands were cold and trembling, and there was moisture on her eyelashes. "Get a hold of yourself," she admonished.

When she was able, Marena opened the closet doors and retrieved some clothes from a lower shelf. She glanced at her watch. He had been in there a long time. She pondered going to check on him. Turning around, she found Coulter was right behind her.

"Jeez," she yelled before bumping into the shelves. "I forgot how stealthy you could be."

Coulter appearing wasn't the only thing that startled her. He was standing there with a towel slung low on his waist. Water slid down his chest, and his hair was wet. He'd also shaved his beard and mustache off. He looked the same as the last time she'd seen him. His chiseled jaw was more pronounced without the facial hair, as were his jade eyes. Marena's stomach twisted into knots.

"Here," she said overly loud before holding out the clothes in front of her as if they were a shield. "Put these on."

Coulter glanced between them at the pair of shorts and T-shirt she was holding. His face was unreadable. "You sure your boyfriend—or husband—won't mind?"

The friendly smile slid off her face, pulling her lips into a tight frown. When she spoke, her voice was toneless. "I suppose they would if I had either. These are *your* old clothes. You left them the last time you were at my house. I guess you don't remember, considering the hurry you were in when you left." She shrugged. "Don't ask me why I packed them with my things and brought them here. It seemed stupid at the time—yet here we are."

"Marena—"

"Let's not. We have more pressing issues."

Silently, Coulter eased the clothes out of her hand. When their fingers touched, Marena noticed his hand shook. Their gazes locked.

"Why don't you sit down and put those on?"

"I'm fine," Coulter replied and slid the shirt over his head.

When he swayed, Marena's arm instantly came up to steady him.

"You're not fine."

She guided him to the guest room. Coulter finished dressing and settled in bed while she went downstairs to get a large water bottle. Filling it with ice and cold water, she stopped before heading back upstairs to grab half a submarine sandwich from the fridge, an apple, and a package of trail mix.

"You need more to drink." She offered him the container while standing at his bedside. She set the food on the nightstand. "I didn't know if you were hungry, but just in case."

"Thank you." Coulter took a few sips before sinking against the pillows. In less than a minute, he was asleep.

She retook his temperature. It was lower, but the fever remained.

"I'll be back soon," she whispered.

Marena went downstairs to get another bottle to hold more ice water. She hoped the medicine would do its job and lower his fever. At least then he would feel better, and she could discover what all this was about and find a way to help him. She may be angry with him, but she would put personal feelings aside and do everything in her power to help. And from the looks of it, whatever was wrong was severe. That thought caused fear to ricochet through her like a ball slamming around in a pinball machine. At that moment, Marena realized that she would do what-

ever was needed to keep Coulter alive. She wasn't about to stand by helpless while another person she cared about died. Not again.

Where are you, Coulter?

Cole Everett, the founder, and chief executive officer of Ghost Town Security, sat with his feet up on the mahogany filing chest behind his desk. His Washington, DC, penthouse condo afforded him an uninterrupted view of the Potomac River, the Washington Monument, and the Washington Channel. As his troubled gaze scanned the skyline, Cole's right thumb absentmindedly pressed the top of a ballpoint pen. The clicking sound it generated was the only noise in the room. He had a bad feeling, and it wasn't going away.

There were three soft taps at his office door.

"Come," he called over his shoulder, not bothering to turn around.

"Sorry to disturb you, sir, but Mr. Maxwell is here to see you."

"Send him in."

Stuart Higgins stepped aside to allow the man to enter.

"David." Cole turned back to his desk. "I didn't expect to see you for another week. Vacation not agreeing with you?" he laughed.

"There's been a development," David Maxwell said severely. "I heard from one of my contacts."

The playful mood was gone. Cole sat up straight in his chair. "Okay, shoot."

"There's been a development in Colombia. Coulter didn't report in at the appointed time. Usually, I wouldn't get concerned because I know how it can get in the field sometimes, but—"

"Coulter is never late making contact."

"Exactly," David replied. "His entire team is off the grid,

and no one at his company can provide a straight answer as to his whereabouts."

Cole frowned. "When was the last time he checked in?"

"Two days ago. Right before Javier Palacios's meeting was scheduled to take place."

Cole nodded. He glanced up at Stuart. "Where's Joe?"

"Unknown, sir."

He got up and paced around. "I want to know where he is by the end of the day."

"Yes, sir," Stuart replied.

After a few moments, Cole stopped and strode to his desk. "Could you two excuse me for a moment?"

Both men nodded and filed out of the office. Cole bowed his head for a moment. Then he sighed loudly before picking up the phone and dialing a number.

"Sonia, it's me."

"Dad? Why are you calling?" Sonia responded warily. "I thought I—"

"Yes, I know. You've been very clear that you don't want me in your life. And I've done my best to grant you that, but there's a problem."

"Your problems don't concern me anymore, remember? They haven't for years now, so—"

"Sonia," her father said sternly, "we don't have time for this. Have you heard from Coulter lately?"

"Why are you asking me about my son?" she hissed. "I told you to stay away from him."

"Answer my question. Have you heard from him?"

"If I have, why would I tell you?"

Cole balled up his fist and slammed it on the desk in frustration. "Listen to me. You're my daughter, whether you like it or not. Even though they've kept me from you and my grandson, I have respected your wishes." His voice shook with emotion. "But right now, I need you to put this hatred

of me aside and answer my question. Have you heard from your son?"

There was a long pause before she said, "I don't hate you. And yes, I have, but it was two days ago."

Cole closed his eyes and took a deep breath. He struggled to remain calm.

"Dad, what's going on?" she finally spoke. "Why are you asking me about Coulter?"

"Because I think he's missing."

"What? No. No, that's insane. Besides, how would you know that?"

He let out a harsh breath and sat down on the edge of his desk. "It's a long story."

When Sonia spoke, the barely restrained note in her voice mirrored his own.

"Then you'd better tell me the short version. Starting with what you had to do with this and where my son is."

By the time David and Stuart joined him again, Cole was sitting at his desk with his head resting on his arms.

Stuart rushed over to his desk. "Sir, are you alright?"

Cole gazed up at both men. His eyes were bloodshot, and he looked like he'd aged several years. "No, no, I'm not." He leaned back in his leather executive chair. "I just had a conversation with my daughter for the first time in twenty years. It went much worse than I expected. I can't blame her. I had to tell her that Coulter is missing and that he was on a mission I hired him to do."

David paled. "I'm sorry, Cole."

He got up so fast that the chair crashed into the chest behind the desk. The sound was like a clap of thunder echoing off the walls.

"I want every resource I have available on this. I don't care what it takes or how much it costs. I want my grandson found and brought home safe."

"We'll find him," David replied. "I promise you that." He paused before he said, "What about Brinkley?"

Cole pinched the bridge of his nose. "I need proof, David."

His friend let out an exasperated breath. "We've been tracking Brinkley's movements for months. Since you put him in charge at Ghost Town, his actions have been questionable at best. Look, I know you've got a host of other businesses to run, but I'm telling you, Cole, Joe isn't looking out for your best interest or even that of the company. He's looking out for himself. Period."

"I won't jump the gun on this. We're accusing Joe of illegal activities, David. I want to be darn certain before I go down that road."

"Stuart, could you excuse us for a moment?" David asked.

The younger man turned to Cole for approval. He nodded his agreement, so Stuart stepped out, closing the door behind him.

"Why are you letting your friendship with him blind you to the facts right in front of you?"

"I'm not," Cole countered.

"For crying out loud, your grandson has gone missing after trying to get you proof about Brinkley. You don't find that odd?"

"I'm aware of that!" Cole shouted. "Joe is one of my closest friends. We were in the army together. He was at my daughter's wedding and Coulter's christening. Heck, I introduced him to his wife. Since day one, he has been here, and I will not take any severe action until I am one hundred percent sure that Joseph Brinkley is guilty of everything in those reports. His future as a free man and that of Ghost Town hinge on the intel we hired Coulter to find. My gut tells me that if we find Coulter, we'll find that smoking gun."

David nodded. "And until then?"

"Until then, keep monitoring Joe and Falconi."

"Cole, what if they had something to do with Coulter's disappearance?"

He looked David square in the eye. "Then only heaven can help them."

Chapter 6

If I don't get a handle on this, I'm a dead man.

Joseph Brinkley paced the confines of the dilapidated room. His salt-and-pepper hair was buzzed short, but that didn't stop him from running an impatient hand through it. He was waiting for Derek Falconi to come in and explain the debacle that had occurred in Medellín. Javier Palacios expected his weapons to be delivered, but the exchange hadn't happened thanks to Coulter and his team's interference. As a result, the guns were destroyed, and Brinkley had a serious life-and-death problem.

Not one to believe in coincidences, Javier had accused Brinkley of setting him up.

Brinkley had done all he could to diffuse the situation before it escalated. However, he had no intention of providing a refund. Instead, he promised that he'd find a new supply to replace Javier's investment with interest, and that was precisely what he would do.

The only thing that appeased Palacios was Brinkley's news that he had secured him a seat at the table when the bidding started for Silent Night.

There was a brief rap at the door, and then it opened. A few men filed into the room, along with Falconi. He got straight to the point.

"Status?"

One of his men stepped forward.

"Colonel McKendrick's men have disappeared, sir."

"Disappeared? Of course, they've disappeared, you bonehead. That's what they're trained to do."

He turned to Derek. "Why wasn't I told about this?" he said with deadly calm.

"I just returned to base myself. I was about to—"

"I don't want excuses, Falconi," Brinkley interrupted. "What I want is the blasted game plan for finding them and what we're doing to keep Javier Palacios happy and off our backs until Silent Night is sold."

Just then, another man stepped forward. "We've been searching for the last forty-eight hours, sir. If Coulter's men are anywhere in the area, we'll find them."

Brinkley pinched the bridge of his nose. "How many times do I have to say it? His team won't *be* in the area. They're trained to disappear, and we don't have time to search the globe for Coulter's men," he snapped. "Forget them. I want McKendrick. I want to know what they were doing at that meeting. Who tipped them off, and what, if anything, does he have on us?"

"What if it was just about the arms deal with Señor Palacios?" one of the men asked.

Brinkley stared at the man like he was crazy. "If you think I believe for one second that a group of former Special Forces soldiers just happened to be in a Medellín jungle and matter-of-factly sabotaged our meeting and destroyed some guns, you're delusional. Coulter always has something up his sleeve. We need to bring him in and find out what that is. If I go down, we all go down, and I'm not about to land first. You got that?"

"Yes, sir," the group replied.

He turned to Derek. "Your team screwed this up, and now Palacios is suspicious. We *need* those guns, Derek.

Do I have to spell out what's going to happen if this deal goes south?"

One of Derek's men shifted uncomfortably. Brinkley zeroed in on the motion.

He turned to Falconi. "What aren't you telling me?"

More silence ensued.

Brinkley scanned the room. "I'm not going to ask again."

One make spoke up. "Uh, the scientist that had the thumb drive with the decryption key is missing, sir."

"What? How is that possible? The one guy responsible for keeping it on his person at all times has just up and disappeared? What about his security detail?"

"They're missing, too, sir—we presume dead in the explosion."

The vein in Brinkley's forehead looked ready to burst. Roaring in anger, he picked up a chair and threw it, not caring how many people had to duck to keep from being hit. "How in the world did this happen? If they're dead, where are the bodies?"

"We're still searching, Mr. Brinkley."

"There is no auction without those codes, and now you tell me that not only are they missing, but the guy carrying them is missing, too? How do we know he didn't just take the codes and run?"

"I handpicked him," Derek replied. "He would die before betraying us."

"So you say."

"Excuse me, Mr. Brinkley?" another man asked.

Brinkley spun on a dime, ready to do battle. "Say the wrong thing," he warned.

"We have a second problem, sir," he said reluctantly. "One of the men shot McKendrick with Silent Night. He may be dead by the time we locate him."

The color drained from Brinkley's face. His expression turned apoplectic.

"What did you say?"

"Colonel McKendrick was injected with—"

"How?" he roared. "How is that even possible?"

"We're sorry, sir," the man behind Derek said quickly. "It was a mistake."

Brinkley turned to face him. His eyes narrowed on the unlucky bearer of bad news before advancing until he was almost nose-to-nose with Derek. The man didn't take a step back but held his ground.

"Are you telling me that some screwup injected the one man I need alive with poison? Is that what you're telling me? And before you say it was an accident, you have to freaking use the activation code to use Silent Night."

"You ordered us to take out his team. We followed your orders to the letter, Mr. Brinkley."

"I said his *team*, you idiot," Brinkley spat. His skin turned a mottled red. "Did any of you hear me say, McKendrick? He was never to be harmed. He's my partner's grandson. That makes him untouchable."

The room was silent.

"And let's be clear," Brinkley snapped, turning to Falconi. "You all didn't take out his team, and you let them get away."

"If McKendrick is alive, there are only a handful of places he can go for medical treatment. So why not begin the search there?"

Brinkley was thoughtful. A minute later, a smile stretched across his taut face.

"You may be on to something." He turned to Derek. "Your gross incompetence in this matter is shocking. But there may be time to fix this mess. If we can't find the scientist and that thumb drive, I want anyone at Beecham who has any connection to Silent Night tracked down. We need another activation key. That will allow us to continue with the auction as planned and buy us time to find Coulter. If

he's alive, I guarantee he's not on his own. He's got help—and I want to know who. So follow the trail, Falconi," he instructed.

"The sale is in two weeks, Mr. Brinkley. Coulter doesn't have that long. He may have four or five days left at best. Is it worth going after him?"

"I want to hedge my bets. I don't believe for a second that the scientist possessing priceless codes just disappeared into thin air or died in a fire. My hunch is telling me that Coulter had something to do with it. We need the thumb drive with the codes back or a new one in its place. Without them, we can't initiate the transfer protocol, which means we don't have a sale. And I have no intention of returning one hundred million dollars to our bidders. Am I clear?"

"Yes, sir," everyone in the room replied, almost in unison.

"I'm sure the people that made this thing at Beecham have prepared for every contingency in the event of something like this happening. And if Coulter dies before I get another key in my hand, I guarantee that none of your jobs are safe—or your lives."

Brinkley turned and stormed out of the room. He missed the slight smile on Falconi's face.

I don't know what happened or why he's back, but you can't let him die.

Coulter may have broken her heart, but he was sick and needed her help regardless of their turbulent past. Luckily, it was early, and there wasn't much traffic, so the ride-sharing service Marena called made it to the health clinic in record time. Deactivating the alarm before going inside, she moved past the brightly decorated waiting area and went straight to the supply room.

Retrieving a large bin from a closet, she sifted through

drawers, carts, and boxes to get everything she needed. Finally, Marena reactivated the alarm and left.

On the way home, myriad thoughts raced around in her mind. What was Coulter doing back after three years of silence between them? Why had he come to her, of all people? And most importantly, how was she going to keep her emotions in check while treating him?

Marena had plenty of things to get off her chest but now wasn't the time. She had to focus. Luckily, her driver wasn't in a talkative mood, and for that, she was grateful. The deafening quiet was soothing. She'd almost drifted off for a nap when her cell phone played a familiar tune. She answered without looking up.

"What are you doing out and about this early?"

"What are you doing calling me this early?"

"Hey, I asked you first," her best friend, Vivica Greenley, replied.

"I had to pick up some supplies from the clinic."

"I know you were at the clinic. Locator app, remember? So, was Dr. John there with you? Hallelujah," Vivica said excitedly. "You finally took my advice and went out on a date?"

"No," Marena said flatly. "I've told you a million times that I'm not dating Dr. John. We're colleagues and friends, and that's it."

"You do realize that my mother has gone on more dates than you—and she's sixty-five."

Marena chuckled at that. "Dating is the last thing on my mind right now. But I, uh, have an unexpected situation that I'm dealing with."

"You can't keep hiding behind work, you know. Sooner or later, you'll have to move on. All you've done since I met you is pine after Carlton. The only thing getting your attention is to-go boxes from your favorite restaurants."

"I'm not pining, thank you very much, and it's Coulter—which you well know. And speaking of—"

"Sweetie, he's gone," Vivica interrupted. "The love story is over, and it's time for a new man. Preferably one that doesn't shatter your heart into a million pieces."

"Vivi, I know you mean well, but you're not helping right now."

"Why not?"

"Because he's here."

"Excuse me?"

"Coulter is at my house."

There was a long silence before Vivica spoke up.

"Well, I hope you gave him a piece of your mind."

"Not yet. He's sick. Some bronchial thing," Marena hedged. "Anyway, our unfinished business will have to wait."

"What unfinished business?" Vivica scoffed. "Marena, he left you. What's left to finish about that?"

"I guess nothing," she said softly. The problem was Marena didn't believe it for a second.

"Vivi, I just got home. I'm going to have to run."

"Okay, but as your best friend, I'm recommending that you send him to urgent care and then tell him to say whatever he came to say, and then hit the road."

"I hear you." Marena felt terrible about not telling her friend the truth. "Don't worry about me. I'll be fine."

"You'd better be," Vivica warned. "Or I'll come over there and kick his butt for you."

Chapter 7

Marena didn't doubt her friend's veracity for one minute. After thanking the driver, she piled everything precariously on top of the bin. Her progress was slow since she couldn't see over the burgeoning pile, but she made it into the house in one trip, though her arms ached from the effort. Then Marena quietly hefted the supplies upstairs and set up the immediate things needed to help Coulter.

After rechecking his vital signs, Marena prepped him for an IV drip. Coulter was dehydrated, so it took several minutes to find a suitable vein to use. She squeezed the IV bag a few times to force the fluids into his system faster. Coulter started shivering, so she eased the covers higher and remained at his side, watching him until his breathing evened out.

She pondered her friend's reaction to hearing that Coulter had returned. She had been just as blown away upon realizing it was him on her doorstep.

Vivica could be relentless when she felt that one of her loved ones needed protecting. Marena was just as loyal, but Coulter was in no shape to go ten rounds with anyone. So, for now, she would acknowledge that there were more questions than answers—and for the immediate future, that was as good as it would get.

Her cell phone rang, so she rushed out into the hallway

so she wouldn't wake him up. Seeing her brother's number and picture flash on the screen, she groaned.

"Hey, Lucas. What's up?"

"You tell me."

Not wanting to disturb Coulter, she went downstairs. Marena contemplated telling him what was going on but thought better of it. Lucas and Coulter had been best friends, but things went south when he called off their engagement. There was no telling what her brother would do if she told him Coulter was there. Decision made, she said, "Not much. Why?"

"Because it's been a month of Sundays since you bothered to call."

"Last time I checked, the telephone is a two-way device."

"Very funny. I guarantee Dad won't be amused."

Her brother wasn't kidding about that. Ever since her mother died, Terry Dash had lost a lot of joy. He was more severe and less playful than before her mother's accident.

"Lucas, what do you want?"

"I was planning to stop in for a visit soon."

"No," she blurted out.

"Boy, that was quick. Spoken like a woman who's dating and doesn't want her big brother cramping her style."

"I don't have a style to cramp," she said dryly. "I'm just busy."

"Since when has that mattered?"

"Vivica and I are planning to take a trip. You know, girls' weekend out."

"Uh-huh. Well, I'm sure she'll have you lined up with blind dates while you're gone. You'd think her whole life's mission was to get a boyfriend."

"Luke, cut it out. Vivica has a boyfriend."

"Ah, the man must be good and desperate to get roped into her train wreck of a life."

"Did you call me to pick a fight? Because insulting my best friend is the surest way to get hung up on."

"Okay," he laughed. "My apologies, but she deserves it after what she pulled."

"It was an honest mistake. Vivica didn't know you'd come for a visit, and if you didn't want anyone barging in on you in the bathroom, you should've locked the door."

"Uh-huh. If that were the case, she'd have averted her eyes and not stood there staring at me as if I were an after-dinner mint."

"Quit exaggerating," Marena laughed. "If all you're going to do is rake my friend over the coals, the conversation is over."

"Suit yourself," he replied before hanging up.

Marena shook her head and plopped down on the couch. How could she be surprised by her brother's antics? His theory was that Vivica had a crush on him, but Lucas thought the same about every woman within ten feet. The fact that he was single, tall, built like a linebacker, and a military man only added to his appeal. Women couldn't help themselves when it came to her brother, and she could honestly say that Vivica was not immune.

Retrieving her laptop from the coffee table, she replaced it with her feet as she got comfortable. Next, she researched Coulter's symptoms to determine how best to help alleviate them. She understood his situation was classified, but if his condition didn't improve, she would insist that he go to the hospital for an evaluation.

Her mind drifted back to years ago when they were inseparable. Marena was used to Coulter being wounded and having to patch him up after he and Lucas got carried away in training or some weekend warrior activity. Not one to hide anything, Coulter even told her about any injuries while on active duty. Marena had experienced him dealing with various emotions over the years, violent nightmares,

and personal loss, but she had never seen him flat on his back sick. This was different.

Thirty minutes later, she went upstairs to check on Coulter. He was asleep, so she knelt by the side of the bed and took his temperature. His fever was down.

Much better. Marena's hand drifted to the side of his face. Without thinking, she rubbed his cheek, then inched closer. "You'll be better in no time," she said against his ear.

"That's not exactly true," he whispered.

Startled, Marena sat back. When their gazes connected, his expression held sadness.

"Colt, what's wrong with you?"

"I've been poisoned, Rena—with Silent Night."

She reared back so fast she almost lost her balance and toppled over. "Poisoned? What are you saying? What is Silent Night?" Marena grabbed his arm in alarm. "Who did this to you, and when? Were you injected, or was it airborne? Better yet, *why* were you injected?" she demanded.

"It's—"

Marena bolted to her feet. "Don't. Don't you dare tell me it's classified, Coulter McKendrick, or so help me, I'll set your dilapidated butt right out on my front porch."

He smiled, despite the obvious pain. "I wasn't going to. You're already familiar with it."

"What do you mean?"

"Silent Night is the antithesis to your Advanced Synthetic Patient Renewal formula."

Marena paled. She sat down on the bed next to him. "Lord, help us." Her breath hitched in her throat. Developing the formula to help save the lives of wounded soldiers was the pinnacle of her career. It had opened up many doors of opportunity for Marena to continue her research in regeneration therapy.

"I knew Beecham Pharmaceuticals was toying with the idea of reengineering A.S.P.R., but—I couldn't do it, Colt.

I wanted no part of it and refused to work on the project. I had no idea that they would create something to take lives instead of saving them."

"So you left."

Marena nodded. "I assumed they'd scrapped the idea after I resigned."

Coulter's expression was grim. "Then you'd be wrong. It looks like they just moved their operation offshore."

"How is this possible? There's a disarmament treaty banning biological and toxin weapons production."

"There are still some states in the world that haven't signed the treaty, and it's difficult to monitor compliance everywhere."

"Yet, you're saying there are entities actively trying to purchase this bioweapon?" Marena countered. "Why haven't they been found and shut down?"

Coulter sat up against the pillows. "I guess they keep changing locations so they can't be pinned down. I don't know. My job was to get proof that this black-market group existed. So, when we were looking into an arms deal, the last thing I expected was to hear Silent Night come up and that it was getting sold to the highest bidder at some millionaire auction.

"What happened next?"

"We got ambushed on the way back, and as far as I know, my team is unaccounted for and presumed dead. I have Liam tapping his resources to see what he can find out."

Marena stilled. "Neil?"

Coulter nodded. "And West."

They were good friends of his, and she knew them personally. Marena reached for his hand and squeezed it. "I'm sorry."

He nodded. "I don't know why I got injected with this stuff when it's worth probably hundreds of millions on the black market. It doesn't make any sense."

"Was it an accident?"

"Hardly. Someone said 'Silent Night' after getting a dart in my neck. Right now, we've got more questions than answers."

"I don't understand all of this. Someone stole my life's work and turned it into a killing machine. One that someone is selling off to the highest bidder?" she said in disgust.

"And probably have. Silent Night can be injected into someone at close range. Or, in my case, a dart delivered by a high-powered rifle. It can be placed in food or liquid and wipe out an enemy before anyone knows the target has something more severe than a flu bug."

Marena placed her head in her hands. "What have I done?"

Coulter touched her hand. "Rena, don't."

"Don't what? This entire thing is my fault," she shot back. "I gave them the foundation for this weapon."

"Silent Night is not what you created, Marena. You designed a serum that would save lives, not kill. Beecham is to blame for allowing someone to steal the research and morph it into something deadly, not you."

"That doesn't matter. I provided the blueprint."

He tightened his grip. "Listen to me. It would've been developed with or without you. Someone wanted this thing made to use on their enemies. It was just a matter of time."

"And since when are *you* the enemy?" she countered.

Coulter told her as much as he could about Brinkley and Falconi and his frustration at not knowing how far up their connections went or who else might be involved.

"I didn't know who I could trust. So I told Liam the truth because I know he would never betray me, and I didn't tell anyone else because I didn't want to take the chance of walking into a trap."

"Liam Forsythe? How is he? Still twitchy?"

"Hey, that twitchiness has saved his life and mine on several occasions."

"Fair enough," Marena capitulated. "As far as Silent Night goes, the lines are blurred now, Coulter. This serum is just a convenient way to remove a threat, regardless of the circumstances—or who's deemed dispensable. Can't you see this could have global ramifications, where no one is safe?"

"I know," he replied.

When he started shivering again, Marena hurried to the hall closet to retrieve another blanket. By the time she returned, Coulter was sweating and had kicked the covers down to his waist. She had been gone less than twenty seconds.

Marena wiped his face with a towel. "Coulter, how aggressive is this poison?"

His breathing had become labored. "Very."

"How long do we have?"

His guarded expression was gone. In its place was one she'd seen only twice before. When her mother died, and the night he told her that he was leaving. The night he ripped her heart to shreds.

Dread dropped into her stomach like a giant boulder. *It would do no good to come unglued now.* Marena touched the side of his face. It was on fire again.

"Coulter—"

His fingers came up and closed over her hand. He shook his head.

Anger flashed in her eyes at seeing the resignation in his. "Stop. You can't give up. Do you hear me, Coulter McKendrick? You came to me for a reason. Because you knew I could help you."

"We don't have time, Rena."

She let out an exasperated breath. "How long?"

"Four days."

Chapter 8

Marena's heart almost stopped, but she wouldn't collapse into a heap. Not now.

She placed her hands on either side of his face and said, "Listen to me. If I'm going to try and find a cure, I need you in a positive frame of mind. Acceptance of this thing won't help you—or me. Do you understand? We have to focus on beating this."

He shook his head. His eyes bored into hers. "That's not why I'm here."

"What are you talking about?"

"I know how this works. I've seen the intel. There's no antidote, Marena. In four days, I'm dead. Game over. I thought there might be a chance, but this thing is aggressive, and it feels like there isn't time. You and I—we need to clear the air."

Marena bit her lower lip. "You did that when you left," she replied in a voice tinged with bitterness.

"That's why I'm here. To say—"

"No," she said quickly. Tears spilled from her eyes. "I can't revisit what happened between us, Coulter. Not now."

"You need to, Rena—I don't have much time."

She shook her head. "I can't," she choked out. "My attention has to be focused one hundred percent on curing you. I have to find out what's in this thing," she said to herself

more so than to him. "Somehow reverse engineer an anti-dote or determine if A.S.P.R. can counteract this agent. I've still got my logs and notes. I'll need to get them. It would help if I could find out who at Beecham created Silent Night. Is there anyone you can contact that can find out? I don't have my clearance or credentials anymore to get me in, but I know a lab I can use to—"

"Marena."

That one word got her attention. Her eyes widened, and she stopped talking.

Coulter raised his hand to her face. His fingers glided across her lips. "You can't save me."

At that, she pulled away from him. Marena ran an agitated hand through her hair and began to pace the room. "No, I don't buy that." Her voice shook. "There has to be a cure, Coulter. We just need to find it."

"You have to accept that we're in a no-win scenario here."

"You don't believe in no-win scenarios, remember?"

Coulter raised himself higher in the bed, his face mirroring the degree of effort.

"Listen to me. We're dealing with the perfect killing machine. It's untraceable and isn't a danger to anyone except whoever's been injected with it. That's why it was designed. There's nothing that can trace it back to the source. You're dead in six days—end of story."

She glared at him with all the rage, helplessness, and fear she felt inside.

"That won't be the end of *your* story. But I need you not to give up. Do you hear me, Colt?"

Their gazes locked for long, agonizing moments.

"Do. You. Hear. Me?"

Determination warred with resignation until finally, Coulter managed a smile and said, "Yes, ma'am."

Relief washed over her face. "Good. Now get some rest."

When Marena went downstairs, she sank into a chair. Her hands were shaking, so she put them under her thighs. *This is a nightmare.* Marena glanced at her watch and then set a timer for two minutes. "Okay, you have two minutes to give in to the fear, and that's it," she said aloud.

She started the timer and cried as silently as she could. Coulter couldn't die. She had to find an antidote. It was one thing for them to be apart, yet he was still somewhere in the world. But for him not to be here at all was not acceptable.

Tilting her head back, Marena stared at the ceiling. Her tears rolled unchecked into her hairline. Her body shook with muffled sobs, and panic began to take root and spread throughout her body like an uncontrolled forest fire. Just when she thought she would become consumed, her alarm went off.

"Time's up," she announced, wiping her face on her shirt sleeve.

Marena compartmentalized the panic and got to work. She sat at the dining table with her laptop, a large mug of coffee, and the brownie bites. Retrieving the project files she'd saved on her secure server was tedious, and sifting through each of the directories was time-consuming, but she finally found what she needed.

Her most outstanding achievement, the A.S.P.R. serum, helped heal patients in record time. All the advanced testing had been promising, but Beecham Pharmaceuticals had decided to scrap the project without warning. She had been devastated because it had worked in every injured test subject that had received an injection. A noncompete clause she'd signed effectively blocked her from taking her serum to any competitor of Beecham's for three years.

Now, she wondered if they'd pulled the plug because they had something more sinister in mind for A.S.P.R. The thought that her work played any part in aiding the development of Silent Night made her sick to her stomach.

Ever since she had been a little girl, Marena had dreamed of helping people and following in her mother's footsteps. Lily Dash had been a scientist and had always encouraged her daughter to pursue her passions in life and to strive for excellence in anything she did.

There wasn't a day that Marena didn't long for her mother. Her sudden and violent death left a hole in her heart that no one could fill.

She thought about Coulter lying upstairs in her guest room, battling the effects of a poison that would take him out if she didn't find a cure. He, too, had caused a void in her life, but there was no point dwelling on sad stories.

Wiping away stray tears, Marena glanced at the clock on the computer. Standing, she stretched a few times before shuffling to the kitchen to make more coffee. It was going to be a long night.

Where are you, Coulter? Why aren't you home?
Sonia paced around her kitchen, alternating between tears and anger. *Where is my son?*

Her worst nightmare was staring her in the face and daring her to say something.

From the moment Coulter had told her he was joining the army, she'd lived on pins and needles. For years she'd been worrying, losing sleep, and praying fervently that he would come home in one piece. But the fact that he had joined the military in the first place was almost unbearable. Being the child of a serviceman was fraught with challenges. There was nothing she enjoyed about relocating every few years, leaving old friends behind, or the awkwardness of having to be the new kid arriving in the middle of the school year. Compounding that was the ever-present stress of wondering if her dad was coming home when he went on long and dangerous missions. That was the worst torture of all. Her mother had taken it all in stride, but she never had.

He had been missing for the important milestones in her life, or when all she wanted was her dad to be home every night like all the other fathers, and it began to eat away at her like acid. As the years ticked by, Sonia felt increasingly at odds with her dad. It was no surprise that when Coulter decided he was going into the military, she hit the ceiling. She was hurt that he had joined anyway, despite knowing how she felt about it.

And then, years later, when he settled on Special Ops, Sonia knew that she was getting paid back for all the animosity she'd shown her father during their tenuous relationship. But cutting her son out of her life wasn't an option. That notion prompted her to give her father some slack.

Cole was floored at his daughter's change of heart and wholeheartedly embraced the new truce.

The first few weeks were more than Sonia had expected. Her father went out of his way to reconnect with Sonia, Alvin, and little Coulter. He had even taken them on a family vacation to Southern California. While there, they visited Calico Ghost Town. At first, Sonia had wondered if her father had lost his mind, but Coulter had loved it. There was so much for him to do, and he loved spending time with the grandfather he'd never known.

Sonia could've kicked herself for thinking that it would last. Instead, her father began excusing himself from their activities to handle work calls. Each time the phone rang, her tension grew. Finally, she'd had enough. She had planned to speak to him, but he had pulled her aside and dropped the news that there was a work crisis and he had to fly home.

That was the last straw. Sonia didn't care that it was a start-up and required a great deal of his time. All she saw was that once again, she didn't measure up when it came to his time. That's when she blew up and severed all ties. That was thirty years ago.

"What are you thinking about?"

Sonia spun around to see her husband, Alvin, standing in the doorway.

Her expression darkened. "You don't want to know."

"Then it must be about your dad," Alvin replied with a shake of his head.

"This is entirely his fault. How dare he go behind my back and hire Coulter's company for some stupid fact-finding mission? How could he endanger my son like that?"

"*Your* son?"

"Alvin," she said with exasperation. "You know what I mean."

"Do I?"

She glared at him.

"Look, I miss him as much as you do, but this misdirected anger has to stop.

"What do you mean?"

"I mean that you can't go your entire life blaming your father for every bad thing that ever happens."

She frowned. "That's not what I'm doing."

"Oh, no?" Let's start with the fact that Coulter is thirty-five years old. He's a grown man and more than capable of making his own decisions about who's in his life and who isn't."

"My father has never cared about anything more than he did work," she shot back. "And now his selfishness has placed our son in danger. The irony is Coulter has no idea he has a connection to Cole Everett."

"And whose fault is that?" Alvin shot back. "Besides, Coulter experiences danger every day. It's his job, and that mission was no different."

"No different?" She threw up her hands in frustration. "He's missing, Alvin. Missing."

"You don't think I'm worried about him, too? But what's the point of placing blame right now? How is that helping

Coulter? Shouldn't we be focused on doing all we can to find him—and using every resource we have at our disposal?"

"By every resource, do you mean my father?"

Alvin sighed loudly. "Sweetheart, I love you, but you have tunnel vision when it comes to Cole. Our son is highly skilled and is exceptional at what he does. I know you mean well, but you can't continue trying to manage every aspect of his life—he needs space. Case in point, Coulter ends up working for his grandfather, despite your best efforts to keep the two of them apart."

"That's because my father forced the issue. He knew what he was doing."

"And so do you. This estrangement needs to end, Sonia. It's time. And we should be working with Cole to find our son, not bickering."

Sonia sank into the closest chair. Tears trickled down her cheeks. "I lost my father to his job. I don't want the same to happen to my baby, too."

Alvin walked over and knelt in front of his wife.

"You have to ease up, sweetheart, or you're going to lose both. Whether or not you like it or even understand it, their jobs are a part of who they are. You railing against them is not going to change that."

She lowered her head. "I get it."

He grasped her hands in his and kissed her knuckles. "Good. Now let me get off this floor before one of my knees locks up," he chuckled before kissing her lips.

"Alvin, I don't know how to fix things with my father or Coulter."

"With one word at a time." He got back on his feet and then squeezed his wife's shoulder before leaving.

Sonia sat there with her thoughts for a few moments. Finally, she stood up and walked over to the table to retrieve her cell phone from her purse. She dialed a number and waited.

"Dad?"

"Sonia," her father replied in surprise. "Not that I'm not happy to hear your voice, but why am I hearing it? After I told you about Coulter, you made it pretty clear that I wouldn't hear from you again."

"I know. But, Dad, I need your help," she admitted. "I would move heaven and earth to get my son back."

"Just like I would do for you, Sonia."

"I can't do it alone. I don't know where to start, who to call."

"It's my fault he's missing. I will do everything in my power to find him, Sonia. I promise you that."

"I know you will." She sighed with relief. The words *I'm sorry* teetered on her lips like a swimmer about to jump off a high dive.

At best, their relationship was contentious, so the most she could muster was a thank-you. Her father graciously accepted. It wasn't the perfect scenario, but it was a start.

Chapter 9

Coulter awoke with a start. He lay against the pillows while he assessed how he felt. Getting up gingerly, he took his time walking down the hall to the bathroom. Poking his head into Marena's bedroom, he was surprised that she wasn't there.

Going downstairs, he found her at the dining room table, slumped over her laptop. Her head was resting on her arms with her hair draped over the keyboard. He sat down in the closest chair and observed her for a moment. He swept her hair out of her face.

Her eyelids fluttered open. She blinked a few times and glanced around.

"Sorry, I didn't mean to wake you."

"It's fine. I needed to get up anyway."

"How's the research going?"

Marena sat back in her chair. She couldn't hide the frustration in her expression.

"From the look on your face, I'd say the prognosis isn't too good."

"I have four days left."

Marena didn't tell him this, but just thinking the words caused her heart to ache. Setting the laptop aside, Marena rubbed a hand over her eyes. Yawning, she wearily glanced down at her watch and groaned when she saw the time.

"How long have you been at this?"

"The entire time you were asleep."

Coulter glanced at his watch. "I didn't know I was out that long."

"I pored over the data after downloading all the notes and files I had on Advanced Synthetic Patient Renewal. All the team's research was turned over to Beecham upon my resignation—except A.S.P.R. Now I have everything needed to duplicate the serum."

"That's good news."

"Yeah, but the problem is figuring out if giving the drug to you while Silent Night is coursing through your veins would help or harm you. The serum wasn't designed to counteract a biotoxin, Coulter. I created A.S.P.R. to heal wounded soldiers in record time from gunshot wounds, internal injuries, cuts, burns, and minor illnesses. If we're not careful, I could just as quickly kill you."

"I'm dead anyway, so what's the harm in trying?"

Frowning, she stretched her exhausted muscles. "That's not funny."

Coulter smirked. "Maybe not, but it's true."

"What are you doing out of bed, anyway? You should be resting."

"I couldn't sleep."

She observed him for a moment. There were a few more lines etched into his face and under his eyes, and if possible, his build was more muscular. But other than that, he was how she remembered. Clearing her throat, Marena leaned over and felt his forehead. "Temperature's down."

"For the moment," Coulter agreed, "but I'm sure it won't last. Fluctuating body temperature seems to be one of the side effects. The body's protection mechanism, I guess."

"Your immune system is trying to fight off the poison." Marena grabbed her laptop and started typing. "What other symptoms have you noticed?"

Coulter shrugged. "Not much, just the fever, loss of strength, appetite, and severe headaches. They vary. Oh, and nausea, too."

"How long do the headaches last?"

"It depends. Some are a few minutes, but others last for hours."

"What about mental clarity?"

"So far, so good, but that will change. As time ticks by, I'll develop impaired motor skills and body strength and degradation of mental faculties."

She made more notes. "Is this based on observation?"

"No. I read through some of the data on Silent Night."

Marena rested her elbows on her thighs before closing her eyes. "I have to find out what's in it. I don't want to risk giving you A.S.P.R. while it's still in your system. I don't know what that will do to you. We don't have time for me to make both, and I can't reverse engineer an antidote until I know for sure what we're dealing with."

She felt Coulter's hand on her shoulder.

"I know you'll figure this out, Rena."

She opened her eyes and glanced at him. "We can't afford for me to be stumbling around in the dark. Being wrong isn't a luxury we can afford."

"I'm off the grid, so I don't have the resources I normally would, but I was able to use other means to find out more about Brinkley and Silent Night. I also checked in with Liam," Coulter added. "He's still trying to find out what happened to the rest of my team. If they made it out alive, and if any of them were injected, too. I have the codes that Brinkley needs to activate the formula for Silent Night for the winning bidder."

"You do? Where?"

"On a secure server. If something happens to me, he'd never get his hands on those codes and sell it as planned."

"Why not?"

"Because Beecham put in a fail-safe. Those codes on that drive are the initiation key to activating each vial of toxin. If any code is wrong or missing, the sequence won't work, and Silent Night would remain inactive."

"But why can't someone at Beecham just create new codes?"

"I don't know, but I know that someone stole the formula and the codes from the pharma company. I doubt they'd be eager to recreate the codes, especially when they're trying to downplay having created them in the first place. So, no, whoever stole it knew what they were doing. They anticipated that Beecham would try to distance themselves from it once it came to light. That would ensure its value and that they had a one-of-a-kind bioweapon that they could sell to the highest bidder."

"I still don't understand how Brinkley got involved in all of this or why. It doesn't make sense that he'd willingly betray his country. He's a lot of things, but I never pegged him for a traitor."

"There has to be a pretty substantial motivator for him to be taking such an enormous risk. If he's caught, he's going down in a rather public way."

"Which makes him dangerous if he's cornered because he may see it as he's got nothing to lose."

"Where were you when all this went down?"

"Colombia."

"How did you escape?"

Coulter stared at the wall. "I passed out for a while after I was injected. When I came to, my team was gone, and I was in the back of a van about to be buried alive."

Marena blanched. "What?"

"It was okay," he assured her after seeing her expression. "The men in the front seat were lax and didn't tie me up—their mistake. It didn't take long to disarm them

and confiscate their truck. Liam helped me get back to the states. I covered my tracks as I went. Eighteen hours later, I landed on your doorstep."

"How did you find me?"

Coulter hesitated. "I called in a favor and got your forwarding address."

She made a face. "Ringing the doorbell would have sufficed."

"Not much for doorbells," he joked.

"I seem to remember that about you. If I recall, you took great pleasure in finding ways to break into my house undetected."

Coulter grinned. "I'm slipping." His boyish smile warmed her in places she decided long ago it wasn't safe to acknowledge.

"Besides, back then, I wanted to impress you. Any man can use the front door."

Coulter had never, ever been *any* man. "That's true," Marena agreed. Without warning, her stomach growled. Her hand instantly covered her middle. Her cheeks flushed with embarrassment.

His smile faded. "When was the last time you ate something?" He perused her face. "Or slept, for that matter? I mean solid sleep, not a catnap."

"I had an energy bar a few hours ago. As for solid sleep—before you showed up on my doorstep."

"Okay, we're going to get you something to eat, and then you should try and get some sleep."

Marena opened her mouth to protest, but he silenced her with his finger across her lips. "No *but*s. You are exhausted, Rena. It's time to recharge."

"Look who's talking. You've been through more of a ringer than I have. Come on, I'll rustle up some lunch," Marena drawled.

Marena decided on turkey and Swiss on rye for her and

chicken noodle soup for Coulter. She figured it would be better for him to eat light and not upset his stomach, but he had other plans. He ate the chicken noodle soup and then fixed himself two turkey sandwiches loaded with all the trimmings. Marena occasionally watched him inhale the food while she tidied up.

"I think I'll place a five-gallon bucket by your bedside. Just in case that meal decides not to stay put."

"No need," he assured her. "I'm good."

"You should try and get some sleep, Coulter."

"So should you," he countered. "I've placed a call, and I'm waiting to hear back. Until I do, there's not much we can do but wait."

"That's dangerous for you," Marena retorted.

"Yes, but I trust my contact with my life. I'm confident he'll find out what we need to know."

Marena looked skeptical.

"Trust me," he replied. "We'll get what we need."

"I hope you're right. In the meantime, I'd like to recheck your vitals before I take a nap."

Back upstairs, Marena examined Coulter and was happy to see his temperature was still less than one hundred degrees, but his heart rate and blood pressure were still elevated. Still, he was no longer dehydrated, and that gray pallor had faded. She left him reading and went to her room. Out of habit, she was about to close the door, then she stopped. She needed to be able to hear Coulter if he called out. Marena kicked off the canvas tennis shoes she was wearing before easing under the covers. Thankfully, she'd purchased blackout curtains a few months ago. Her room was dark and cool, and the sleigh bed welcomed her into its embrace like an old friend.

Closing her eyes, Marena listened to her breathing for a while, willing herself to relax.

"I have no clue what tomorrow will bring," she said aloud.

"But I pray it isn't another setback." After a few rounds of breaths, Marena drifted into a deep, exhausted slumber.

Coulter bolted upright in bed. Something was wrong.

Kicking off the covers, he swung his legs over the side. His head pounded, and his mouth was as arid as the Sonoran Desert, but that didn't matter. He glanced around the bedroom. His practiced eye missed nothing. His cell phone chirped twice and then vibrated. He scanned the text message and then reread it. Without making a sound, Coulter bounded off the bed and retrieved his gun from the rucksack he'd placed under the bed. He checked the gun's magazine clip before advancing toward the door.

Coulter crept toward Marena's room, slipped in, and went straight to the bed. Seeing that she was still asleep, he knelt beside it.

"Rena, we're in trouble," he whispered into her ear.

Marena's eyes popped open, but she remained still.

"We've got about two minutes before we have company. We have to go."

By the time he had finished speaking, she was off the bed and in motion. Marena threw on a pair of jeans over pajama shorts and a T-shirt over her camisole before slipping on sneakers. Next, she threw clothes and toiletries in a backpack.

"What can I do?"

Marena secured her gun and ammo to her gun belt and tossed a backpack to Coulter. "Take as many medical supplies as you can," she called over her shoulder before bolting out the door.

Coulter slung one bag over his shoulder before helping Marena downstairs with the rest of their gear. He took the lead, with Marena following close behind. They were walking through the living room on the way to the back door of the kitchen when a man grabbed Coulter and shoved him

against a wall. The parcels he was carrying scattered to the ground.

Coulter recovered and grabbed the man's arm as he advanced. He flipped his attacker over and onto the floor before following up with a blow to the jaw.

Not waiting to see if the man was conscious or not, he grabbed Marena's hand and rushed toward the kitchen. Suddenly, a man came up behind Marena and yanked her away from Coulter. His arm snaked around her neck, holding her securely.

"That's far enough," he warned. "I don't want to hurt her, but you know by now that I will."

Coulter's eyes narrowed at the man's familiar distinction. "Why are you here? Did Brinkley send you? Are you working for Ghost Town Security? He's a traitor and won't hesitate to throw you to the wolves. You know that, don't you?"

The intruder drew Marena closer to him. "Don't bother negotiating with me."

Coulter eased forward. "Let her go, and you walk out of here."

"No can do. We're taking a ride." He glared at Coulter. "All of us."

Marena glanced at Coulter. He saw her take a deep breath and go rigid. Then, staring at her intently, Coulter shook his head slightly. When he saw her relax, he turned his focus back to her captor.

Chapter 10

"We won't try anything," Coulter said calmly. "You can release her. We'll cooperate."

Unexpectedly, Coulter let out a shuddering breath, and his face contorted in pain. He doubled over onto the countertop and let out a moan.

"Please, you have to let me help him," Marena said, quickly turning as much as she could to face her captor. "He's not well. I've got to take a look at him." She tried to pull away.

The man took his eyes off Coulter. Seconds later, Coulter grabbed a kitchen knife and flung it at the man. It whirred past Marena and embedded itself in his leg. Releasing Marena instantly, he howled in pain. She headbutted the assailant, then jabbed him in the stomach with her elbow knocking him to the ground. The moment Coulter heard gunshots, he grabbed Marena and flung them both to the floor.

He used his body to shield her at first but then rolled to the right to raise his pistol and return fire. Marena's ears rang, but there was too much adrenaline coursing through her veins to be affected by it.

When it was quiet, Coulter got up, motioning for Marena to stay put. Cautiously, he left the kitchen and slowly advanced toward the living room. The moment he spotted his

target's leg pop out from behind the couch, Coulter aimed and fired. The bullet landed in the assailant's calf.

The man yelled in pain and jumped up from his hiding spot. His face was a mask of pain and rage. Coulter intercepted him and knocked him out.

Marena was at his side in an instant.

"Let's move," he told her.

They stepped over the men littering the floor to grab the supplies they could carry.

"Stay here," he instructed. "I'm going to check the perimeter."

Marena watched him slip out the back door. Agitated, she looked over again at the motionless bodies. She hurried to retrieve their supplies, glancing at her watch for the third time. When Coulter hurried in the door a minute later, she sighed with relief.

"It's clear. I took out the other guy patrolling the back of the house. I don't see any more, but we need to go."

Marena picked up the bags and followed him out.

"Where's your car? Do you have the keys on you?"

"I don't have one."

He stopped in his tracks. "What?"

"I don't have a car," Marena repeated. "I haven't driven since—since Mom died."

A surprised expression crossed his face.

"How'd you get here?" she inquired.

"I hired a driver." Coulter's mouth pressed into a thin line. "Stay here."

He returned to the house. A few moments later, he came out holding a pair of car keys. Moving his hand from left to right, Coulter kept pushing the unlock button on the remote. Finally, when they heard a chirp, he shoved it into his pocket.

"There it is. Let's go."

He stopped in front of a black Chevrolet Suburban. Un-

locking the doors, Coulter began loading their gear into the back seat.

"All set. Get in."

Marena stood rooted to her spot.

"What's the matter?"

Marena was as still as a Greek statue. Seeing the dark sports utility vehicle reminded her of her father's old car. Then, without warning, she was transported back to the fatal night when her mother died.

"Marena?" Coulter called her name a second time. When she didn't answer, he ran back around the car. He stepped in front of her. "What's wrong?"

A chill ran down her spine. Fear gripped her body, causing her to tremble. In her mind, she heard the explosion that ripped through the night air. The shockwave that followed hurled her father, brother, Coulter, and her across the restaurant's parking lot. Next came the unbearable heat and blinding light, and finally, the horrific smell. They had all escaped with minor injuries. Her mother had made it to the car first and started the engine. She died instantly when the vehicle erupted into flames.

Coulter shook her. "Rena, we've got to move. Now. They'll be sending another team."

The terrifying memory held her captive as tight as a vise grip.

She turned grief-stricken eyes to Coulter. When she spoke, her voice was shrill. "I... I can't get in."

Realization dawned on Coulter's face. He wrapped his arms around her and eased her into his embrace. "It's okay, Marena," he whispered against her hair. "This is a car we're borrowing, and it's all clear."

She shook her head. Her eyes were wide with fright. "No. I can't. How can you be sure?"

"Stay here."

Coulter retrieved a miniature flashlight from his pack

and got down on the ground to look under the car. He swept the entire vehicle inside and out before dousing the light.

"We're good," he announced.

"Maybe something was overlooked?" she questioned, wringing her hands. "You could have missed something."

"Rena, I didn't. This is what I do, remember? There are no devices anywhere. I promise you. There are no explosives."

She didn't budge.

"Sweetheart, we are in more danger out here in the open. I'm going to start the car. You stay here."

"No," she hissed between clenched teeth. She clawed at Coulter's arm when he started to pull away. "Don't get in the car, Coulter—please, don't."

Slowly, Coulter peeled her fingers from his arm. He rubbed her shoulders rapidly with his hands.

"Marena, we have to leave, and the only way we're going to get to safety is on foot or in that car," he reasoned. "We can't waste time we don't have, so I am going to get in the car and start it, okay?"

She grabbed his shirt in her hands and shook him. "Come back."

He tilted her face so that they could make eye contact. "I will. I promise."

Coulter released her and headed back to the car. Marena stood, shifting her weight from foot to foot with her arms wrapped protectively around her waist. Her gaze riveted to his every movement. She stopped breathing when he slid into the seat and shut the door behind him. After the engine started without incident, she allowed the breath to escape her lungs with a whoosh.

Leaving the car running, Coulter returned to open the passenger door. "Time to go."

She nodded and hesitantly got in.

He shut her door and then hurried around to the driver's side. Once behind the wheel, Coulter fastened his seat belt and pulled off.

There was silence in the car for a while. Eventually, he glanced over. "How are you feeling?"

"Better."

Coulter returned his gaze to the road. "You wanna talk about it?"

"I'm sorry I freaked out. The nightmares are one thing, but this hasn't happened since the accident."

"Hey," he said quickly. "Don't ever apologize for your feelings, Rena. Your fears are completely warranted."

Marena recalled the trauma of losing her mother. When authorities retrieved an incendiary device from her father's mangled Suburban undercarriage, her family realized that her mother's death was no accident. That realization only intensified their grief and her father's rage.

In the weeks after the funeral, General Terry Dash, USA, Retired, began to change. Convinced he was the target for the explosive and that his wife had been collateral damage, he worked relentlessly to discover his wife's killer, but to no avail.

"I'm not sure why the memories came flooding back right now."

"We were fighting for our lives a few minutes ago. Maybe that triggered the memory. Your loss changed your family forever."

She stared at him. "We weren't the only ones altered by my mom's murder."

Coulter let out a harsh sigh. "Marena—"

Before he could continue, his cell phone rang. He took it from his pocket and answered.

Marena turned her attention to the window and listened

as Coulter spoke in hushed tones. It gave her the time she needed to compose herself.

"That was my contact," he said after hanging up. "He's come through for us."

"How?"

"In addition to warning me about Brinkley's men earlier, he just told me who was in charge of Project Silent Night."

She perked up. "Really? That's a good start. Now we just need to get a phone number."

"You have it already," Coulter replied. "Rena, it was Cutty."

Marena stared at him. "Frank?"

"Yes. He headed up the project after you left. If we get to him, we can get him to help you create an antidote."

"Frank? No." She placed a hand over her mouth. "I can't believe he could have a part in this nightmare."

"I agree, but we need him on our side and cooperating."

"I'm sure if we can talk to him, we can get everything I need to engineer it."

"I don't know about that," Coulter warned. "My source told me Frank hasn't been seen or heard from in about six weeks. He was supposed to have taken a few weeks off and then reported back to the lab. He never showed up. Right now, he's MIA."

Marena crossed her arms and bit her thumbnail while contemplating their next move. "We've got to find him—and fast."

"I've got some men on it, but first things first—we need to find a place to lie low. Preferably not in the immediate area."

She pondered the question for a moment. Finally, she snapped her fingers. "I know a place. It's remote. Stay on this street. Turn right on Cedar in about half a mile. We're going to take Route 70 for about twelve miles."

Coulter focused his attention on the road. "Good. Do you have any cash?"

Marena blinked. "About fifty dollars on me. Why?"

"We'll use the money I have. We shouldn't use any of your credit cards more than once. They'll be monitoring your transactions, so we don't need a paper trail highlighting our trip."

"*They* who? The police?"

"No."

"Why not? There are several men in my living room. Someone must've heard the gunshots and called the police. My house probably looks like a shooting gallery."

"No men will be there."

"How can you say that? What if some of them were dead?"

"The third guy was only wounded."

"I'm telling you, reporters and news trucks are probably swarming my house by now. My neighbors are beyond nosy, so I'm sure it's been videotaped already and gone viral."

"Trust me, Brinkley can't afford to have his men exposed. The house will be empty, and the media won't hear a word about what happened."

"How can you be so sure it's Brinkley? Don't they think you're dead?"

"I didn't kill the men that took me. I just knocked them out. My guess is they reported back, and now he knows I'm onto him. He may have guessed that you're helping me." His expression was pensive. "I'm sorry, Rena. That's not what I wanted."

"There's no need to apologize, Coulter. We're in the thick of it now and have to make the best of it."

"Still, my job is to protect you, not bring firefights to your doorstep."

Marena turned to say something to him but stopped. She touched his arm. Her eyes widened in fear. "Coulter," she said loudly, her hand flying to her mouth in shock.

He turned and glanced her way. His puzzled expression met her horrified one.

"What?"

"What do you mean *what*? Stop the car. You've been shot!"

Chapter 11

Coulter didn't spare it a glance. "It's just a flesh wound."

"I need to examine it." She had already undone the seat belt, turned backward, and rifled through one of the bags on the back seat.

"We'll deal with it later."

Just then, Marena's cell phone rang. She turned back around and stared down at the bag by her feet. "Should I get it?"

"Uh-uh. Turn it off."

"Why?"

"Because your location can be tracked. We need a place to get some supplies and a new cell phone. Any suggestions?"

She checked the time on the car's console, trying her best to ignore the loud ringing.

"At this hour, we'd better make it the Walmart Supercenter in Morehead City."

After a few moments, Marena saw Coulter flex the fingers on his right hand.

"I need to look at that arm."

Coulter's jaw clenched. "I'm fine."

"No, you're not. We were just in a gunfight, Colt. You've exerted the most energy I've seen since you got here, and

now you're shot. You need to pull over so I can treat that arm, and you can rest."

"You can worry over it later," he said doggedly. "This is hardly my most extensive injury. I've had much worse—you know that."

"Yeah, well, not while being poisoned," she muttered.

Marena went to turn on the truck's GPS. He grabbed her hand. "No GPS," Coulter said quickly.

"Let me guess. They'll track that, too?"

"We're not taking any chances. You'll have to give directions, old school."

They were silent for a few minutes, but eventually, Marena couldn't help but ask, "Why are they after me?"

"In hopes of getting to me."

"How would anyone know you'd come looking for me?"

"I'm sure Brinkley realized I'd need medical help after being poisoned."

"Then he'd also know that I didn't have any involvement with Silent Night and that I'd resigned before it was created."

"Maybe he's playing the odds. My seeking you out would be the most logical choice."

"That's a stretch."

Coulter scoffed. "You don't think creating A.S.P.R. and being tapped to produce its converse wouldn't put you back on the radar?" He glanced over. "Among other things?"

"It might," she admitted, "and what…other things?"

"I'm sure he knows our history."

Though it was dark, Marena still blushed. She turned her face toward the window. "Aside from the fact that we're ancient history, there's nothing to know."

She looked back in his direction. Their eyes briefly connected before Marena resumed her fascination with the blurs speeding by her window. Her arms were crossed protectively around her like body armor.

Coulter observed her profile for a few seconds before focusing his attention on the road. "Yeah, ancient," he said softly.

After the trip to the supercenter, Coulter drove to a nearby gas station to fill up. While there, Marena used the new phone they'd purchased to check her messages. Her father's voice boomed into her ear. He asked how things were going and hoped that all was well before requesting she return his call. She dialed Burt next and waited for him to answer.

"Hey, Marigold," he said affectionately. "What's up?"

"Hi, Burt, I'm sorry to call so late, but I need a favor."

"Anything," the man replied. "What do you need?"

"Can I borrow Crystal's place?"

"Sure."

"I mean tonight, Burt."

"Are you okay, Marigold? You sound off."

"Not really, but I will be. But you should know that Coulter's back."

"Say what now?"

"He came to see me, and he's not well. So, I'm trying to help him as best as I can. I thought Crystal's would be a good place for him to recoup. It's remote, beautiful, and on the water."

"What's mine is yours, Marigold—you know that."

Marena sighed loudly with relief. "Thanks, Burt."

"Use it as long as you need. And Marena?"

"Yes?"

"I'm not one to be jumping into other people's business. But I know what he put you through. So you let that boyfriend of yours know that he and I are going to have ourselves a long talk when he's feeling better."

"He's not my boyfriend, Burt. That's ancient history."

"When it comes to lovers, darlin', there ain't no such thing as *ancient*."

"Thank you," she said while trying to ignore his comment.

"My pleasure. And don't forget what I said."

"I won't." She smiled before ending the call.

Marena leaned her head against the door frame. She knew Burt well enough to know that he meant every word. He and Coulter would be having a "Come to Jesus meeting," as Burt called them. She didn't envy Coulter one bit. Her friend was a straight shooter and seldom held back what was on his mind.

She had also missed several texts and messages from Vivica, so she called her back.

"Where have you been?"

And so the next few minutes went almost identical to her conversation with Burt.

"I don't like this," Vivica replied after a considerable bout of silence. "I'd hate to have to kill him for playing with your heart again—though honestly, I'd probably enjoy it."

"He's not playing with anything. This is serious. Coulter is sick, and it could prove fatal." Her voice trembled on the last word. "No matter what's gone down between us, I can't not help him, Vivi. That's not who I am."

"I know," she agreed. "You've always been a saint when it comes to helping people. I love that about you, but truthfully, I'm worried. I'm sorry he's sick, but you're too kindhearted sometimes. I don't want you falling back under his spell."

"Quit worrying," she replied. "*Kind* doesn't mean doormat."

"It better not."

What if Coulter doesn't improve? She dismissed that thought. *Practice what you preach.* She scolded herself.

"Vivi, I have to go. I'm sorry to worry you. I'll be out

of pocket for the next few days trying to get him better, so don't take my absence personally."

"Since when do I—"

"Since every time," Marena quipped.

"Fair enough," Vivica laughed. "I love you, Marena."

"I love you, too."

She hung up when she spotted Coulter at the counter.

"Perfect." She hopped out and raced to the driver's side before Coulter returned from paying the cashier. She took a moment just to get acclimated. She hadn't driven in years, and it felt strange to be sitting behind the wheel.

Her skin felt a bit prickly, and sweat was forming at the base of her neck as her trepidation rose. Taking a deep breath, Marena closed her eyes and refused to let it take hold. "You've got this."

Then, slowly, she turned the key in the ignition. The car immediately started. Relieved, Marena released the breath she'd been holding and sank back against the leather seat.

When Coulter returned and noticed where she was sitting, he glared. She flashed him a broad smile and motioned toward the passenger seat. Coulter got in and shut the door with more force than was necessary.

"Don't get all huffy," Marena retorted before driving off. "I did it for your own good."

"It's not you that's annoyed me," Coulter countered, pulling his seat belt into place. He gazed her way. "Truthfully, I'm starting to feel like crap again."

The smug smile slid off her face.

"Is your fever back?" Marena scanned over his face as she touched his forehead.

Coulter shook his head. "I don't think so." His face wrinkled in concentration. "This is—different."

Checking her rearview mirror, Marena eased over into the right lane when it was safe and looked for the next exit. "Different how? And be as descriptive as you can."

"There's an awful taste in my mouth. Like metal, but different. I don't know. I can't explain—"

Before he could say more, Coulter started shaking violently. His head hit the passenger window more than once.

"Coulter?" Marena yelled. She grabbed hold of his shirt to keep him upright. She called out again, but he was nonresponsive.

Marena pulled off the road and onto a side street. Throwing the car in Park, she jumped out and bolted to Coulter's side. She yanked the door open and had to duck to keep from being hit in the face by Coulter's flailing arm. She slowly reclined the seat and turned his head to the side. With one arm braced across his middle, Marena drew his seat belt tighter around him to keep him secure. It took several tries, and one of those times, his upper arm nailed her in the jaw. She blinked back the stars forming behind her eyes at the unexpected blow.

With Coulter partially braced against injury, Marena watched over him.

"It'll be okay," she soothed as his movements grew less violent and eventually stilled. "I've got you."

Seconds turned into minutes, and he still hadn't come around. Marena was beginning to worry when suddenly, Coulter's eyes fluttered open. He stared at her. Confusion etched across his face. He blinked several times and attempted to speak but only mumbled intangible words.

"It's okay, Colt. I'm here."

Marena stroked her hand down the side of his face.

"We're still in the car. You just had a seizure, but you'll be fine. Just relax, Colt. You'll be less disoriented shortly, I promise."

Coulter's breathing evened out before she had finished her sentence, and he stilled. He fell asleep minutes later.

Marena shut the door and returned to her side of the car. Before getting in, she leaned her back against the side. Her

hand shook when she raised it to her mouth to stifle the crying. She couldn't lose it now. Not when his symptoms were so unpredictable.

"Okay," she said aloud. With a deep breath, Marena spun around and got in. Coulter was resting comfortably, so she drove off.

Thirty minutes later, Marena veered off the main road and down a long graveled path. It was pitch-black save for a lone light post. After she turned the car off, Marena turned sideways in her seat.

"Colt, are you awake?" She tapped his shoulder.

"Mmm-hmm," he responded groggily, trying to sit up.

"No, wait. Let me help you."

Before she reached him, Coulter had the door open and was getting out. Luckily, when his legs buckled, she was right there to help. Stooping, Marena came up under him so his arm draped around her shoulder. She braced herself against the added weight.

"This sucks," Coulter said with difficulty.

"You had a seizure. You have to give your body time to rebound. You're not in the field, you know—let me help you."

He nodded.

It was a slow procession to the house. Marena had to take several breaks to rest. Coulter was all muscle and extremely heavy. The darkness swirled around them like a heavy canopy threatening to fall. The one perimeter light did little to keep Marena's nerves from being on edge. Was someone out there watching them? Ready to strike? *Of course not*, she scolded. Nobody knew where they were. They were completely safe. *That's what you thought at your house, and look how that turned out.*

There was also the matter of each ominous, unidentifi-

able sound floating through the air as they walked. Around this time, she also pondered her brilliant idea to cut the headlights off on the car.

Chapter 12

When they finally made it to the house, Marena sighed with relief.

"I'm better now. I got this," Coulter spoke up.

Marena almost jumped out of her skin at hearing his voice.

"Let me help you. We're already dealing with a biotoxin. The last thing we need is you injuring yourself by stumbling around in the dark and falling."

Coulter placed one hand on the rail. "I'll go first. You can watch my back."

Marena shook her head. "Stubborn man. If you feel dizzy—"

He lowered his other arm from her shoulder. "I'll let you know."

Marena hung back two steps to track Coulter's progress. Not once did he sway, but when she reached the top and stood next to him, she could hear his labored breathing.

"That was disgraceful," he gasped out.

"Are you kidding me? You've been poisoned and shot in the arm, and you suffered a seizure forty-five minutes ago. You're complaining about how well you climbed a flight of stairs?"

"You have no idea what this is like," he complained. "I'm always in control."

"If I weren't so worried about another episode, I would hit you myself," she snapped. "Now, if you can stay here without trying to kick in the door like the awesome soldier that you are, I've got to find the hide-a-key."

Marena stomped down the stairs. Five steps down, she stopped. Then, instantly regretting the outburst, she backtracked up the stairs, went straight into Coulter's arms, and hugged him tightly.

"I'm sorry. You're right. I don't know what this is like for you."

She gazed up, trying to see his face in the dim light. "But I know that I'm going to do whatever it takes to save your life, but you have to help me. You can't let your frustrations push you to do things that may cause you harm or set you back."

Coulter's chin rested on the top of Marena's head. "I'll try, Rena, but I can't make promises."

"I know." Marena smiled into the darkness. "I know."

"Where are we anyway?"

"My friend Burt's family retreat."

Marena walked cautiously to the car and flipped on the headlights. Locating the rock hiding the spare key was easy now that the area was illuminated. Taking a few of their bags with her, Marena returned to unlock the door. Coulter flipped the light switch as they entered.

The three-bedroom and two-bathroom bungalow was on the Intracoastal Waterway in Morehead City, North Carolina. Marena had been there only once, but it had left quite an impression on her. The sunrises and sunsets on Bogue Sound were incomparable. The house had a shaded back deck that was a short walk to the boat dock. The interior was elegant in its simplicity. Dove-gray walls, bright white cabinets, and stainless-steel appliances made the kitchen warm and welcoming. Three ample bedrooms fed off the

main hallway. Each had a coastal theme tying in the living and dining area's blue, green, and white decor.

"This is a very quaint home."

"Yes, it is. Since Burt's wife, Crystal, died, it hasn't been used much. It's a shame that it's sitting empty. This house screams *family fun*."

"True," he replied, looking around.

"I'll go back to get the rest after I get you settled," she told him while walking around, turning the lights on as she went.

"I'll help you."

"No, you won't. You'll be going straight to bed, Colonel. Doctor's orders."

She guided him down a short hallway to the first bedroom. "Here we are." Marena sat his rucksack on the floor, followed by her bag. "You can't see it, but there's a small deck out there. Now have a seat. I need to dress that arm."

Surprisingly, Coulter didn't argue. Instead, sinking to the bed, he unbuttoned his shirt. Marena helped him remove it before going to wash her hands. When she returned, she donned a pair of rubber gloves and gently prodded his arm.

"It's just a scratch."

"True," she agreed. "It just grazed your arm, but I still have to clean it."

Retrieving supplies, she applied antiseptic before placing a thick pad on the wound. Next, she wrapped gauze around Coulter's arm before securing it with medical tape.

"There. All done."

"Thanks, doc."

"I'll be back to check on you shortly."

When Marena moved past him, Coulter raised his arm to stop her and pull her back to his side. "Wait." When he stood up, he towered over her. His mouth stretched into a thin line.

She looked bewildered. "What's wrong?"

Coulter placed a finger under her chin and tilted the other side of her face toward him. "What happened?"

"Huh?"

His hand caressed her cheek. She flinched away from his touch.

"There's a bruise on your face." His expression turned murderous. "Did one of the men that broke in hit you?"

"No," Marena told him evenly. "It's nothing. I'm fine."

"You're not fine."

"I am. It's no big deal." Marena would have moved past, but he was like a brick wall.

"Start talking."

She let out a sigh. "You did it."

Coulter's hand dropped to his side. "Say what?"

She watched several emotions play across his face. She reached out for him, but he stepped back.

"I hit you?"

"It's okay, Colt."

He rubbed a hand over his face. "It's definitely not okay."

"You were having convulsions. This wasn't your fault. I was trying to tighten your seat belt and wasn't paying attention. Don't worry, I'm fine, really," she said brightly.

Coulter closed his eyes for a moment. "Marena, I'm sorry," he said hoarsely before eyeing her cheek. This time his touch was light. "It's turning reddish-purple. We need to get ice on it to keep the swelling down."

"I will, but I want you to rest. I'll take care of it."

He remained in his spot.

She touched his arm. "I promise," she said in a soothing voice.

Marena knew him well enough to know that he struggled with his emotions. In truth, she was having a difficult time as well. For so many years, she had done what she could to remain emotionally neutral where Coulter was concerned. Occasionally, she'd slip up, but all in all, she had had a grasp

on her feelings. But with him here in person and so much at stake, Marena felt the caution tape around her heart unraveling by the hour. It was almost as scary as the thought of not finding an antidote.

She turned her attention back to Coulter, who sat heavily on the bed. His elbows were resting on his thighs.

"Do you have any leads on where to start?"

Marena was used to Coulter's abrupt conversation shifts when he was troubled. She sat next to him. "With Cutty?"

He nodded.

"I have a few ideas about Frank's location. I'll try the numbers that I have. We'll find him, and then he'll tell us what we need to know to save you. If he doesn't help us, I swear I'll kill him."

Despite himself, Coulter smiled. "Now you're just trying to make me feel better."

"Maybe," she teased.

"Finding Cutty is a shot in the dark, Rena. Like trying to find a needle in a haystack."

"You found me, didn't you?"

A strange expression crossed his face.

"True, but Cutty doesn't want to be found."

She arched an eyebrow. "And I did?"

He gave her a boyish grin. "Touché."

"I know it's a calculated risk, but it's one we have to take. I can't lose you, Coulter—I can't."

He took her hand and entwined their fingers. He stared at their joined hands.

"Why? When I've brought you nothing but pain since we met?"

"That's not true. You made me perfectly happy. I had no regrets that we got together—"

"Until I left," he supplied.

"Yes, until you left." *And broke my heart into a thousand pieces.* "It seems *forever* just wasn't meant to be."

"Rena—"

She shook her head. Releasing his hand, she rose. Her guard was firmly back in place. "Get some sleep, Coulter. I'll check on you soon."

"Doctor's orders?"

"Yes." She smiled, but it didn't reach anywhere near her eyes.

After Marena left, Coulter showered as best as possible and got into bed. He crossed his arms behind his head and stared at the ceiling. The move caused his injured arm to hurt, but he ignored it. *If you survive this mess, what will you do about her?* he asked himself. It bothered him that there was still wariness and a wall separating them. Not that he could blame her. Three years was a long time. Though it was awkward at times, there was still familiarity, too. He had forgotten what it felt like to be with Marena. It was easy to converse with her, share meals, smile and laugh with her over things. Though he'd damaged her trust, that connection was still there underneath the surface, like a beacon of light calling out, imploring him to fix what he'd destroyed. *What you purposefully threw away*, his inner voice added.

He balled up a fist and slammed it on the bed, sucking in a breath because he'd used his injured arm. This was about the time when he'd work out or shoot something up at the practice range to release pent-up tension. Now, he was on a medical roller coaster as his symptoms alternated between receding and coming on with a vengeance.

Coulter hated being helpless. He had prepared for many scenarios in his life and career that dealt with overcoming adversities of every kind. But this was different. There was no roadmap to tell him how to navigate this uncharted territory. That was the most frustrating part of all. He couldn't gauge when he'd feel better or if even the littlest thing

knocked him on his butt. He was a man of action, but lately, Marena had been doing all the heavy lifting, which bothered him more than he could verbalize.

Coulter's cell phone vibrated on the nightstand. Retrieving it, he scanned the screen.

Are you still alive?

You're texting me, aren't you?

Good point, mate. How's it going?

Don't ask.

Right. I do have a spot of good news.

I'm listening.

Several of those aliases you gave me panned out. There's been some movement on a few of the checking accounts you provided, but nothing major. A few in your team, though in hiding, have resurfaced.

Coulter grinned in relief.

Which names were used?

Katmandu, White Dwarf, Gold Digger, and Farmerville.

That's it?

That's it for now, Colt.

He noted that Neil wasn't among the men that had checked in.

Thanks, Liam. Keep me posted.

Are you going to send messages back?

Coulter was thoughtful for a moment.

No, I'm not. Better if I stay off the grid for now.

Understood. I can assist with logistics when you're ready to roll, mate.

Thanks, man. I owe you my life.

Nonsense, you've given me mine ten times over, Colt. Tell you what. You live, and we'll call it even, eh?

Working on it.

Coulter placed his phone on the nightstand. His friends, Tanner and West, had made it, and so had two other team members. He was relieved to hear that they were still alive but worried about the rest that hadn't checked in.

His team always had contingency plans and protocols in place if an op was compromised. They would have access to credentials, money, and travel to get them off the grid and in safe havens worldwide. But for now, he would have to trust that if they were alive, his men were at least safe.

He stared at the ceiling. "Where are you, Neil?"

Eventually, Coulter's eyes drifted shut, and he fell into a troubled sleep.

Chapter 13

Derek Falconi walked into his office and slammed the door shut, causing the picture of a cheetah chasing a gazelle to go crooked on the linen-colored wall. Then, striding across the floor, he yanked the brown leather high-backed chair out from under his executive desk and sat down. Leaning almost as far back as the chair went, Falconi plopped his feet on the desk.

"What do you mean they got away?" he yelled into his cell phone.

"I'm sorry, sir, but we missed the opportunity to bring them in."

His chair snapped back upright with a loud thud reverberating off the walls like a gunshot. "How many chances are you going to give one dead man to get away? Did you sweep the house? Please tell me you at least got that right."

"Yes, sir. We left no traces behind."

"Any casualties?"

"Our men were wounded, but no fatalities."

"Then McKendrick was generous," he concluded. "I want a full report on my desk first thing in the morning. And let me be clear—I don't want anything leading back to us, do you understand? As far as anyone knows, McKendrick has lots of enemies that want to see him dead."

"Understood, Mr. Falconi."

Derek ended the call and tossed the phone onto the desk. Leaving Coulter alive didn't fit into his plan. He wanted a clear shot at taking over at Ghost Town, and overhearing Cole Everett tell Brinkley that he was leaving his company and its assets to his grandson was a wake-up call. Drastic measures were needed to secure his position, and now was the time to strike. Thanks to Cole's vast government and private-sector contracting connections, Ghost Town was a multimillion-dollar company. Its outlook was golden, but Cole was getting old. He'd probably be retiring soon, and any thoughts of him handing the reigns over to Brinkley just went up in smoke. Coulter stood to inherit everything, which meant Falconi and Brinkley would be out on their ears—and maybe even in prison, if Coulter had his way.

Falconi knew they were scraping the tip of the iceberg on their side business deals. And now, with Silent Night in play, there was no limit to their earning potential.

Not if you play your cards right.

"Sorry, Mr. Everett, but you just became expendable." Getting up, he snatched his briefcase and cell phone before dousing the lights on his way out. During the elevator ride to the parking garage, Derek thought about Brinkley. His mentor was ambitious, but he was getting old, not to mention cocky and making too many mistakes.

His arrogance was becoming a liability, but that's what made Brinkley the perfect fall guy. The thought made Derek smirk.

The elevator lurched violently. Thrown against the back wall, Derek rushed to the control panel and hit a few additional floors. They lit, but there was still no movement. He picked up the emergency telephone and tried dialing the fire department.

"Great, the line is dead," he muttered.

The elevator shook again, but this time dropped at a high rate of speed.

Derek was pushed against the wall. He banged his hand against the stop button several times, but the speed only increased.

"Hey," he yelled before slamming his eyes shut. *This can't be happening.*

The elevator stopped suddenly. The force threw him to the floor. Spread-eagle on the carpet, he was still trying to get his bearings when the door chimed and slowly opened.

Glancing up, he saw two men in suits watching him.

"Mr. Falconi?"

"Yes," he panted, wiping the sweat beading on his forehead with the back of his hand. "You don't know how glad I am to see you. I thought I was a goner."

"Come with us," one of them said.

Pulling himself off the floor, Derek swatted at the dust on his pants.

"I'm doing no such thing. I could've died just now. So, unless you work with the elevator company and you're here to apologize for this near-fatal mishap, we got nothing to say."

One man retrieved a gun and pointed it at Derek. The red laser dot hovering on his chest was a sharp contrast to his navy blue shirt.

"That's not exactly true," his counterpart replied. He grabbed Derek by the arm, and none too gently forced him out of the elevator and down to the parking garage.

"I don't know what this is about, but whatever it is, I'm not about to go along with it."

The men remained silent as they walked toward a black limousine. Then, opening the door, one man stepped aside while the other shoved Derek inside.

"I'm getting tired of being pushed around," he snapped as the man shut the door. He was alone except for a laptop. The screen showed live video feed of an empty chair. After a few moments, a man he recognized sat down in it.

"Hello, Mr. Falconi."

Javier was staring at him from the screen.

"Mr. Palacios? What's going on?" he demanded.

"How did you enjoy the elevator ride? Thrilling, wasn't it?"

"It certainly wasn't. What is the meaning of all this?"

"I'd have thought it was apparent by now. Wherever I choose, I can get to whomever I want—wouldn't you say, Mr. Falconi?"

Derek's face turned a mottled red, but he merely said, "Yes, I'd say so."

"Good. Because I want Silent Night, and you're going to get it for me—unless you need additional demonstrations of my resolve to get what I want?"

"That's not necessary, Mr. Palacios," Derek said calmly. "You'll find that my loyalties are completely transferrable."

"I look like I have a cat sitting on top of my head."

She let the cold water run for a few seconds before pooling the chilled liquid into her cupped hands. After splashing her face, Marena stared at her reflection in the square-shaped mirror. Her hair was flying, bags were under her eyes, and the ugly purple bruise Coulter mentioned was still a prominent feature on her face.

"Glamorous," she chuckled before going to check on Coulter. When she peeked in and found him asleep, she tiptoed over and placed her hand on his forehead. Happy to find his skin cool to the touch, Marena retraced her steps and returned across the hall to her bedroom.

There were books and papers scattered across the thin blanket. Marena had been studying for hours, and the lack of sleep was starting to take its toll. She picked up the mug of cold tea and took a few sips, hoping the caffeine would wake her up. It didn't. After the third time of waking up with one letter typed across the screen in several neat rows,

Marena acknowledged she should quit and rest awhile, but having made no progress, she forged ahead.

If they couldn't find Dr. Cutty, she would need a backup plan. There had to be a way to enhance the properties of A.S.P.R. to counter the effects of Silent Night. It had to work. A few frustrating minutes later, Marena set her laptop aside.

"This is getting me nowhere fast." Annoyed, she went to get the new cell phone from her purse.

If she called Frank and he didn't recognize the number, he wouldn't answer. Still, Coulter's words of caution that time was running out replayed in her head. Decision made, Marena called. When the number was not in service, she dialed an alternate. It rang several times before the line connected.

"Hello?" a man said in a wary tone.

"Dr. Cutty?"

"Who is this?"

"Frank, it's me. Marena."

There was a pause. "Marena? My gosh, how are you? It's been years since we've spoken. How have you been? Honestly, I'm surprised to hear from you."

"I know. I'm sorry to call you at this hour, but it's a matter of urgency, Frank. Someone's life depends on it, and if you don't help me—he'll die."

After Marena had brought him up to speed on their predicament, Dr. Cutty said, "Marena, what you're asking for is difficult."

"You helped create Silent Night, didn't you?"

"Yes, but—"

"Then I'm not asking the impossible, Frank. *Difficult* just isn't acceptable."

"Who's sick? Is it your father?"

"No."

"Your brother?"

"No, it's not Lucas, either—it's Coulter."

"Seriously?"

Marena's voice shook when she answered. "Yes. He was injected, and we don't know why. He doesn't have much time, Frank."

"I'm sorry to hear about Coulter, but—"

"I can't let him die—do you hear me? I won't."

"I know what Coulter means to you, Marena, but I can't help you with this. I began work on an antidote, but—"

"What do you mean *but*?"

"I never finished it, and I'm not at liberty to work at my lab anymore." He lowered his voice. "I'm being watched very closely right now, Marena."

"By whom? Frank, what's going on?"

"Let's say that making an antidote to the biochemical weapon you created that was recently stolen and sold to the highest bidder isn't exactly something Beecham wants getting out," he explained in a rush. "Can you imagine the blowback if it's known that they designed this thing in the first place? This would break so many international laws."

"Then why do it?"

"Because regardless of whether it should've been created, there's a market for it. So now there's an extremely lethal bioweapon on the loose with no known counteragent. Doesn't this read like something out of a movie to you? And not one where everyone lives to the end."

"You had a hand in creating this thing, Frank. I don't care a fig about the politics involved. This is a life we're talking about."

"Yes, but it could be my life, too," he countered.

Marena struggled to keep calm. She refused to take no for an answer. "I understand the stakes for you, but I can't do this without you."

"I know," he said after a few moments of silence. "Heaven help me, but I'll do what I can to assist you, Marena."

She closed her eyes in relief. "Thank you."

"The antidote you need to create is DNA specific. You'll need the infected patient's blood—in this instance, Coulter's."

"Okay. What can you tell me about Silent Night itself?"

"It's one of a kind," Frank said, almost proudly. "It reacts based on the person's biology, so it affects everyone differently. Some symptoms will cause violent reactions in the host. Other times not so much. What is Coulter experiencing?"

"Fever, nausea, vomiting, flu-like symptoms, and pain. His energy level has been compromised, too."

"How many days does he have left?"

"Three."

"Marena—"

"I get it. We don't have much time."

"You'll need a biocontainment lab."

"Okay."

"With a *minimum* of biosafety level three," he warned, "just in case."

"Gotcha. I just have to locate one we can use."

"Let me see what I can find."

"I'll make some calls, too."

"There's one thing you'll need that you can't get—emylanoroc."

"What?" Marena placed her head in her hands. "You've got to be kidding me. Frank, that chemical's unstable."

"I know, but not when it's paired with monosodium hexahydrate. It acts as a stabilizing agent."

"But I thought that—"

"You have to trust me, Marena. It'll work. We've tested it. We just haven't used it on anyone in the field yet. But, as I said, all of the scenarios involving the use of Silent Night were meant to be—permanent."

"Frank, can you get it?"

"Yes, I should be able to, but I have to go through back

channels. Do you still have access to the cloud storage we used?"

"Yes."

"I'll download the formula there with the list of what you'll need. If I can get emylanoroc, I'll need at least twenty-four hours."

"Twenty-four hours? Frank—"

"It's the best I can do, Marena. They don't just have the stuff lying around, you know. As you say, if Colt has days left, we can't afford to wait. But, Marena, you're not leaving any margin of error."

"I can't understand how you could help create this thing."

"I know," he said. His voice was heavy with regret. "You may not believe me, but I realized that we shouldn't have tampered with nature, but it was too late by then. I wanted to make my mark in our field, you know? The lure of notoriety was intoxicating, Marena, but I realized too late that Silent Night was a horrible way to be remembered."

"Because of that, I started working on the antidote, but the suits found out, and I was kicked off the project and reassigned. My biggest regret in life is my part in developing this killing machine." His voice shook.

"Frank—"

"Check there in an hour," he said, effectively cutting her off. "You'll have everything you need."

Tears came to Marena's eyes. "I can't thank you enough."

"Save his life. That'll be enough."

Chapter 14

"I'm doing everything within my power to do so," Marena replied. "Please be careful, Frank."

"Always am."

The moment Marena hung up, she dialed another number on her cell phone.

"This is Dr. Dash," she said when the line connected. "Yes, I know what time it is. This is an emergency. I need a favor. Right now."

It was almost dawn when Coulter awoke to go to the bathroom. He took his toiletry bag and a change of clothes with him. Later, after showering, he dressed in jeans and a plain gray T-shirt. He peeked into Marena's bedroom on the way back and found her lying sideways across her bed with her cell phone headset still attached to her ear. Sitting next to her, Coulter watched her for a few moments.

The faint sunlight shining through the window cascaded over hair that slightly blocked her face from view. Gently, Coulter slid it behind her ear before tracing the swollen area on her face. Having caused the angry bruise marring her otherwise flawless cheek made him sick to his stomach. The yellowish-purple mark was a stark contrast to her bronzed skin tone.

Before thinking better of it, he leaned down and kissed her cheek. She didn't stir.

He watched the intermittent bright blue light from her Bluetooth headset. He removed the small device from around Marena's head and retrieved the cell phone lying next to her. When he saw which phone it was, Coulter stuffed it in his pocket. His eye caught a steno notepad partially under her on the bed. He retrieved it with a slow and steady tug, stood and grabbed a chenille throw from a nearby chair. He placed it on top of her and left with the notebook in tow.

While on his way into the kitchen, Coulter doubled over in pain. His gut felt like it was on fire. Holding on to the wall, he struggled to get a handle on his breathing to ride out the pain. In minutes, the intense feeling subsided, only to return seconds later.

"You're going out of your way to kill me, aren't you?" he panted. Taking a deep breath, he continued his pain-management techniques until the wave subsided. Then, cautiously, he resumed walking.

Coulter poured a glass of water and downed it. Splashing more cold water on his face, he ran his hands over his stubbled jaw and the back of his neck before dabbing his face with a paper towel. With a yank on the refrigerator handle, Coulter peered inside, taking inventory of the food. Settling on eggs, bacon, and fresh fruit, he commenced making breakfast.

When fifteen minutes had elapsed, and the pain had not returned, he allowed himself to relax. He was pouring himself a cup of coffee when Marena entered.

"Smells heavenly."

She still wore baggy pajama pants and T-shirts to bed. Coulter made himself focus on the conversation instead of how beautiful she looked first thing in the morning.

"Smell isn't taste," he joked.

Pouring the steaming liquid into a mug, he went to hand it to her. She met him in the middle.

"Black, just like you like it."

"Actually, I like cream in my coffee now. Burt had me try it one time, and it sorta stuck. My favorites are the French vanilla or hazelnut creamers."

Coulter watched her go back to the refrigerator to retrieve a small container of creamer. Marena took a spoon out of the drawer and mixed the white liquid into her cup. He watched, fascinated, as an expression of unadulterated bliss suffused her face. It took his breath away and made him wish that he was the cause of that high-wattage smile instead of a source of heartache.

"Thank you."

He snapped out of the daydream and gave her a boyish grin. "Hope you're hungry. I made breakfast."

"You didn't have to do that. I should've been making you breakfast."

Marena went to sit down. Coulter followed.

"From the looks of it, I'd say you only recently went to sleep."

"I've had a few hours," she hedged.

Coulter raised an eyebrow.

"Well, at least three," she defended.

She saw her notepad on the table next to him. "I see you've had plenty of reading material to keep you occupied."

"I hope you don't mind my taking it. I was curious what had you up so late."

Her eyes lit up. She leaned forward in her seat, barely able to contain her excitement. "Coulter, I reached Frank."

He stopped chewing. "You spoke to Cutty? How is he? *Where* is he?"

"He wouldn't say, but he gave me the formula to Silent Night and his notes on the antidote he'd started." She

grabbed his hand and squeezed it. "We have almost everything we need for me to get started."

Coulter didn't allow himself to become overly excited. "Really?"

"Yes," Marena said, helping herself to the food on the table. She dug into it with gusto. "Frank sent the formula to one of the electronic drop boxes we shared. I downloaded everything last night. All the ingredients I'll need, the list of chemicals, other agents, and all the measurements. He has saved me countless hours of stumbling around in the dark. We have a chance now, Coulter. But, unfortunately, there's one we can't get on our own, so Frank will get it."

Coulter digested this information. "You don't find that strange?"

"Why would I?"

"He's been MIA for who knows how long, hasn't even reported back to work yet, and suddenly, he's going to meet us with a chemical that his company might arrest him for if they found out—or worse."

She eyed him. "How'd you know he hasn't been to work?"

"I have resources, too, you know."

She shrugged. "No, I don't find it strange. He helped cause this nightmare we're in. So why not help us fix it? Bottom line is, I can't do it without him, Colt, and there isn't enough time to do this piecemeal."

"It seems too convenient."

Marena's smile faded. "Colt, Frank has been sticking his neck on the line to save yours, and you're questioning his motives?"

"I'm just curious why he's helping when, as you say, it's risky."

"He doesn't want to see you die any more than I do. So, can we please just focus? We have a lot to do in a ridiculously short amount of time."

He finally capitulated, though it still made him uneasy. He leaned back in his chair. "So what's the next move?"

"We need a research laboratory with a containment lab at biosafety level three."

"Oh, that'll be easy," he quipped.

Marena gave him a look. "We're working on it."

"Really? How?"

"I contacted another colleague of mine. We've kept in touch. He's out of the country for the next few weeks, but said I could use the space whenever I needed it. I'm waiting to hear back to confirm."

"He?"

"Yes, he. I made a few calls last night," she said, ignoring the question and the stare that came along with it. "I'll have to make a few pickups today, but the rest I can get delivered to the lab. Unfortunately, I'm missing the emylanoroc, which is what Frank will be delivering, and diprenzemine, which he's going to see if he can track down."

"I'm not even going to pretend I know what either of those is or does."

"The short version is, I need them for the serum. Without those two chemicals, we don't have an antidote."

"You don't have any female colleagues?"

Marena arched an eyebrow. "What can I say, Coulter, another scientist friend of mine happens to be male," she said with exasperation. "What's the big deal?"

He returned his attention to the plate of half-eaten food. "Nothing."

"Good. Now, have you seen my cell phone? I need to get a number and—"

"You mean the cell phone that hostiles could have used to track our location?" he said after digging in his pocket to retrieve it. "The one that you used to make an unauthorized call?"

"Unauthorized?" she chuckled. "Isn't that a bit extreme?"

"Everything about our current situation is a bit extreme, Rena, and this isn't helping."

"Coulter, I had to use it. How else was I supposed to get in touch with Frank?"

"By using the phone we just purchased."

"I couldn't risk him not answering because he didn't recognize the number. Don't you get that you'll die without his help?"

"I still might," he countered. "Nothing is a guarantee. Now there could be enemies zeroing in on our location, which puts you in danger, Rena."

"It was a calculated risk," she countered. "Look, I know it's not ideal, but we have to deal with this stuff as it comes and pray we get the results we need."

"As in me surviving the next three days without dying?"

"Yeah, that's the plan."

Their eyes connected across the table. They both allowed themselves a moment of levity while they ate.

About to take another bite of food, Coulter stopped and set his fork down. He closed his eyes.

"What's wrong?"

"My stomach has been acting up."

She leaned forward. "Are you nauseous? Are you experiencing any abdominal pain right now?"

Coulter bolted out of his seat and to the sink. He made it just in time before he threw up the contents of his stomach. Marena was right by his side.

"Is this the first time this has happened?"

"No. There was intense pain earlier, but it went away."

"Why didn't you tell me?"

"I just did."

Marena hurled a barrage of questions at him while he rinsed his mouth out with water. Then, clutching the notebook, she found a pen in a drawer and furiously scribbled notes. It took her a minute because fear was causing her

hand to shake. She knew that his condition would deteriorate as they got closer to the time limit on the toxin, but it was happening too fast for Marena. She thought she was fine and could use her training to focus and do the job she needed to do, but it was a struggle. This wasn't anything like working on A.S.P.R. At Beecham, she had worked with military personnel, too, but this was Coulter. Their connection was personal. Intimate. It was hard to remain objective and keep her emotions at bay. The violent reactions and the rapid decline of his condition scared her to death.

Coulter watched various emotions play out across Marena's face. She was so easy to read. It was one of the things that he loved most about her, but sometimes her transparency was a curse instead of a blessing. Like right now. Her expression relayed worry, fear, and another emotion that caused hope to flutter. Before he could think better of it, he laced his fingers through hers. He almost sighed with relief when Marena didn't pull away.

"I'm sorry I didn't mention it when you came in," he apologized.

She nodded. "I have to know everything, Coulter. I need to know about any new problem that crops up, if you feel differently, if there's more pain, less pain, anything at all."

He rubbed the palm of her hand. "Roger that."

The moment slipped away faster than a person running across the ice in smooth-bottomed shoes when she started asking him about bodily functions. Coulter's gaze flew to the ceiling.

When he remained silent, Marena looked up exasperated. "Coulter."

"Okay, yes, there is a discoloration in my urine that I just noticed this morning."

She stood up and held out her hand. "Let's go."

Coulter got up and took it. "Where?"

"I need to take your vitals, give you something that will hopefully keep nausea at bay while helping you with the pain. Then, I need you to rest while I'm out stocking up. When I get back, I'll need to draw a few vials of blood."

"So, where is this man you're meeting?"

Marena pushed him toward the bedroom. "*She* is back in Beaufort, near the hospital."

Suddenly, he turned around, causing Marena to stop short. She glanced up at him in alarm.

"Whoa. What's wrong?"

Marena, I love you. My life is never the same when we're apart. I long to touch you, talk with you, share your thoughts, your food. I miss everything about you, and I want you back. In my arms and in my bed. Forever. Instead, Coulter said, "I don't want you going without me. It could be dangerous."

Internally, he called himself a coward for not leveling with her that he was struggling with everything. Since he'd been back in Marena's life, he hadn't had an opportunity to be frank with her about how much this illness was robbing him. How severe his body was reacting as the clock wound down. How being fearless and acting like Silent Night wasn't affecting him was a smokescreen. In truth, he was scared about the uncertainty he was facing. The pain was much worse than he let on, and he knew he should be truthful, but seeing her upset and fearful was eating him up inside.

In his line of work, facing death was a daily occurrence, so dying didn't scare Coulter—living without Marena did.

Chapter 15

"Hey," she said, misinterpreting his look. "It won't be a problem, I promise."

He scowled. "That's not a promise you can make. We don't know what you're stepping into, Rena. We need to be careful and have a plan."

"I'll be fine. I'll get what I need and be right back. That's the plan. Plus, I'll have my gun with me. I know how to take care of myself, which you know firsthand."

He rubbed the side of his thumb along her jaw before backing her up against the wall. Marena's eyes widened in surprise at the sudden move.

"I know you are more than capable of taking care of yourself, but you'll do it much better if I'm there with you."

As hard as it was to concentrate when he was so close, Marena struggled against the familiarity. She and Coulter had always had chemistry. It was evident from the start and had only increased over time. Her mother would tease them by saying that she and Coulter were the north and south poles of a magnet. The attraction was that strong.

It was foolish to think that the years had dulled the spark between them. She assumed it had for Coulter, but she knew him too well. The rapid staccato his pulse was beating could be seen in one of the jugular veins in his neck

and was a telling sign that he, too, wasn't unaffected by their closeness.

"It's still here, isn't it?" he said more to himself than her. The bewilderment on his face echoed the awe in his voice. "Even after all the time, space, and silence between us."

"Coulter," Marena croaked out. She was trying not to focus on how his words made her knees weak. Clearing her throat, she tried again. "I don't want you getting worse. For once, please be sensible. This illness is volatile. There's no telling what will happen from one moment to the next. You have to rest up when you can."

He released his hold on her waist and retreated a few inches. "It's not negotiable, Rena. I'm going with you, or you don't go."

She blew a breath out in exasperation, but it also helped to clear her foggy brain and the butterflies swirling in her stomach.

Marena crossed her arms over her chest. "You're so stubborn."

"And you're not?"

After a few moments, the standoff was over.

"Okay," she capitulated. "But we're not leaving until I take your vitals and give you something for that upset stomach."

"Fair enough."

They returned to his bedroom, and Marena instructed him to lie down while she went to get what she needed. Carrying a vial of clear liquid when she returned, Marena rolled up his sleeve up and tied a rubber band around his arm before swabbing the area with alcohol.

Finding a vein, she inserted the vial into the plunger and pressed the lever until liquid shot out of the needle to ensure there weren't air bubbles.

"Okay, this will make you feel better," she informed him as she slid the needle into his skin.

Marena administered the medication. Once done, she covered the puncture wound with a small gauze pad and Band-Aid and lowered his arm to his side. "All done."

"Great," Coulter replied before lowering his sleeve. He went to sit up and swing his legs over the side of the bed. He made it halfway up but stopped.

Marena looked at him. "What's the matter?"

"I'm feeling—woozy," he replied in a slurred voice.

Coulter's gaze flew to Marena. She sat on the bed next to him and rubbed his shoulder. "It's fine. Just try and relax."

"Wh… Rena. What. Did. You. Do?"

"Close your eyes, Colt."

As if by the command of her voice, his eyelids lowered. He let out an even sigh. "You—tricked me."

Marena leaned in until her mouth was inches from his left ear. "Yes, I did. You rest now, and I'll be back before you wake up. Scout's honor."

Her lips gently brushed his cheek before lowering to graze his lips for a hesitant kiss.

"*Now* you kiss me?" Coulter accused before drifting into a drug-induced slumber.

Marena eased the sheet over him before sitting on the bed for a few minutes. While she watched him, she tried to get her bearings. It was hard not to feel like she'd been thrust onto a speeding train with no knowledge of its destination or clear path on how to jump off.

That's not exactly true, her conscience piped up. *If you don't save him, you know where this train ends.*

Marena observed Coulter in his sleep. He'd aged a bit, and there were lines around his eyes that hadn't been there before. But the sight of him still caused an electric current to ricochet through her body. That hadn't dulled over time. Nor had the residual pain from his breaking off their engagement.

Normally, the hurt would take precedence, but until

Coulter was out of danger, that well-used baggage that was her pain would have to wait.

Unable to help herself, Marena placed a finger on his cheek and followed the sharp line of his jaw. "You sure know how to make an entrance, Colonel McKendrick."

Coulter had come to her despite how he had arrived because he needed her help. A moment of panic overtook her thinking about the sheer enormity of his condition and the obstacles they were facing. *Am I even the right person for the job?*

Marena wondered what her mother would have said about her being thrust in the middle of this situation. "Mom would have said, 'It doesn't get easier—it's you that gets stronger.'"

Marena glanced down at Coulter a final time before she got up and left.

Joseph Brinkley was seated on the black Italian leather sofa going over a mission plan. The multicolored, hand-knotted Persian area rug in front of him was a bold palette of red, black, navy, and gold that echoed around the room in various paintings or decor items he'd picked up from his travels. He had just picked up his sparkling water glass and took a hefty sip when someone knocked on the door.

"Come in."

He looked up to see Falconi. He set the glass back on the end table next to the couch and motioned for Derek to sit. "You'd better have good news."

"I believe I do, sir. We've got a lead."

"Now you're talking. What is it?"

"Two scientists that worked on Silent Night. I've sent a team to surveil each one."

"Good. I don't want anything or anyone slipping through the cracks. Am I clear?"

"Of course. There's one more thing."

Annoyance crept into Brinkley's expression. "It better not be a problem."

"It's something you'll find interesting," Falconi replied before sliding a manila folder across the desk.

Brinkley leaned over to retrieve it. He sat back in his chair and flipped open the folder. After a few moments, he glanced up at Falconi. "Are we sure about this?"

"Yes, I confirmed it before bringing it to you."

Brinkley stroked the stubble layering his chiseled jaw. "Good work. This may pan out. I want you to handle this yourself, Derek, understand?" He glanced down at the papers again and back to his subordinate. "I don't care what it takes—you find her."

"Yes, sir," Falconi responded. "Are we still on schedule for the Silent Night auction?"

Brinkley didn't bother to look up. "Yes, why wouldn't we be?"

"We don't have the codes."

"Nobody needs to know that but us. Either we'll have found Coulter by the auction and gotten those codes, or we'll keep leaning on our operative at Beecham to provide new ones. Either way, our bases will be covered, so there's no sense rocking the boat now and causing a panic."

"I hope you're right, sir. Seems a risky move."

Brinkley shrugged. "What's life if you can't take some risks, Falconi?"

The intercom on Brinkley's desk phone clicked on.

"I'm sorry, sir, but Mr. Everett is here to see you."

"Take a message. I'm in a meeting."

Before Brinkley could reply, his partner and CEO, Cole Everett, walked into his office and shut the door behind him.

"Hey, Joe. Hope you don't mind me stopping by."

"Not at all, Cole. I was just in the middle of a meeting," he began.

Cole turned to Falconi and back to Brinkley. "This won't take long."

He sat down across from Brinkley and waited.

Brinkley flushed a bit before he turned to Falconi. "Thanks, Derek. Get started on that project for me, though. It's a high priority."

"Right away, sir," Falconi responded before glancing at Cole. "Good to see you, Mr. Everett."

When Cole didn't respond, Derek excused himself and left.

Coulter stretched his legs out in front of him. "You're a hard man to pin down, Joe."

"You know how it is," Brinkley laughed. "I just got back from meeting with a potential client."

"Really? Who?"

"An owner of a tech start-up. He's the newest millionaire out there and will be traveling out of the country for some important meetings. He wants added security. It's a pretty standard contract."

Cole nodded. "If it's standard, why are you involved? I'd think one of our other managers could handle things."

"Well, he asked for me by name. He's pretty skittish, so, you know, kid-glove treatment." Brinkley chuckled.

"Can you believe it's been thirty years already, Joe? It wasn't that long ago when we first started. You were the first employee I hired."

"And I've been your partner ever since." Brinkley smiled. "Through every type of storm known to man."

"And we've braved them all."

"Yes, we have. That speaks to our staying power," Cole pointed out.

"Either that or we're both adrenaline junkies that love a challenge." Brinkley chuckled.

"There's one lesson that I'll always remember—there is

nothing more important than family. There's no substitute, whether it's by blood or design."

Brinkley leaned forward. "That's been our mantra since day one, hasn't it?"

"It sure has," Cole replied and then stood up. "I've talked your ear off enough. I'll let you get back to it. Why don't you come to dinner sometime soon, and we'll get caught up? There are some things I'd like to discuss with you."

"Sure," Brinkley replied. "I'm sorry I've been hard to reach lately. I've just had so many deals going on. The business has been booming, Cole. Ghost Town has never been better."

"I've seen the financials, Joe. You've been doing a stellar job. But then, I never doubted your abilities. You've always had a sixth sense about business ventures that has paid off well."

"Thanks, buddy. I know that you appreciate me, but it's nice to hear the accolades occasionally, am I right?"

"Believe me, nobody knows what you've been doing at Ghost Town more than me."

Brinkley beamed under the praise. "We're in it to win it. Always have been."

"No truer words, my friend." Cole stood up. "It was good seeing you, Joe."

"You too, Cole."

A few minutes later, Falconi knocked and then came in. "Everything all clear?"

"Of course," Brinkley responded. "Why wouldn't it be?"

"It's not every day that Cole Everett darkens your doorstep. So what did he want, if you don't mind my asking?"

"He was on a fishing expedition." Brinkley smiled. "Nothing I can't handle."

"Does this change our plans?"

"No. We continue as scheduled. Silent Night will be sold to the highest bidder," Brinkley replied. "And that, my friend, means you and I will be in a whole new tax bracket."

Chapter 16

"All our hard work is going to pay off big-time, Derek. I'll be the CEO of a new company, and then it's goodbye Ghost Town—and Cole Everett. So, you'd better find Coulter because I don't want any surprises getting in my way."

After leaving Brinkley's office, Derek headed down the hallway to his own. He sat at his desk and made a call on his cell phone.

"Señor Palacios, please. Derek Falconi calling."

"Do you have good news?" Javier said without preamble.

Derek undid the top few buttons on his shirt. "Not exactly. We have a problem."

"We don't have a problem, Mr. Falconi, *you* do."

"Brinkley doesn't have the codes that activate Silent Night. It won't work without them."

"That's not exactly true, is it? Wasn't one of your associates injected with it just days ago?"

Derek didn't bother asking how he knew that.

"The details don't concern me. Either you make good on our agreement, Mr. Falconi, or I'll make good on mine."

Derek found himself on the receiving end of a dial tone. Hanging up the phone, he pondered Javier's not-so-veiled threat. Either get him Silent Night or Derek was dead.

How had this situation gotten so far out of control? One

minute, he was in the driver's seat. The next, he was getting run over by a bulldozer.

Derek knew for sure that if he wanted to stay alive, he needed to convince Brinkley and Palacios that he was on their side and working for them. It would take some strategic maneuvering, but he would come out on top in the end. If there was one thing he was, it was a survivor.

Six o'clock. Marena groaned after checking her watch. She started the truck and backed out of her parking space. She was still an hour away. That meant that Coulter would be awake when she returned.

"And probably as mad as a wet cat," she noted aloud.

The moment Marena shot him with a sedative, she knew the ramifications. Coulter had a hard head, but they'd need to do things her way if he wanted to stay alive. She would not apologize for doing what she thought was medically necessary to save his life. With that bolstering thought, Marena turned her attention back to the road.

An hour later, she eased her car down the dark path toward the house. It was no surprise that the second her truck's wheels stopped rolling, Coulter headed out the door and down the steps. Marena cut the engine off, slid the key out of the ignition, and dropped it into her purse. Then, taking a deep breath, she opened the door. "And here we go."

Coulter's speed was impressive. He was at her car door before she shut it.

"I see you're up," she said in a conversational tone.

"Earlier than you expected, I bet," he said calmly.

Too calmly. Marena knew that his *calm mad* was much, much worse than his *emotional mad*. She was in a lot of trouble.

"Not really," she countered. "How are you feeling?"

Coulter's jaw ticked rhythmically. "How do you think I'm feeling? I have a sedation hangover, thanks for asking."

She started to walk toward the house. "Any more vomiting?"

Coulter grabbed her arm and spun her around to face him. "You drugged me, Marena. Don't ever do that again."

So much for good intentions. Marena yanked her arm out of his grasp. Her ire skyrocketed to match his. "Don't do what, Colt? Keep you from setting yourself back because you're trying to be a hero?"

"I was trying to help you."

"I don't need your help," she shot back. "*You* need *mine.*"

Coulter froze in his spot.

Marena pinched the bridge of her nose. "I know you don't want to hear it, but, Coulter, I know what's better for you right now than you do, so you'll have to trust me."

Her elevated voice reverberated around them. The silence that followed was just as loud. They stood there glaring at each other. Her chest rose and fell in time to her rapid breathing. This time, Coulter was the first to move.

He threw his hands up in defeat. The sigh he let out caused some of Marena's hair to blow across her forehead. Coulter absentmindedly flicked the strands back into place.

"I guess it's my turn to apologize."

Marena shook her head. "No, I should. I spoke too sharply."

"No, you didn't. You were right, and I needed to hear it. I've spent my entire adult life serving my country and helping other people out of life-and-death situations. It's hard for me to sit back and let someone else call the shots. I'm sorry, Marena."

"Apology accepted. Colt, I don't want us fighting anymore—it won't help. We must be on the same page if there's any chance of pulling this off. You have to—"

"Trust you?"

Her eyes sought his. "Yes, you do."

Coulter nodded.

"We should go in," she said. "I have to get back online."

"You go ahead. I'll be in shortly."

Marena didn't argue. Instead, she grabbed some of her stuff and headed into the house. Before going in, she peeped over her shoulder. Coulter was walking toward the water's edge. She observed him for a few moments before going inside.

Edgy after their altercation, Marena dropped the supplies she'd purchased on the dining room table and headed straight for her room. Throwing her stuff on the black wicker rocker in the corner, Marena tried to relax. She did some stretches to remove the tightness across her shoulders.

Being in such a calming environment helped. To Marena, the room looked like a photo shoot for a home-decor magazine. The entire house could've been on the front cover, for that matter. There was no way Burt could've managed the home's interior design on his own. At times, he was so focused on his projects that he would forget to eat. Not for the first time, Marena wondered who had helped outfit his house after Crystal had died into the extremely cozy home it was now. She figured that maybe Delores had something to do with Burt's suddenly impeccable taste.

The large black sleigh bed with the white sheets and down comforter had a calming effect—it drew her like a giant stuffed animal. Marena's legs propelled her to the bed. She flopped onto it and sprawled out across the firm mattress. Lying on her back, Marena stared up at the soft blue ceiling. Her emotions were a jumble. Guilt had her regretting the harsh words she'd spoken to Coulter.

What would you do if you were in his shoes? Lying there, she pondered what she would do if she had only days to live unless a past lover saved her. Would she feel as out of control as she knew Coulter did? He was an elite soldier who was used to relying on a team and heavily on his capabilities. *Just like your dad and brother.* "I'm such

a dolt," she admonished herself. "I didn't consider how you'd feel, did I?"

Marena sat up. *Should I go to him?* she contemplated. *No.* Her instincts warned her to leave him alone. To give him some space to sort out what must be hell on earth for him. Decision made, Marena got off the bed and walked over to grab her laptop. She returned and stretched out on the bed, stuffing a few pillows behind her head to prop herself up. Opening her computer, she tried clearing her mind of everything except Silent Night.

Sonia and Alvin drove up the circular stamped-concrete driveway and stopped in front of the four-car garage.

It had taken them two hours to drive to Chesapeake, Virginia, from their home on the Eastern Shore in Maryland. Sonia used the time to prepare herself.

"Here we are," Alvin said as he cut the engine.

"Yep, here we are."

"Are you ready for this?"

"As I'll ever be," she replied, glancing up at the large custom-built home. Her hands twitched nervously.

Alvin leaned over and kissed his wife. He rubbed her shoulder reassuringly. "Sweetheart, it'll be okay."

"I'm seeing my father for the first time since Coulter was young. There's a gap between us the size of several football fields, and I—"

Her husband squeezed her hand. "Will take it one yard at a time."

She smiled. "Yes."

Getting out of the car, Alvin walked around to the passenger side and opened the door. He held out his hand. Sonia clasped it in a death grip and got out.

They walked up the eight steps to the mahogany wood front door. It was an arched double door with a hammered

wrought iron design. By the time they reached the threshold, one side had opened.

Cole was transfixed in his spot for a few moments, just staring at his daughter. His expression was almost desperate as he glanced over her as if committing her to memory. Sonia was immobile. Finally, Alvin cleared his throat.

"Thank you for inviting us over, Cole."

Cole snapped out of his trance and turned to his son-in-law. "My pleasure. Come on in."

He stepped aside to let them enter.

They followed him into a bright and spacious family room with floor-to-ceiling windows that allowed an uninterrupted view of the outdoor living space and lake.

"Can I get you all anything? I know that was a long drive from Maryland.

"No, we're fine," Sonia replied.

They sat down on the couch, and Cole jumped right in.

"I don't know where Coulter is yet, but I have an idea who does."

Sonia leaned forward. "Who?"

"Joe Brinkley. He's likely responsible for Coulter's disappearance."

"How can this be possible? Joe's your partner and a family friend that we've known for years."

"I know, but Coulter was investigating Joe and his sidekick, Derek Falconi, when he went missing."

"Why?"

"Because Joe's been dabbling in illegal activities. That's why I hired Coulter. I wanted proof that he was betraying me and his country."

Coulter's parents digested that information.

"Is he aware of your suspicions?" Alvin asked.

"No, not yet."

"Well, what are we waiting for? Dad, if he has any information that can lead us to Coulter, we need to get it."

Sonia batted at the tears sliding down her cheeks. "You can sort out his shady business dealings after he's home safe."

Alvin reached into his pocket and handed her a handkerchief. She thanked him and dabbed at her eyes.

"He's under surveillance, and my team is following the paper trail. But don't worry, Sonia. We'll find out what Joe knows about Coulter's whereabouts."

"What if he doesn't tell you?"

"That's not an option," Cole barked. "This is my fault. I'm responsible for Brinkley using Ghost Town for his self-centered agendas, for not keeping an eye on what was happening in my company, and putting my grandson's life in danger. I'm sorry. I swear to you that I will find him."

He reached out and took Sonia's hand and squeezed it. She looked down at their entwined hands as though she were looking at a foreign object. Then, finally, she returned the squeeze.

"I want to be there when you interrogate Brinkley."

"No," Alvin and Cole said simultaneously.

"That's not something you need to see," Cole added.

"Fine, but I want him to pay." She looked her father in the eye. "Painfully and repeatedly."

"Finally, things are looking up."

Marena moved the computer from her lap to the bed. For the first time in hours, she allowed herself the luxury of a smile. Granted, she had been up most of the night, but her perseverance had paid off. Thanks to a facility director colleague, Marena had secured a biosafety level three biocontainment lab in Sedona, Arizona. She glanced at her watch. It was eight o'clock in the morning. If they left for the airport immediately, she could set up and be well underway by nightfall. That galvanized her. Bolting off the bed, she started packing.

After finishing, she started in Coulter's room. Though

she hated to overtax him, she realized that having his help would speed the process along. Decision made, she set the bags by the front door and went to find him.

Coulter wasn't in the house, so Marena went outside. She spotted him down by the water's edge again.

Marena yelled his name and took off running. Coulter turned, and when he saw her barreling down on his location, he moved to intercept her.

Chapter 17

Coulter's long legs devoured the ground while his eyes darted around the perimeter searching for hostiles. When he reached Marena, his gun was drawn. She froze.

"What's wrong?" he said, jumping in front of her. He moved in a circle with Marena behind him as he scoped out the yard.

"Nothing," she quickly assured him. She placed her hands on his shoulders. "I'm sorry. I didn't mean to startle you. We've got a lab, Colt. It's in Sedona, completely remote, and has everything we need. We just need to finish packing up and call to request the jet."

Coulter was still on alert. "You're sure nothing's wrong?"

"Yes, positive." Marena's cheeks flushed red. "I was just excited by the news, that's all. You can stand down, Coulter—we're safe."

Though he harnessed his weapon, he still kept her behind him as they picked up the pace back to the house. With his assistance, Marena could load the truck in record time. Next, she did a final cleanup and walk-through of the house before locking up. Then, with the key tucked safely back in its hiding place, they toted the last of their gear back to the car.

"Do you want me to drive?" he asked.

"No, I'm good." Marena turned to him. "It's been so

long since I've driven anywhere. I didn't know how much I missed it. Besides, I want you to rest."

"I feel fine. I haven't had any symptoms in a while."

"Yes, but we have no idea what's next. So you shouldn't be behind a wheel when it happens."

He gave her a mock salute. "Fair enough, doc."

Marena waited until they were back out on the main road before she spoke again.

"What did you do, sleep out there?"

"Not exactly, but I figured I'd do us both a favor and give you some space. Besides, I needed to think. I haven't done much of that lately. Most of the time, I've been in reaction mode."

Marena glimpsed over at him. "And now?"

"I've come to grips with not calling the shots this go-round."

"That can't be easy for you."

"No, it's not."

"Coulter, I'm sorry about earlier. After you left, I realized that having to rely on someone else this heavily goes against your training."

"In the field, we aren't just responsible for ourselves. We must watch each other's backs, too. We have to operate as a unit, so the concept isn't exactly foreign to me."

"Still, it can't be easy when your life is on the line."

"I'm in danger all the time, Marena. But that wasn't it."

She gripped the steering wheel in frustration. "You mentioned giving me some space. It hadn't occurred to you that I've had three years of it already?"

The long sigh that reluctantly left his mouth floated around the truck's cabin, leaving the air drenched in tension. It was almost a full minute before he spoke again.

"I could always count on how good it felt to be with you. It was easy, you know—like breathing. I didn't have to think about it or censor myself. We just were. And now,

that's gone. And I'm left trying to figure out how to orbit around you again without hurting you more or causing painful memories to resurface. I know it was because of me that we're in this jacked-up predicament, Marena, but if you think that makes it any easier, you'd be wrong."

"Coulter—" Marena began but stopped. Finally, she said, "Thank you for that. Because I did think it was easier."

"We've got less than three days left, Rena." Coulter ran a hand over his face. His fingers grazed the stubble on his jaw. "I don't want us to spend the time being at odds with each other or trying to avoid land mines."

The analogy made her smirk. "Nor do I," she admitted and placed her hand on his face.

Marena's fingers moved lightly over his skin. When she slid them down the side of his neck, Coulter's right hand came up and stilled her fingers.

"Are you trying to take my vitals?"

Unable to help herself, Marena burst out laughing. She returned her hand to the steering wheel. "Not too subtle, huh?"

"About as much as a kid shaking gifts under the tree at Christmas."

They shared a chuckle at that. Eventually, both got quiet. Finally, the strain between them evaporated.

After getting everything loaded on the jet of her client, Alejandro "Dro" Reyes, Marena took a moment to close her eyes, exhale and relax. The flight to the Sedona airport would be four and a half hours, during which she planned on taking a much-needed nap.

"You should try and get some sleep," she called out to Coulter. "I'll wake you when we get there."

Her hand snaked out to rest on his left thigh protectively. His muscled leg felt as pliable as granite.

"Woo. There's no doubt that you still work out," she joked.

When she spared a glance, it was to find that Coulter was already sound asleep. Suddenly, her mind produced snapshots of their time together. Her stomach fluttered and a lump lodged in her throat at recalling some of the memories. His truthful declarations earlier had done crazy things to her equilibrium. *Stop it. You have to stay focused*, she warned. *Any misstep could prove fatal for Coulter.* "And my heart," Marena whispered aloud.

Her borrowed research lab turned out to be a large state-of-the-art facility in Cottonwood, Arizona. Thanks to Alejandro's team, a driver was waiting to take them to her new workspace. Sedona had always appealed to Marena. The red-rock buttes, steep canyon walls, and plentiful pine forests in the desert town enticed tourists worldwide, as did the lore behind it being the home to four of the earth's energy vortexes and spiritual enlightenment.

Marena left Coulter sleeping while she and the driver lugged in as much stuff as she could carry. She was startled to see Coulter closing the back door and toting the last of their supplies on the third trip back.

"Thanks," she told him. "I was trying not to wake you until it was done."

"I see that," he replied, following her into the building. "Wow, this place isn't what I expected. It looks more like someone's gigantic mansion in the mountains than a biocontainment laboratory."

"Looks can be deceiving," she agreed. "But it's got everything we need." She grabbed his hand. "There's a lab and workrooms, three bedrooms, a kitchen, and an exercise room. Outside, there's a pool and a greenhouse, too."

Coulter walked around, taking it all in. The space was bright and inviting, and it did its best to bring the outdoors inside. The back of the building was mostly glass to afford a vantage view of the mountains from each room. Everything

was neat and orderly. He watched Marena move around with the same delight that a child has in the candy aisle at the grocery store. Her enthusiasm was infectious. "It appears you have everything you need."

"And then some. The house operates on solar power. It's off the city grid and purely clean energy. I'm not sure if you remember that solar farm we passed on the way in, but that belongs to this place," she said with excitement as she read through the notebook in her hands. "There are motion sensors and high-tech security measures. I'm eager to get started," she gushed.

"It sounds like it's a well-designed, environment-friendly house."

"Oh, it is. Also, I've downloaded the formula Frank provided. Now, the only thing missing is the emylanoroc. Let's hope we can get it soon."

Coulter arched an eyebrow. "The what?"

"Let's just say it's the star in this cast of characters. I call it *emmy* for short."

He shook his head. "You are such a geek," he teased.

"You'd better count your blessings over that fact," Marena countered. "Granted, when I first discovered we'd need a biosafety lab, I was worried about calling too much attention to ourselves."

"Why?"

"Because if I started asking around for a biosafety level three lab, authorization would be required to reserve it. That might raise some questions as to what I was working on and for which organization. I didn't want to get attention from the wrong crowd."

"Brinkley." Coulter sneered. "I know he's out there searching for us."

"Well, good luck finding us here," she said confidently.

Just then, Marena's cell phone rang. She retrieved it from her purse.

She glanced nervously at Coulter. "It's my old one."

"Don't answer it."

She stared down at the phone. "I have to, she called over her shoulder. "It's Dad."

"Rena, someone could track our location."

"You know my father, Colt. If he doesn't get a hold of me, he'll be on the first plane to Beaufort. I have to answer."

"Fine, but you need to be off that call in thirty seconds, or I'm hanging up."

Marena nodded and hit the talk button. "Hi, Dad."

"Hey there, sweetheart. How are you?"

"Just fine, and you?"

Coulter pointed to his watch.

"Great. I haven't spoken to you in a while and wanted to see how you were."

"Dad, I called you last week."

"I know, but is calling your old man too much to ask?"

"Of course not," she replied.

"So, how's Beaufort?"

"Great." Marena grimaced at having to lie.

"So, what have you been you up to lately? I'm not disturbing you, am I?"

Coulter gave her a look.

"Actually, Dad, I'm on my way to the store. Some problem with inventory."

"At this hour?"

Marena could've kicked herself. She'd forgotten about the time. "Yeah, well, I want to get it straightened out before I open up tomorrow. I hate to cut this short, but you know how I hate driving and talking on the phone."

"Since when did you start back driving?"

Marena frowned. "I haven't been at it long. Just short distances. I thought it was time."

"Good for you, honey. Just call me later, okay?"

"Sure thing. I love you."

"Love you too, sweetheart."

She pressed the end button and placed the phone back in her bag.

"That was over a minute," Coulter accused.

"You were here and heard the whole thing. So you tell me what I was supposed to do—hang up on him? You know my father."

"Yeah, I do. And, if memory serves, the general's last words to me were, 'If you ever come within one klick of my daughter again, I'll blow your face off.'"

"You deserved it," she countered. "All the more reason not to give Dad any excuse to worry."

"Trust me. I'd just as soon give General Dash as wide a berth as possible. Besides, I can't begin to imagine what he's going to say if he finds out you're trying to save my life instead of ending it."

"Don't be silly," Marena said, suddenly serious. "My father never wanted to harm you, and he certainly wouldn't want to see you die."

Coulter closed the distance between them. He took her hand in his and held it to his chest. "I wouldn't be too sure of that. I've caused his only daughter a great deal of heartache—and I'm still doing it."

She slipped her hand out and touched his jaw. "Don't say that."

"It's true, isn't it?"

"The only heartache I'm feeling is at you talking like your life doesn't mean anything when you know it does—especially to me."

"Why? Marena, I left you. And the only reason I came back is that someone I don't know and can't get to is trying to kill me. That's about as selfish a motive as I can think,

yet you've placed your life on hold and put yourself in danger to help me." Unshed tears caused his eyes to sparkle like emeralds. "And that's eating me up inside, Rena. How can I ever repay you for the kindness that I don't deserve?"

Marena stared at him in absolute shock. "Do you honestly think I would've said no? That I would've turned you away and let you die?"

He couldn't look her in the eyes.

"Coulter, answer me."

"I wouldn't have blamed you if you had."

She leaned in and placed her hands on either side of his face. She didn't budge when he tried to step away.

"I would never, ever have done that—I couldn't. Regardless of what you did or what you said, if the situation was reversed, would you have let me die?"

"You know the answer to that."

Marena stared him in the eyes. "I need to hear you say it."

"You need to hear me say what? That I would give my life to save you until the end of time? No matter what happened between us? I would—without hesitation."

"As I would give my life trying to save you."

"That's just it. I wouldn't want you to because I don't deserve it."

"So you're saying that I'm a terrible judge of character?"

"What?" Coulter stared at her in confusion. "I never said that."

"You implied it when you said that you don't deserve me trying to save you. I will never agree with that statement. You deserve every chance to live, just like anyone else. And I'm going to see that you get it."

Another layer of wall between them crumbled as Coulter grabbed Marena and hugged her like the lifeline that she was.

"I'm scared, Rena. Not of dying, but of losing you."

"You will never lose me, Coulter," she vowed, crying right along and hugging him just as tight. "There will never be an outcome of this I will accept if it means your death. Never."

Chapter 18

"What?" Marena called out as her elbow slid from under her, causing her head to slide off the hand supporting it. It took her a few seconds to realize that she'd fallen asleep. She let out a loud yawn and blinked to clear her vision.

Four hours had passed since Marena began mixing two chemicals that would help make the antidote adhere to the necessary cells. If any of her calculations were off, it wouldn't work and would cost a significant amount of time.

Tiredness seeped into her body, but she fought it off, along with the aching muscles and burning eyes. She'd lost track of how long she and Coulter had stayed locked in each other's embrace. Both were terrified of letting go, but eventually, they had to because time was running out. None of the bodily discomforts would cause her to quit. Instead, she promised herself a break once she had the foundation in place.

At times, it was challenging to keep focused, because her mind wandered to thoughts of Coulter. He would never admit it, but she could tell he wasn't feeling well again and that the frequency of the episodes was getting worse. He hadn't had another seizure, but he didn't have much appetite, and his nose had started bleeding earlier when he was helping in the lab.

The sound of shattering glass snapped Marena out of

her reverie. She glanced down at the mess at her feet. Her mind had wondered, causing her to drop an empty vial onto the floor.

"Great," she muttered. Marena walked across the room to a metal storage cabinet. She retrieved a small broom and dustpan before sweeping up the mess.

Her heart raced. What if that had been the antidote?

"Come on, Marena. Get your head in the game. You can't afford these setbacks," she scolded aloud.

After completing the task, she dumped the broken glass into a trash can. When a piece slid onto the floor, not thinking, she bent down to retrieve it. When she grasped the tiny shard, she cut her finger.

"Dang it," she said with exasperation. She flicked the glass remnant into the trash before eyeing her bleeding index finger. "I don't have time for this. Coulter's dead if I don't get this formula right, and I'm standing here dealing with a stupid cut."

A burst of anger suddenly consumed her. She threw the broom and dustpan across the room. "Two days. I've got two days to produce a miracle. This whole thing sucks," she cried. Her foot connected with the trash can. "No margin for error, huh?" Marena whacked it again. "All I have are what-ifs.

"What if I'm not good enough? What if I can't get the calculations right?" she yelled at the inanimate and now-dented trash receptacle. "What if he dies? I'm just floating along on a river of possible disasters. If I screw up, Coulter's dead. If I don't get the antidote right, he's dead. If the bad guys looking for us find out where we are, he's dead." She gave the dented trash can another kick before picking it up and lobbing it across the room—the projectile connected with a table.

The impact caused an ear-piercing boom that reverberated around the room before the metal can rolled off and

landed on the floor on its side. It felt good, but the pain in her heart was still there.

The next thing to suffer Marena's wrath was a storage closet. She banged her hand on its front until it throbbed with pain. The tears flowed down her face as she gave in to fear, anger, and frustration.

It took Marena quite some time to register the strong arms that encircled her middle. Coulter's grip was firm enough to keep her from lashing out at the closet doors again. When she struggled, it was against him and not something that could do her any physical harm.

"Marena, stop. This isn't helping."

"I don't care," she cried.

"You're going to break your hand," he said calmly. Coulter backed away from the cabinet when she continued to lash out, dragging her with him. "Hey," he soothed. "Rena, it's okay."

"No, it's not okay. It may never be okay again," Marena rasped. She was crying in earnest now. Her shoulders shook in violent spasms, and still, Coulter held her.

"I've got you. Let it go."

"You shouldn't have to have me because we shouldn't even be in this jacked-up situation. You shouldn't be fighting for your life, and I shouldn't be trying to save it. We shouldn't be running out of time, and people shouldn't be coming after us. None of this should be happening at all," she wept.

"But it is, and we have to play the hand we're dealt."

"I want a new hand," she sobbed. "This one sucks."

He kissed the top of her head. "I know." Suddenly, he stilled. "I'm sorry, I shouldn't have—"

"Don't you dare say it," she warned, wrenching herself around to face him even though he still held her in his arms. Marena's eyes flashed a mixture of hurt, fear, and anger. She poked her finger in his chest. "Don't you say that you

shouldn't have come or that you shouldn't have involved me in this. If you do, Coulter, I swear I won't talk to you again—ever."

When her movements finally stilled, Coulter released his hold. His finger tilted her face to meet his, and his thumb caressed her tear-stained cheek.

"Putting you under this much stress wasn't my intention. I just recall desperately wanting to see you before I ran out of time. I knew if anyone could find a cure for this mess, you could, but just in case—" Coulter paused as though struggling to find the right words. "Forgive me, Marena."

She clung to him in desperation. Then, her tears started all over again.

"Sorry," she laughed pitifully, wiping her face on her lab coat. "Hysteria was not the look I was going for this evening."

"You have absolutely nothing to apologize for because, I said earlier, this is my fault."

She reared back. A look of disbelief plastered on her face. "Your fault? How can you say that? Did you ask to be injected with a biotoxin trying its best to kill you?"

Coulter shrugged. "Not exactly, but it's one of the risks I face every day. It's my job."

"I know," she said sadly.

He grasped her hand and turned it around. "Your finger is bleeding."

Marena didn't bother to look up or comment.

Coulter raised her finger to his lips and kissed it.

She yanked her hand away. Suddenly, her red, tear-filled eyes turned accusatory. "Why did you leave me?"

The words hung in the air like a thick cloud of smoke. Coulter lowered his hands to his side. When Marena moved away, this time, he didn't follow.

"You know why."

"No, I'm pretty sure I don't. You'll need to spell it out,

Coulter, because I went over it in my head repeatedly after you left. Lord knows I had enough time, and I couldn't come up with anything that made one lick of sense. I meant everything I said earlier. I would go to my grave trying to save your life, but I just can't get past the fact that these last three years should've been spent in marital bliss, not silence, heartache, and regrets."

He sighed. "I wanted more for you than this."

"Than what?" she shot back.

"You deserved better than wondering every time you saw me if it would be the last time. I knew that you didn't want to be with a man with the same background as your father and Lucas. That type of life is hard on a family—on those left behind."

"Are you kidding? That had nothing to do with it," she dismissed. "That's a cop-out, and you know it. Do you think I didn't understand the ramifications of falling in love with a soldier and all it entailed? I know what you do is dangerous, what all of you do, but it's important work, Coulter. I would never want to take that away from you. I could have handled it."

"You shouldn't have to."

"I'm not your mother, Coulter."

That sentence brought him up short. He stared at Marena as though she'd switched to a foreign language midsentence.

"Look, I know how hard it's been for your mom to deal with her way of life growing up and how it must've been a slap in the face for her when you decided to join the military. But I don't share her idiosyncrasies, Colt. I would never have grown to resent your career choices as she did. But somehow, you've painted me with that same brush—which is ridiculous."

For a few moments, he stared at her in stunned silence. Eventually, Coulter found his voice. "Marena, I saw what

losing your mom did to your father—to your family. It's a hellish nightmare that he'll never wake up from—none of you will. That's what shook me to my core. The thought of your mother's needless death haunted me. She had everything to live for, and it was ripped away from her in a second. All I could think about was what if that were me—it could've been me. And if I'd lost you like that, or you'd lost me, how would we go on?"

"Coulter, listen to me. I've accepted that my mother was killed in a despicable act by some faceless coward, but this isn't about me. Not really. It's about you and the fact that you didn't trust me."

"What are you talking about? Of course, I trust you. I trust you with my life," he said vehemently.

"Then you wouldn't have left."

"You aren't hearing me. I left to protect you, Marena."

"No, you didn't," she argued. "You left to protect yourself. You were the one shaken up and unsure how to handle it. We all were affected by mom's death, but I would've dealt with it much more easily had you been there by my side and not using her death as the catalyst to leave me. That's when I needed you the most—and you just weren't there."

"You're right, Marena. It scared me to death, and I just lost it. It was a wake-up call that hit home for me in the worst possible way. It was hard to accept that sometimes the bad guys bring the fight to our front door. Sometimes, innocent people who didn't sign up for this way of life become collateral damage. What then? Can't you understand why I didn't want you in danger?"

"*You* left me in nothing but danger," she said bitterly. "Danger from wanting you beyond anyone—or anything. Danger from losing my mind and my heart breaking like glass against ice every day for the last three years. You were my world, Coulter, but you abandoned me." Her voice

caught in her throat. "You left me falling without a parachute."

He rubbed his hand over his face. "My God, Rena. That was never my intention."

"Then I'd say you failed miserably."

Marena studied him, anger making the lines in her face rigid. "So, if you wanted to spare me so much heartache, why did you come back? Surely I'm not the only person you could think of to save your life? You could've tracked down my brother or my father. Granted, they don't like what you did, but both would've been able to help you get the medical attention you need. So why did you need to show up and throw my life and feelings into another purgatory? You didn't rip me to shreds enough the first time? You thought you'd try it again?"

Coulter opened his mouth to respond, but she cut him off.

"You say you didn't want your career to jeopardize my life, but can't you see it's too late? Your career *has* jeopardized my life, Coulter, because we're not together."

"But at least you're alive," he reasoned.

She recoiled like she had been struck. "Alive?" she laughed harshly. "Oh yeah, I'm alive. I go about my day-to-day activities, trying my best to forget how I feel. I'll never have the husband and family, and how much that loss has ripped me apart inside. Sometimes I see someone that reminds me of you, and I'm paralyzed." Marena threw her hands up in frustration. "Now you're dying, and I've been tasked with saving your life, and if things don't work out the way we hope, your career will have done more than jeopardize *my* life, Coulter. It will have destroyed it because I'll lose you all over again." Her laugh was brittle. "You don't see the irony here? And what's to stop you from doing it again?"

He frowned. "Doing what again?"

"Leaving. How can I ever trust that you won't up and leave me for my own good again? You did it once. What, am I just supposed to take you at your word that it'll never happen?"

Coulter went to her. Tentatively, he placed his hands on her shoulders.

"Lord knows I've hurt you, Marena, and I'm so sorry. I realize that I have to earn back the trust that I broke, and I promise you that I will."

Her face mirrored her pain. "Don't make promises you can't keep."

"This one I can—and will. When I discovered I had days to figure this thing out or die, I realized that if I failed, yours was the last face I wanted to see because I love you that much." He tightened his grip and waited until she made eye contact to continue.

"Sometimes love isn't enough to keep two people together," she murmured.

Coulter placed his hands on either side of her face. "You *are* enough." His voice cracked. "Just because I left doesn't mean that you stopped occupying my every thought or weren't here," he said, tapping his heart. "Do you understand what I'm saying? I never stopped wanting you, Rena—then or now. All the rest was just camouflage. I was hiding against the truth. I shouldn't have assumed your feelings were similar to my mother's. For that, I'm truly sorry. I just saw how much she hated not having my grandfather there. His job kept him from being there for her. I didn't want that for you—to do that *to* you."

Coulter's eyes held remorse and unshed tears. "I shouldn't have made that call on my own. I realize that I had no right to do that for you—for us. And now with Silent Night. If I could've kept from bringing you into all this, I would have."

Marena gasped as if he'd struck her. "You would rather have died than have seen me?"

Before he could answer, she turned away from him. Coulter could feel the walls going up around her like a shield.

"You know that's not what I meant."

"Yeah? Funny. I think it came out exactly the way you wanted it to."

He noticed her ramrod-straight back and her hands clenched at her sides. Her body language screamed *leave me alone*. A wise man would've heeded her external warning. Coulter never claimed to be that smart.

"Then you'd be wrong," he said to her back.

Chapter 19

When she didn't reply, he strode over and spun her around to face him.

"There hasn't been one day since I left that I haven't thought about you. What you were doing, how you were, where you were. Do you know how many nights I've spent going over every memory we've ever created together? All of them. From the moment I first met you that summer afternoon when Lucas invited me over to his house to do homework right up to the moment I left three years ago. Nothing has run through my mind more than you, Marena. What we had together. What I caused us to lose—all of it haunts me. But, despite the danger, I had to see you again. If you imagined that my last thought this side of the grave wouldn't be of you and how desperately I love you, then you'd be wrong."

Marena's mouth hung open in shock. She frantically searched his eyes for something that she needed, something her soul needed. The moment she saw it, she threw herself into Coulter's waiting arms. He caught her in a tight embrace and hauled her up against him. The two drifted together into a kiss as natural as air blowing over grasses on a summer day. Coulter tightened his hold when Marena's arms wrapped around his neck.

Everything that made Coulter who he was wrapped it-

self up in that kiss. Strength. Passion. Determination. It was all there for her to see, along with one emotion that she hadn't felt in years—promise. As their kiss deepened, one of Coulter's hands came up to hold the back of her head while the other rested possessively on her hip.

Marena felt lost in a dream that felt better the longer it played out. So, when she felt herself being lifted through the air and placed onto a nearby table, it barely registered in her rational mind, and it certainly wasn't enough to make her want to break their kiss. The wild horses on Carrot Island couldn't have dragged her away from his kiss.

Coulter's mouth traced a line from her neck to her waiting lips. Her hands gripped his head, locking him in place. She kissed him as if her life depended on it. Marena tilted her neck upwards to allow his roaming lips better access while her hands raked through his hair. When he reached the sensitive spot on her neck that he had discovered years ago, she shivered.

"I know I have no right, but if any man has ever touched that spot, I'll kill him," he growled against her ear.

"You're right, you don't," she agreed, smiling at him. "And no. No one ever has—but you."

Pulling her back into his arms, Coulter hugged her tight. There wasn't an inch of space between them. Closing her eyes, Marena allowed herself to be comforted by the man that had never ceased to bring her great joy and heartache in equal measures.

"It's no different for me, Marena. It's always been a two-edged sword. We're two halves of the one thing."

Startled, she glanced up at him.

"From day one," she murmured, the tears in her eyes shining like flecks of diamonds.

"From day one," he agreed.

The desire to never leave Coulter's embrace was so pow-

erful that Marena felt consumed by it. That unguarded moment of fully transferred emotions between them where words weren't even necessary scared her sober. It shocked her system like a splash of cold water on a grate of coals. Marena instantly pulled away, and Coulter let her go.

She was out of her element. She'd never felt this way before, where it was a struggle to get herself back to normal. She raised shaky hands to smooth her hair back into place.

"That—"

"Yeah, it has never happened before," he said in awe.

Her gaze connected with his in surprise at his revelation.

"Coulter, I—as much as I still love you, there's just so much we're dealing with right now. We should concentrate on saving your life. That has to be the priority. Anything else would complicate things between us."

"You're right," he agreed. "Dying would definitely rank high up on life's complicated list."

"Will you be serious?"

"I am." He hugged her as she was about to protest. It warmed his entire soul when she returned the hug with equal force. "Bookmarked for now?" He murmured into her hair.

"Yes," she agreed, rubbing her face against his. "For now."

When Coulter opened his eyes and blinked away sleep, two things came to mind. The first was that Marena was nestled up against him like a body pillow, and the second was that he felt like leftover boiled crap. His body ached, he was burning up, and he felt like a two-ton elephant had stomped on him from head to toe.

He glanced down at Marena. After they'd cleaned up the lab, she'd gone back to work for a few hours. Coulter had been working on his laptop when she had popped her head

in earlier that night. She'd sat down on the bed and talked about the test runs that evening and her findings. Both had been emotionally drained, so they had fallen asleep fully dressed at some point.

Careful not to wake her, he eased himself out of bed. His shirt was soaking wet from sweating. He grabbed a replacement and was about to go to the bathroom to freshen up when he heard a noise.

His gaze flew to Marena. Coulter dropped the shirt and went for his gun. He tiptoed out of the room and closed the door.

Ignoring the pain, Coulter took a deep breath to clear his head. Silently, he crept along the passageway, sticking close to the wall. With his senses heightened, he was ready for anything. That's when he heard it. A stifled groan was followed by something dropping on the floor nearby. Zeroing in on the target, Coulter moved with lightning speed down the hallway toward the back of the lab. Someone had likely entered the building from the rear through either the window or the exit door. That someone was about to wish they'd found another building to burglarize.

Though it was dark, and Coulter was without the aid of his night-vision goggles, he was used to engaging the enemy devoid of light. He was moving in the direction of the noise when the hair on the back of his neck stood up. Coulter spun around, coming face-to-face with his target.

"Drop your weapon," a voice growled into the silence.

"Not a chance," he replied in a clipped tone that echoed his annoyance at the man's getting the jump on him.

"Now, or I'll make you drop it," the man warned.

Coulter smiled at that. "You can try."

"Where is she?"

The smile faded from Coulter's face, and a fierce pro-

tectiveness caused his body to shake with fury. "Where's who?"

"I swear if you've hurt her, I'll kill you," the man threatened.

"Wait." Coulter lowered his weapon. The other man did not.

Coulter's body tensed. "Luke?" he whispered after another moment.

Backing up, he slid his hand along the wall till he found the wall plate and flipped a switch, bathing the small hallway in light. Coulter stared in surprise at Marena's brother.

Lucas Dash was a tall, well-built man. At six foot four, he towered over most men and, when he was dressed in full military gear, like he was now, engendered both fear and respect, depending on his intention. Marena's brother was standing with a SIG Sauer M17 service pistol aimed at Coulter's chest.

Lucas never broke eye contact with Coulter, his chest rising and falling with each angry breath as he assessed Coulter. His body was poised to spring like a lion about to pounce on its prey.

"Why are you here?"

"There's a rational explanation for all this," Coulter said calmly.

"I asked you a question."

"I'll answer when you lower your weapon."

Engaging the safety on his gun, Lucas harnessed it. He stared at his former best friend in shock. He shook his head as if to clear it and frowned when, after blinking several times, the person standing in front of him remained the same.

"Start talking."

Before Coulter could reply, Lucas's gaze turned murderous. "You don't have any clothes on."

"I don't have a shirt on. That's not what I would call

naked. Besides, I didn't exactly have time to throw one on," Coulter told him. "I thought you were an assailant and was on my way out here to kill you."

Lucas eyed him with contempt. "Where's my sister?"

"She's in bed, asleep."

Before Coulter could say more, Lucas's hand connected with his chest. He shoved him hard. "Wrong answer."

Coulter staggered backward. "Hit first and ask questions later must be a Dash family trait."

"Only where you're concerned," Lucas said menacingly. "You didn't break her heart enough the first time? So you wanted to try it again?"

"It's not like that. Let me explain."

"There's not one thing I want to hear from you—except goodbye. You were my best friend." He charged Coulter again. "I trusted you."

Using Lucas's weight against him, Coulter shoved him to the side.

"I supported you. When you told me you loved my baby sister, I believed you, and you made me look like a fool."

"Luke, I'm not going to fight you, man. I'm still your friend, and nothing between us was a lie. I do love Marena. I never stopped."

"You got a funny way of showing it. Did you take advantage of her? I swear if you forced her into anything— I'll kill you."

"I'll kill both of you myself if you don't stop bickering," came the warning from behind them. "Now, knock it off."

With a slight turn of his body, Lucas glanced behind him. He saw his sister wearing Coulter's T-shirt with her legs and feet bare.

"I knew it." His expression turned murderous.

Marena jumped in front of her brother. "Lucas, stop. Nothing is going on. I went to take a shower and heard all the commotion, so I threw on something and ran out here."

"So, you *were* in his bed?"

"Yes, but not the way you think. We just fell asleep. Nothing happened."

He smiled without humor. "If I handle him now, that'll save Dad a lot of trouble."

"You won't be handling anyone. Coulter did not take advantage of me," she stressed. "He needs my help, and we're running out of time."

"Yeah? He needed to get you naked for you to help him?" he raged, glaring back at Coulter.

"Of course not," Coulter snapped. "You're out of line."

Lucas pushed past his sister and got in Coulter's face. "Oh, I'm out of line? You're the one that called off your engagement and broke my sister's heart, so don't you dare talk to me about who's in the wrong." He turned to his sister. "Did he feed you some line to get you to go along with whatever he's planning?"

Marena's anger was good and stoked. "I think I'm smarter than that, Lucas. A lot smarter."

Her brother snorted. "That's not the view I'm getting. I've been here for the last three years, Rena. I know what this idiot's leaving did to you."

"She's telling you the truth," Coulter replied.

Lucas clenched his fists. "Stay out of this. When I want *your* opinion, I'll ask for it."

"Enough of this," she snapped. "Luke, Coulter's been poisoned, and if I don't save him in two days, he'll die."

Lucas noted the frantic look in her eye and the edge to her voice. He took a step backward. "What?"

Marena rushed to Coulter's side. "Are you alright?"

"I'll live—for the moment."

Her face darkened. "That's not funny." She touched his arm. "Colt, you're burning up again."

"Okay, okay, he's fine," Lucas said impatiently. "Now start talking. Marena, is what you said true?"

"Why would I lie about someone dying?" she shot back. "Of course, it's true. Coulter was injected with Silent Night, and unless I can make an antidote, he's not going to make it. Now, are we done with all this? Are you going to help us or continue standing there scowling like a—"

Suddenly, Marena stopped talking and turned to her brother. She stared at him as if recognition had just dawned.

"Wait a minute. What are *you* doing here?"

"Dad sent me to find you," her brother said matter-of-factly. "When you lied about being in Beaufort, he asked me to check on you to make sure you were okay. Luckily, I was on leave, so I hopped a jet, and here I am."

Marena nodded. She was helping Coulter back down the hallway when she halted again. "How did Dad know I lied?"

Lucas stood there staring at her. His brown skin tone did nothing to camouflage the sudden burst of red that suffused his face. He looked decidedly uncomfortable.

Chapter 20

"Lucas Dash," Marena warned. "Answer me. How did you find me?"

He glanced toward Coulter, who smirked back at him.

With a loud sigh, Lucas came clean. "Dad… Well, he sort of bugged you."

Marena blinked. "He what?"

"He, uh, inserted a tracking device into a piece of jewelry years ago—after Mom died. That's how he knew you weren't in Beaufort. The device led me straight to you."

Marena's mouth dropped open. "He's been tracking me?"

Her brother nodded.

"All this time? Where is it?"

Lucas looked down at his boots.

"Where?" she yelled.

"Mom's pendant."

Her hand flew to the locket that she always wore. Her fingers outlined the gold and garnet heart-shaped pendant that her father had given their mother for an anniversary present.

"He knew you'd never take it off."

"Clearly," she said sarcastically and then turned her attention to Coulter. She pinned him with an accusatory stare. "Did you know about this?"

Coulter's eyes connected with Lucas. This time it was

his friend's turn to smirk. With resignation, he turned to Marena. "Yes."

"Is that how *you* found me?"

"Yes."

"I see. So, the menfolk had a meeting and decided that this frail, helpless female couldn't defend herself without their interference."

"That's not exactly—"

Marena held up her hand to stop her brother's explanation. Disgusted, she stormed off.

"Rena—"

She spun around. "Don't *Rena* me," she replied in a tone that could have frozen boiling water. "And to be clear, I'll deal with the three of you myself when this is all over. Until then, you—" she pointed at Coulter "—get back to bed because you look like you're about to drop. I'll be in shortly to give you something to bring down that temperature. And you—" She pinned her brother with a withering look. "You come with me. I need your help."

Marena left the two of them standing there. Coulter exchanged glances with Lucas and moved to walk by, but Lucas stopped him.

"Wait. I'm sorry I tried to take your head off earlier."

"No, you're not."

Lucas grinned. "Not really, no. You had it coming. So, how'd all this happen, anyway?"

Coulter brought him up to speed on Brinkley's betrayal and the events leading to his being injected with Silent Night.

"Well, that sucks."

"Gee, you think?" Coulter said dryly.

"I have to brief Dad about what's going on. Whatever you stepped into is bigger than just the three of us, and we'll need help."

Coulter's eyebrows rose. "The three of us?"

"Yes. When you get one Dash, you get them all," Lucas explained. "Look, I may be angry at you, but I don't want you to die, Colt. And once Dad finds out what's happened to you, he'll do whatever it takes to fix this."

"I doubt it. I'm sure he's still pretty pissed at me, too."

"Yeah, he is, but you deserve it. Still, if anything happened to you," Lucas said, tilting his head toward the direction Marena had stalked off in, "it would devastate her. We all know that."

Coulter looked resigned. "This may not come out the way either of us hopes, Luke. You have to prepare her—for the worst."

"You know my sister as well as I do. You also know that Marena won't stop until she finds a way to cure your sorry butt. Well, if you had to pick one woman scientist on the planet to fall in love with and subsequently save your life, you picked the right one."

"Gee, thanks," Coulter said wryly.

"You know what I mean."

"What you need to know is that I love her, Lucas. Regardless. And, if I make it through this alive, I won't be walking away from her again—not ever," Coulter said with meaning.

Lucas looked skeptical. "Time will tell. Besides, it's not me you have to convince."

"Lucas." Marena's voice barreled down the corridor like the report of a gunshot. "Move it."

He turned to Coulter. "Get some rest," he stated grudgingly. "You look like you've been dead for three days already."

"I see you've got jokes," Coulter called after him. Walking back to his room, he closed the door and sagged against it. He gritted his teeth and tried to refocus himself as he struggled with the intense pain coursing through his body. It took a series of several deep-breath exercises before Coul-

ter was able to ride out the discomfort. Finally, the pain ended. Relieved, he shuffled across the room.

Kicking off his shoes, Coulter returned his pistol to the nightstand drawer before stretching out on the bed. Lying on his back, Coulter draped an arm over his eyes. He let out a sigh of exhaustion. A faint whisper of Marena's perfume permeated the bed. Unable to help it, his eyes drifted shut, and moments later, Marena's form drifted into his mind's eye like a luminous cloud. The familiar tug of sleep beckoned to him, but Coulter fought it to hold on to her image a bit longer.

"This antidote has to work, Rena. I need a shot at forever—with you," he murmured. Seconds later, Coulter drifted off into an exhausted sleep.

"Marena," Lucas said, watching his sister while he swirled around in a desk chair. "It's been two hours now, and you haven't said anything except for—"

"Hand me the sodium citrate."

"Exactly," he replied as if that proved his point. Then, when Marena scowled at him, he said, "Where is it?"

"Over there, on the table. It looks like salt. It's next to the ethanol. Oh, and bring back a volumetric flask while you're at it," she said before diving back into the notebook on her worktable. Marena alternated raising each leg a few moments to ease the pain in her feet from standing too long.

When Lucas returned, Marena waved her arm in an arc. "Thanks. Just set it over there."

Placing the flask on the table, he stretched his muscles before straddling the nearest stool to watch his sister work.

After a few minutes of silence, he said, "When's the last time you ate? Or slept, for that matter?"

Marena glanced up over her glasses and pinned him with an exasperated stare. "Why does everyone keep asking me that?"

"Oh, I don't know. Maybe because you're the backbone of this whole operation? If you land yourself in the hospital, Coulter is—"

"You don't have to say it. I know. I'm fine. I rested my eyes for fifteen minutes an hour ago. I'll worry about how much sleep I get when we know Coulter won't die. As for food, I had an energy bar earlier, so I'm good."

"I have to admit, while all the scientist stuff has never been a fascinating proposition for me, I do admire your dedication. All things considered."

"Thanks, but regardless of where Colt and I were—or are—I'm not about to let him die. Not when I can help save him. Can you get me the hexahydrate?"

"The what?" he said, hopping up.

"Monosodium hexahydrate. It's a stabilizing agent," she replied while carefully measuring the citrate.

He looked over his choices. "Easy for you to say, I don't speak chemist."

"Everything's marked, Luke."

A muted ring invaded the silence. Marena's head popped up. "It's my cell phone—the old one."

She rushed across the room and retrieved the phone from a small desk.

"What old one?"

"Long story. Coulter thinks my cell phone is being tracked."

Lucas intercepted her and grabbed it. "Wait, then why are you answering it? As much as I hate to agree with anything he says, Coulter is right. It's ridiculously easy to find anyone by their cell phone. It shouldn't even be on, Marena. You know this."

"I know, but it could be from Dr. Cutty."

"So?"

"So, I can't miss his call. He's the one that developed an antidote to Silent Night. Okay, more like he started de-

veloping one. Anyway, Frank's been secretly helping me. He gave me the notes on his formula and provided a few of the ingredients we need. Now I just need to create it." She snatched the phone from his hand and hit the talk button.

"Hello?"

A second later, Marena tossed the phone onto the desk. "Great, now I've missed it."

"Well, maybe he'll call back," Lucas reasoned.

They heard a *ding* next. Marena picked up the phone and read it.

"It was a message from Frank," she confirmed, reading it over. Then, she let out a loud yip. "Great. He has the emylanoroc."

Lucas shot his sister a baffled look. "The what?"

"Emylanoroc. It's one of the major components that I need for the antidote. Unfortunately, I couldn't get it, but it looks like Frank came through for us," she said with glee. "Now I need to meet him for the pickup."

"Oh no, you don't." Lucas took the phone. He read the message. "You're not going anywhere by yourself."

Marena tried to get her phone, but Lucas held it away from her.

"We don't have time to debate this," she replied with frustration. "I need that chemical. We're dead in the water without it."

"And you'll get it," he promised. "But I'm going for you. So, you stay here and continue working."

"You can't go," she replied. "Frank thinks I'm coming. If we change the plans midstream, he'll get skittish."

"Marena. Think. You need to be here to finish the formula. Coulter is in no shape to go anywhere. He looks like he'd drop into a heap before he got to the car."

"Plane," she interrupted. "Dr. Cutty is in Jamestown, Rhode Island."

"What? Then I'm the only choice here. My medical

skills aren't enough to help Coulter if he takes a turn for the worse. Besides, if something goes down, I can handle it. Army of one, remember?" He winked and went to grab his gear. "Text Cutty and let him know that you're sending me to get the package and to text you back with the details on where and when."

Marena leaned against the table. She nibbled at her thumbnail while pondering her brother's plan.

"I don't know, Lucas."

"What's the issue here?"

"Dr. Cutty was specific. I have to be there. He only trusts me at this point, and we can't afford for him to get cold feet about this. He could call off the meeting, and then Coulter is as good as dead."

"Fine. Then we're all going, but I'm running point on this. Having you go in alone would be a tactical error that we can't risk."

"Fair enough." Marena tapped a message on her phone and handed it back to her brother.

They waited almost a minute before Cutty's response came through.

Lucas smiled. "He agreed."

He turned to leave, but she stopped him. "Thanks."

Lucas tweaked her nose. "Hey, don't worry. Everything will work out. This is a walk in the park compared to what I normally do."

"I know, I know. Tough guy and all that."

"You got it." He winked before kissing her cheek. "I'm going to prep."

After Lucas left, Marena went to check on Coulter. She'd given him some medication to bring his fever down earlier, but it was time for another dose. Opening the door, she peeped into the room. Coulter was sound asleep. Marena entered as quietly as she could.

Sitting on the side of the bed, she took his vitals.

"They've been better," she whispered. Then, retrieving the needle from the pocket of her lab coat, Marena prepared his arm for the shot. She was administering the medication when Coulter's eyes shot open.

"Easy," she soothed. "Don't move. I'm just giving you some meds to help you feel better, okay?"

Coulter looked at her with a glassy-eyed stare.

"Colt? Do you understand?"

"You're an angel. A beautiful angel sent to watch over me."

Marena eased the needle out of his arm and replaced it with a cotton ball and Band-Aid. Smoothing his damp hair away from his forehead, her fingers brushed his cheek before she kissed him softly on the lips.

Chapter 21

"You're right. I am here to watch over you, but I'm hardly an angel. I'm just a woman who—loves you," she said tearfully.

"My angel," he sighed, closing his eyes, but opened them again. "Don't cry, beauty. It kills me when you cry."

Marena took a cloth and wiped the sweat from his face. "I won't cry if you promise to get some rest. Deal?"

"You won't float away, will you?"

She kissed his lips and bent down to whisper in his ear. "I'm never leaving you."

"Good to know." He touched her cheek. His eyes were bloodshot, with dark, puffy circles under them. He also had intermittent tremors. "I had an angel once—her name was Marena."

Marena closed her eyes. "Really? That's a great name," she told him.

"She was a beauty. I fell in love with her instantly. Bet you didn't know that."

"No, I didn't." Marena stroked his arm. "But I'm sure she returned your love."

"Yeah. We had it good for a while. You remind me of my Rena. She loves to help people, too."

"She sounds like a wonderful woman." Marena got up and went into the bathroom. She rinsed the washcloth in

cold water a few times. Returning to his side, she wiped his face and neck before placing it on his forehead.

Coulter's hand found hers. Marena felt the heat seep through her skin.

"Thank you."

She squeezed his hand. "You're welcome. Try and sleep. I will be here when you wake up."

He closed his eyes as if the effort to keep them open was too great. "Promise?"

"I promise."

Moments later, Coulter's head lulled to the side. Marena watched him to ensure that his breathing evened out. She let go of his hand when it did and placed it at his side. On the way back to the lab, Marena retrieved a water bottle and an energy drink from the fridge. She downed the pick-me-up in a can and half the water. She put her glasses back on at her table and cued up a song on her cell phone playlist. A soft, soulful tune piped into the room. Placing her head on her desk, she started crying so much that she had to remove her glasses.

Seeing Coulter in a state of delirium was expected, but it was troubling nonetheless. He was deteriorating, and time was running out. She cried for a few more moments before drying her eyes and blowing her nose. *Frank, you'd better come through as promised.*

Putting her glasses back on, Marena grasped the beaker she'd just filled and got back to work.

It paid to have friends with an abundance of resources. Alejandro Reyes owned a crisis management company in Chicago. Marena had done work for him, creating various chemical and technical gadgets used in his work line. So, when she called him for assistance, he was happy to help.

"How's Coulter? Any improvement?"

"Not yet. He's in rough shape, Alejandro. One of the

drugs I need is in a lab outside of Washington, DC, Bio-dyne. We need access, and it's a high-security facility. I can't go through the red tape. There's just no time."

"Understood, and consider it done," Alejandro replied. "I'll spec it out and contact you when everything is ready."

"Wait, just like that? Letting us use your jet was favor enough, but this is huge, Dro."

"Well, it's not just like that." He chuckled. "I have to call in several favors, and there will be several moving parts to make this happen. But I promise you'll have what you need."

Marena released the breath she'd been holding. "Thank you, Alejandro. I appreciate everything you're doing to help."

"Anything for my number one scientist. I spoke to Alexa earlier. She mentioned that you two had spoken and she's on standby, waiting to help wherever you need her."

"You two are wonderful."

"Hey, glad to be of service. Normally we're the ones calling you, asking for your help. So it's our turn to return the favor."

"I appreciate that."

"Whatever you need, Marena. All my resources are at your disposal."

Overcome with emotion, she fought to hold back tears. "This means the world to me—and Coulter."

Hanging up the phone, Marena turned to find Coulter standing there. He appeared as if he hadn't been at death's door just hours before. To Marena, it just reiterated that he was fighting against the illness with a Herculean effort.

"Are you okay?" he asked.

"Yes, more than okay."

He hugged her. "It's coming together, Rena."

"I know." She touched his forehead. "I just pray we have the time we need."

"I know we will," he assured her. "I came in to tell you that Liam's sending a jet to take us to Jamestown. It'll arrive at the Sedona Airport in two hours. How'd you do?"

"I was on the phone with Alejandro. He's provided resources and access to Biodyne. Alexa's on standby to help where we need her, too."

"Who's she?"

"Oh, I'm sorry, I forgot to tell you. Alexa King is a colleague who's an expert at close-contact protection. She owns her own company. I've done some consulting work for her and Dro."

"At this point, we need all the help we can get."

"Yes, we do. Luke is coming with us to Jamestown. He and I will go meet Cutty." Marena looked hopeful. "This has to work."

Coulter rubbed her shoulder. "It will. We should get going."

They went out into the main area to find Lucas eating in the kitchen. He glanced up as they walked in.

"Did you bring Colt up to speed on our game plan?" he asked between bites of his club sandwich."

"Yes, and I'm going to be there to meet Cutty, too."

Lucas's gaze traveled to Coulter.

"Do you think that's wise?"

"Whether it is or isn't, I'm not about to let Marena roam around getting in and out of dangerous situations with just you. We don't know what we're jumping into, so it's better to be prepared with a contingency plan."

"Thanks a lot," Lucas said.

"That's not what I meant. I'm talking about there just being two of you," Coulter corrected.

"Your worry is unfounded. This is my sister we're talking about, which means I will always watch her back. I protected her long before you came into the picture, after you two broke up, and I will be again when you leave."

"What's that supposed to mean?"

"Take it however you want, Colt. I'm just saying that she's suffered more from you than any external danger she's been up against."

"I would never intentionally hurt Marena. I left to keep her safe. You know that."

"Do I?"

"Okay, enough!" Marena bellowed. "We are all on the same team, remember?"

Coulter and Lucas eyed each other but remained silent.

She observed them both. "I'll take silence over bickering any day."

Lucas cleared his plate from the table before clapping Coulter on the back. "She's right. My bad."

"Yeah, sorry, man," Coulter replied.

"It's cool. Dad texted me earlier. I'll go call him back. He'll be anxious to hear what's going on. Never in a million years will he see this coming."

She closed her eyes. "You're right about that."

"I'm sure Terry won't like hearing that I'm back."

Lucas snorted. "That's the understatement of the century."

"No, he won't," Marena agreed. "But he'll have to get on board because I'm not changing my plans."

"I get it. Just thought I'd give you a heads-up."

She went to hug her brother. "Thanks, Luke."

He grinned. "Hey, we're family. That's what we do."

"I'd hate to be a fly on the wall during that conversation," Coulter replied.

"No kidding. But when you look at it, you *are* the fly on that wall," Marena pointed out. "I can't even imagine what dad is going to say."

"True," Lucas said. "You haven't exactly been his number one person since you two broke up."

"That's understandable. But your dad is flat-out scary.

Honestly, I should be happy I've been on borrowed time this long."

Marena had to laugh at that. "You've got a point."

A few minutes later, Lucas went out to the backyard, sat down on one of the patio benches, and called his father.

General Terry Dash was sitting in a recliner, watching television. When his cell phone rang, and he saw who it was, he turned down the volume.

"There's my boy," he answered. "We've been playing phone tag."

"Hey, Dad."

"So, how's it going? Did you get to the bottom of what's going on with your sister? Does she have a new boyfriend that she's keeping from us?" he inquired good-naturedly.

"Not exactly," Lucas hedged. "She's been a little tied up lately working on a—uh, project."

"Project? What's so important that she's been evading her father and lying about where she is? That's not like Marena."

"You're going to need to sit down, Dad."

Terry frowned. "I am sitting down. Now quit beating around the bush and give me a sitrep, Lucas."

"Coulter is back."

Terry bolted upright in his recliner so fast that when the footrest closed, it made a snapping sound. "Repeat that?"

"That's not going to change the answer," Lucas replied.

"I'm going to kill him."

"He's been injected with a biotoxin, Dad. And if Marena doesn't create an antidote in a few days, someone will have beat you to it."

Lucas filled his father in on the rest of the details and their location. When he ended the phone call, Terry leaned forward and buried his head in his hands. He was utterly silent and still for a few minutes before sitting back heavily in his chair.

"My God," he said aloud.

He rubbed his hand across his face before he picked up his cell phone again and dialed a number.

"Hello?"

"Cole, it's me."

"Terry, what are you doing calling so late?"

"We have to talk. Where are you? Chesapeake or DC?"

"I'm at the condo. What's up?"

"I'm on my way. I'll tell you when I get there."

Coulter had started going downhill by the time they arrived at Sedona Airport. His temperature was elevated, he was beginning to wheeze, and could only keep liquids down. He also had a violent case of the shakes.

"I was afraid of this," Marena fretted to herself more than anyone else.

After ensuring that he was resting comfortably on the plush leather sofa, Marena sat next to Lucas.

"He's in bad shape," Lucas noted.

"Yes, he is."

"Is he going to make it?"

"Luke, really?" Marena chastised.

"What? You know I'm a realist. I'm just wondering if, at some point, we'll be waking up to a corpse."

"What is wrong with you?" she hissed. "Coulter used to be your best friend. Why are you so cold?"

"You're right. He was—and then things went south between you two. So now I'm indifferent to the whole thing."

She eyed her brother. "That's not true. You talk a mean game, Luke, but I know you. You used to say that Coulter was the best friend you'd ever had. Regardless of what happened between him and me, you two were like brothers."

"Yeah, well, brothers or not, he wasn't there for you when you needed him the most. That's not something I can easily forgive and forget—and neither should you. Which

is why I don't understand why you're here risking everything to save his life."

"Like I wouldn't do the same for you, Dad, Vivica, or Burt?" Marena countered. "Whether I thought the person deserved it or not, I'm still going to do whatever I can to save a life. I would never let someone die when I have the power and the know-how to help them."

Chapter 22

"I'm not saying let him die. I'm talking about taking him to the hospital. They have specialists they can tap to deal with this kind of thing. So why does it need to be you?"

"Colt used up valuable days to get to me, Luke. He's here, and I'm not about to turn him away to waste even more time he doesn't have. For better or worse, I'm the one he came to, and I will see it through. I suggest you think about that when you're trying to keep your heart hardened against him."

With that, Marena got up and left Lucas to his thoughts.

Coulter had not woken up by the time the aircraft had landed in Rhode Island.

"Let him rest," Lucas said. "We'll likely be back before he wakes up, anyway."

Marena lingered. The worry was evident on her face. "We have to hurry."

When they got off the plane at T.F. Green International Airport, there was a black Mercedes sedan waiting for them. After they settled inside and the driver pulled off, Lucas said, "I want you to know that I heard you earlier—every word."

"Then you know that there's no talking me out of this."

"Yeah, I do." He grimaced. "I just want you to protect your heart, Rena. You've always had blinders on when

it came to Coulter. I just—I don't want to see you hurt again, sis."

"I'll be hurt worse if he dies, Lucas. I can handle anything going on between Coulter and me. As long as he is alive and well." Marena struggled with her composure when she said, "I'm just not ready to live in a world that doesn't have him in it."

Lucas stared out the window as they rode along the highway on Interstate 95. Marena had agreed to meet Dr. Cutty at Beavertail State Park. The New England coastline was majestic, but he did not have time to appreciate the rugged beauty. There was too much on his mind. The driver mentioned it would be just under forty minutes to their rendezvous. Letting out a long sigh, he turned to face his sister.

"I'm sorry for how I've been lately. But despite being angry with Colt, you know I'll do whatever I can to help you save him—no matter the cost, Marena."

Lucas grasped her hand and squeezed it before pulling her into his arms.

She leaned against him. "Thank you," she croaked.

He held her tightly. After a few minutes, he said, "Are you sure about this plan? How do we know no one's tailing Cutty?"

"We don't," she admitted, finally trusting her voice. "It's a chance we'll have to take."

"Don't get near him," Lucas instructed. "If he has something to give you, have him drop it, and then I'll pick it up. I don't want you getting caught in a cross fire if something goes down."

"Okay," she agreed.

The driver dropped them off at a park and waited.

Lucas got out first. "Stay here while I have a look around."

A few minutes later, he tapped on the window, and Marena got out and scanned her cell phone message.

"The instructions say to go down the path and head to the right. We'll see a park bench. We're to sit there and wait for him."

"Roger that," Lucas replied. "Stay behind me."

It was late afternoon, and there were a few joggers and people walking dogs. When they arrived at the bench, Marena sat while Lucas stood guard.

Her gaze swept around the tree-lined area. "It's lovely here. Did you know this park has the third-oldest lighthouse? There's even a museum."

"Yeah, I did. Came across that scoping out the mission." He checked the time. "Cutty's late."

"He'll be here," Marena replied confidently.

Marena spotted Dr. Cutty coming toward them from another trail a few minutes later.

"He's here."

When Cutty saw Marena, he picked up his pace. He'd gotten halfway there when Lucas called out.

"Stay where you are. I'll come to you."

When Lucas got there, Cutty handed him a small, square container. He began speaking to Lucas, but Marena couldn't hear their conversation.

"This is crazy," she complained.

Getting up, Marena began walking toward them. She was almost there when shots rang out. She dropped to the ground. The impact took her breath away.

Marena watched in shocked horror as Cutty's body lurched, and then he pitched toward the ground face-first. The metal briefcase he had been carrying flew out of his hand and landed in the grass.

"Frank!" Marena screamed as Lucas drew his weapon to return fire. He stopped after determining there was no clear shot.

When she tried to get up and run to them, Lucas yelled, "Marena, stay down."

Not about to lie there and wait, she crawled on her belly, doing her best to keep low as she hurried to check on Cutty.

"Frank?" she exclaimed, checking him over. When she noticed that he was wearing a bulletproof vest, Marena let out a sigh of relief. "He had a vest on, Luke."

"Can he move? If so, we need to get out of here. I swept the area and didn't see anyone. There must be a sniper. We need to get to the tree line, Marena—now."

She tried to revive Cutty.

"He must've fainted."

"Or hit his head when he fell. Either way, we can't wait." Lucas handed Marena his rifle. "Let's go," he commanded. "Stay low."

Bending down, Lucas picked Dr. Cutty up from under his arms. He half dragged, half pulled Cutty to the safety of the trees. Grabbing the briefcase, Marena quickly followed behind Lucas while crouched low. Her gaze was darting around as they went. Lucas placed Cutty in the back seat when they arrived at the car before hurrying Marena inside.

"Don't spare any gas," he told the driver.

When they reached the airplane, Coulter was down the steps instantly. The moment he saw Lucas pulling someone out of the car, he ran across the tarmac. He spotted Marena getting out of the car and slowed down, but he didn't stop.

"What happened?" he asked when he reached their side.

"Frank was shot," Marena told him.

His practiced eye raked her over. "Are you alright?"

"Yes, I'm fine. No one else got hurt. We need to get moving so I can examine his injuries."

Once on the plane, Lucas informed the pilot they were ready to take off while Coulter laid Cutty down on one of the sofas at the back of the aircraft. He unbuttoned Frank's jacket and gently eased off the bulletproof vest.

Coulter reviewed it. "Where'd he get this thing—online? It's not very good quality."

"Maybe not," Marena said, pointing to where the bullet had lodged itself in the strong material, "but it stopped the bullet and saved his life, and that's what counts."

Tapping the side of Frank's face, she shook him gently. "Frank? Can you hear me? If you can, open your eyes and blink a few times."

Eventually, he awakened. When he saw Marena, Cutty asked, "What happened?"

"Someone tried to kill you," she replied. "Thank goodness you were wearing this vest, or you'd be dead. Has anyone contacted you lately? Did you check to make sure that you weren't being followed?"

Frank tried to sit up but stopped. His breathing was labored as he tried to handle the pain. "No, I didn't see anybody. I took precautions, though."

"Not enough," Lucas said as he came in and sat down. Marena shot him a withering look, which he ignored.

"What am I going to do now?" Frank said suddenly. "If someone tried to kill me, they know who I am—where I live. I can't go back there. I'm not safe."

"He's got a point," Coulter pointed out. "He needs to disappear for a while."

"How long is that?" Frank protested.

"Until nobody else wants to kill you," Lucas said matter-of-factly.

"Luke, you're not helping."

"I'm telling him the truth, Rena. Someone knows who he is and has likely already been to his house and ransacked it. We can tell by the bullet hole in his vest that whoever it is doesn't want to get a hold of him just to ask him questions. They wanted him dead."

Lucas turned to Coulter. "Someone is going through a lot of trouble to make sure Dr. Cutty doesn't help you, and that Silent Night runs its course."

"I have no idea who," Coulter said with frustration. "I don't know who'd have an ax to grind against me that's this sharp."

Turning to Coulter, Marena said, "We have to do something. If he hadn't been helping us, he would've been able to stay under the radar."

"If he hadn't helped create Silent Night in the first place, none of us would be in this predicament," Coulter said testily. "And I wouldn't be on a countdown to death."

"I'm sorry," Frank said quickly. "I didn't know what they planned to do with it."

Coulter glared at him. "What did you think someone would do with a bioweapon, Cutty—play with it? Brinkley is getting ready to auction it off to the highest bidder as we speak. And you had no clue this was one of the possibilities that could happen with such a dangerous weapon?"

"Coulter," Marena whispered.

"What? Cutty needs to know the extent of the damage that he's wrought. Thanks to you, there are global ramifications for Silent Night. And you, what, just decided for the heck of it to try to make a weapon that kills people without any accountability?" He glared at Frank. "The list of potential cowards you're empowering with this thing is frightening. And you know what else, Frank? It's mind-boggling that not once did you stop and think about what would happen if it fell into the wrong hands. You're a scientist who wants to make a creation and soak up all the accolades and recognition, aren't you?"

"No, of course not," Cutty sputtered.

"Coulter—"

"Uh-uh, Marena. He doesn't get a pass. This disaster is on him—all of it. Someone taking a potshot at him is the least of his worries today. And if that person is bold enough to come after him in a park in broad daylight, then I'd wager

they know who he was coming to meet. That means that none of us are safe."

Coulter turned and stomped off.

"He's right," Frank said quietly. "I deserve a lot worse than this. But, Marena, I swear to you that I'll do whatever I can to make this right."

"Kind of late for that, don't you think?" Lucas reasoned.

"No, it's not too late," Marena said quickly. "Frank, think back on anyone new you may have come in contact with during the last few days. Did someone call you? Drop something by your house? Anything that can help us determine who's after you—and, by extension, us?"

"Okay," he said quietly. "I'll try. There's one more thing. I wasn't able to get enough emylanoroc. We need more, but the only place that has it is in London."

"What?"

"I can give you a contact there that you can meet for the exchange, but he's going to want something in return."

"Name it."

"Fifty thousand dollars."

Marena's mouth dropped open. "Are you serious?"

Frank nodded. "And it's on sale only for the next twenty-four hours. After that, the deal goes away."

Lucas whistled. "How are we going to be in two places simultaneously? DC and London?"

"We're not. We'll have to split up. Coulter and I will take DC, and you'll go to London."

Chapter 23

A big smile was plastered across Marena's face.

"I have an idea who can help you."

"Uh, hello, army of one," Luke replied.

"Not this time, big brother. Time is critical. Things will go much faster if you have a partner."

"Well, who? And don't tell me that guy," Lucas replied, tilting his head toward Cutty.

Marena frowned. "No, but I'll let you know as soon as I have the plans confirmed."

"They'd better not slow me down." He gave Frank a final glare before leaving.

"I'm sorry about that. I know this isn't what you need after being shot at earlier."

"Are you kidding? It's because of all of you that I'm alive right now. Besides, I deserve their animosity. Yours, too."

She sat down. "I'll need to get more intel from you later about who Lucas will be meeting in London. I don't want any more surprises, Frank."

He nodded and then struggled to sit up. "Oh, there's one more thing. In the container with the emylanoroc, you'll find three vials of medicine. For Coulter. They won't cure him, but they will help slow down the poison's progression."

Opening the case, Marena's fingers slid over the glass tubes. "Oh, Frank," she said in surprise. Her eyes misted

over with tears. She dabbed at them with her shirt sleeve. "Thank you." Squeezing his hand, she got up to let him rest.

When she found Coulter, he was sitting in one of the window seats staring at the horizon.

Marena sat down next to him. "Guess what? Frank gave us three doses of something that will help slow Silent Night's progress. Of course, it's not the cure, but at least that helps us manage the symptoms quicker."

"Thanks. I appreciate that."

"Your facial expression says otherwise."

"All the brains in the world, and yet no common sense whatsoever," Coulter said wearily. "He's going to be a danger to everyone on this mission."

"No, he's not. When we land in DC, I'll call Alejandro and make arrangements to get him someplace safe." When Coulter didn't respond, Marena touched his leg. "Colt, I need you to calm down," she instructed. "Stress is not good for you. The last thing I need is you agitated and this poison coursing through your veins even faster."

"I'm calm," he replied. "And that's a nice plan, but you should know that if at any time I feel like Cutty's double-crossed us or put you in harm's way, I promise you I'll put a bullet in his head."

"I second that motion," Lucas replied, coming up behind them.

"There's one more thing," she told Coulter, ignoring his threat. "There's been a change in plans."

"Good grief, now what?" Coulter muttered.

"We'll need more emylanoroc, and it's in London."

Coulter pinched the bridge of his nose. "Of course it is."

"We're going to split up. You and I will take the DC facility while Lucas rendezvouses with Alexa King to get it."

"She'd better know how to handle herself. And don't forget the fifty grand," Lucas said sweetly.

She gave him an exasperated look before turning back to Coulter. "That's how much it'll cost us to get it."

"Rena, I don't have access to that much cash, not this fast. I'd have to contact Liam and—"

"We already have it. Alejandro is going to wire it to Alexa in London. She'll have it by the time Lucas arrives."

"Are you sure? That's a ridiculous amount of money."

"Yes, I'm sure. We don't have time to haggle over the price, Coulter. We have to take things as they come. We'll worry about the rest after you're cured."

Glancing out the window, Coulter was thoughtful. "There are so many moving parts to this, Marena. I don't know if this is even going to work."

"Yes, it will," she said with conviction.

He stared at her. "How do you know?"

She laced her fingers with his. "Because it has to."

Joseph Brinkley was heading to his car when his cell phone rang. Glancing at the screen, he quickly answered it.

"Bad news, sir," Falconi said. "Our contact at Beecham can't create a new encryption and decryption key for Silent Night."

"Can't or won't?"

"Can't," Falconi clarified. "The vials created can be activated only by the asymmetric encryption algorithm created with it. No other key will work. Plus, there are no additional vials. We have all the Silent Night there is—period."

Brinkley's anger skyrocketed. "Is he certain?"

"Yes, sir. If we don't find the key that Colonel McKendrick stole, we're going to be looking at the most expensive, nonlethal paperweights in the world."

"We did not come this far to fail," Brinkley yelled into the phone. "As long as the auction can happen as scheduled, I don't care about the minute details."

"Minute details? Joe, Silent Night is dead in the water

without that key. It's not a matter of 'it would be nice to have.' It's just liquid in a vial without it. If we had some paraffin wax, it could be a lamp," Falconi said sarcastically.

"I don't need you being part of the problem," Brinkley snapped. "We need solutions. We move forward as planned and continue to track down McKendrick."

"If you say so."

"Yes, I do. We'll get those codes before the auction, and no one will be the wiser."

"One more thing," Falconi added. "Our new client has requested that we push our meeting tonight to eleven o'clock. He has a business meeting he needs to attend first. If it's inconvenient for you, I can handle the meeting myself and—."

"No," Brinkley said quickly. "I am at all initial meetings, Derek. You know that."

"Understood. I'll alert his assistant that the time change is acceptable."

"Thank you. And, after we get Silent Night, Derek, see to it that our scientist is properly chastised for his sudden change in our agreement."

"I'll see to it personally, Mr. Brinkley."

"Good."

Derek hung up the phone and turned his attention to the laptop on his desk.

"He'll be there as scheduled, Señor Palacios."

"*Excelente*, Falconi. Thus far, you've kept your end of our bargain, and I intend to do the same. Once Brinkley is dead, and you have taken over all his business holdings, we can talk about further advancements on a more global stage."

"Thank you, señor. I appreciate your trust in me."

"My trust is earned, Falconi. Continue moving me closer to my end goal, and you can enjoy the promise of a long, healthy life."

Brinkley was all smiles as he got into his Range Rover.

He threw his briefcase onto the seat next to him and called his wife on his cell phone. Then, after letting her know that he would be late coming home, he hung up and placed his phone in his cupholder.

He was about to put his key in the ignition when someone grabbed him around his neck and placed something over his mouth. He struggled with his unseen attacker as he was forcefully pulled toward the back seat. His leg hit the horn several times to draw attention to his situation, but it was too late. As the drug he had inhaled began to take effect, Brinkley could feel himself slipping into unconsciousness, and there was nothing he could do to stop it. As darkness surrounded him, the last thing that came to mind was *Silent Night*.

"I'm not waiting indefinitely for him to wake up."

Two men stood side by side in a darkened, windowless room. The only light was hanging over one of the two wooden chairs in the room. Their captive was tied to the seat with two thick leather straps, one across his chest and the other at his shins. He was wearing dress slacks, a disheveled dress shirt, and a tie.

A roll of duct tape sat on the floor by his feet along with his suit jacket.

"It's only been twenty minutes."

One man gazed at his watch and then back to the unconscious man. "I think he needs some incentive."

His partner nodded. "What do you suggest?"

"Hand me that knife."

Brinkley's eyes popped open, but something was over his eyes, keeping him in the dark. He attempted to speak, but it was unintelligible because of the gag in his mouth. Livid, he tugged fiercely against the rope binding him to the chair.

"Look at that. He was awake, after all. I told you he merely needed some motivation."

"That you did."

A man reached out and yanked the blindfold off Brinkley's head. The sudden movement stood his already messy hair on end.

Brinkley blinked several times as his eyes adjusted to the light. Finally, when he saw the two men standing in front of him, his eyes practically bugged out of his head. Several times, he attempted to speak, but it was useless.

Cole Everett leaned over and peered into Brinkley's confused face. "How's it going, partner? Now, I bet you're sitting here wondering what's going on, aren't you?"

Brinkley struggled for a moment but then stilled and nodded.

"Come on now, Joe. I'm sure if you put your mind to it, the answer would present itself."

The two men waited for a few seconds, staring intently at Brinkley. Eventually, he shrugged his shoulders and shook his head.

"No?" Cole asked. "Hmm. That's too bad."

The other man reared back and hit Brinkley in the face. The force of the blow sent him and his chair reeling to the floor like a tree being chopped down. The back of Brinkley's head connected with the concrete floor, causing him to let out a loud moan. His body shook from the effort of trying to escape the restraints.

General Dash bent down and tilted his head to the side to look their prisoner in the face. His mouth curled upward into a smirk. "Did that jog your memory?"

Cole reached over and hoisted the chair upright. Instantly, Brinkley struggled, trying to break free.

"I don't think that will work," Terry offered. "Cole tied you up pretty good. Now, are you going to answer, or are we going to kick it up a notch?" He leaned in. "Personally, it doesn't matter to me. Either way, I'm going to get the an-

swers I want. Now, how long that takes and how painful it will be is completely up to you."

"So, Joe, are you ready to tell us about Silent Night?" Cole asked.

Recognition darted across his face for a few seconds before a blank expression replaced it.

This time, Terry delivered a front kick to Brinkley's chest. He fell backward and connected with the floor a second time. He closed his eyes and grimaced with pain.

"Still don't know what we mean?" Cole squatted down so that he wasn't towering over Brinkley. "One of the perks of having a partner is getting to know that person over the years. You develop a rapport with them, learn how they operate and what makes them tick. And not just what their likes or dislikes are, but other, more personal details that they don't share with people." He leaned over until they were eye to eye. "Like what they're afraid of."

This time, when they set him back upright, his expression was apprehensive. His gaze darted around the room before settling back on Cole. Sweat glistened on his forehead as he tried again to loosen the slack on the rope binding his hands.

Brinkley moved his head around to prevent Terry from placing the blindfold back on, but it was in vain. His muffled tone grew angry now that he couldn't see.

"Your mind must be working overtime trying to guess what's coming next," Terry chuckled. "Don't worry, Joe, we won't keep you in suspense."

Sauntering across the room, Marena's father returned with a large sack. He untied the knot at the opening and sat it on Brinkley's lap. Brinkley jumped upon contact, but eventually, he settled down. It took a few moments for the first snake to make its way out of the bag.

Cole and General Dash watched as it slowly exited the bag. But then, meeting no resistance, it cautiously journeyed

up Brinkley's arm. When he realized what was in his lap, Brinkley almost turned the chair over himself, trying to get away from the serpent.

They removed his blindfold so that he could see what was coming. Brinkley was practically hysterical by the time the fifth snake was out of the bag. Terry removed his gag. Brinkley gulped in the air. "Get these things off me!" he roared. "Get them off!"

"Not a chance. There are plenty more where these came from to ensure you stay motivated to tell us the truth."

Chapter 24

One snake slithered up his chest and wrapped itself around Brinkley's neck like a scarf. He was almost in tears.

"Okay, okay. I'll tell you what you need to know. Now take them away," he demanded. Then, when no one moved, he said, "Please."

"Why don't you start by telling us what we want to know, and then we'll consider removing the snakes," Cole advised. "Let's start with why you'd betray your country by selling our weapons to foreign adversaries—and using my company to do it."

Brinkley looked at Cole as though astonished at the question.

"Why does a person do anything they shouldn't? For money. For power. These guys would get the weapons they needed with or without my involvement. So, why not make a profit off them in the process?"

"You were using Ghost Town to do it," Cole bellowed. "Exploiting my connections, damaging my good name and the relationships it's taken me decades to foster, and for what? A few million dollars?"

"I never tarnished Ghost Town or your precious name, Cole. No one knows about my business dealings. It's all done by a third party."

"You're lying," Cole snapped. He walked over to a table

and retrieved a folder. When he returned, he threw it on Brinkley's lap. "If I could find out about it, Joe, anyone could. I've been having you investigated for months now. Coulter was investigating you, too, which leads us to Silent Night. Where are you hiding the bioweapon, Joe? And what have you done with my grandson?"

"I had nothing to do with Silent Night, Cole. That was all Falconi. I swear to you, I would never harm Coulter— ever." He was crying in earnest now as the snakes continued writhing around him.

"I may be guilty of many things, but I'm not dealing in bioweapons or killing anyone."

Terry stepped up and hit Brinkley across the jaw. One of the snakes reared back as if to strike.

"Stop it!" Brinkley was apoplectic. "Are you insane? Do you want to get me bitten?"

"Cut the crap, Joe. We know you injected Coulter with Silent Night. We know you're after him and that he has days to live. And I'm sure you know my daughter, Marena, is doing everything she can to save him. Unfortunately for you, when you messed with Coulter, you messed with Marena and by extension me. And I don't play nice or fair when it comes to traitors—or anyone that messes with my family. A quick death or rotting in a nice, cushy prison is not on the table for you. No, I'll make sure you disappear where no one will know where you are, and you'll never see a familiar face—or this country again. Now, I suggest you quit playing games and tell us where he is."

"If you find Derek, you'll find Coulter and Marena. He knows where they are. He's after them because there's a bid for Silent Night in a few days. He needs the access codes that Coulter stole to activate the bioweapon. It's useless without them." Brinkley turned to Cole. "You have to believe me. I didn't do this. Falconi is the one you want."

Cole reached over and grabbed the collar of Brinkley's jacket. "If I find you deceived us—"

"I'm not, Cole. I'm not."

"Let's go," Terry said and motioned to the door.

Cole stared at Joe as if he were a stranger. "You're fired. And if we discover you tipped Falconi off that we're coming, or if you try to run, we'll have you arrested and prosecuted within an inch of your life."

Terry's smile was genuine. "I hope you do run. It'll make my plans for you so much more exciting."

They turned to leave.

"Wait, aren't you going to untie me?"

"No," they said in unison.

"Wait a minute. You can't leave me like this. Come on, I cooperated and told you everything I know. You gotta get me out of here, Cole," he pleaded. "Cole?"

They walked out, and Terry slammed the door shut. He turned to a man standing on guard at the door.

"Give him another fifteen minutes, and then send medical in to give him the water bottle and patch up his face." Terry reached in his pocket and retrieved a small manila envelope. "Make sure they use this Band-Aid, understood?"

"Yes, sir."

"You certain it'll work?" Cole asked as they headed upstairs.

"Of course. The tracking device is passive and won't be detected. He'll lead us right to Falconi. In the meantime, I'm going to rendezvous with Lucas. You sure you don't want to come?"

"No," Cole said firmly. "This isn't how I want to reintroduce myself to my grandson. I'll stay anonymous. At least for the time being. You can take my company jet."

Terry nodded. "Thanks. I told you years ago that you were plumb crazy for not telling him the truth."

"It's the way Sonia wanted it," he said with a pained expression. "I was respecting her wishes."

"If you ask me, you've indulged her too much over the years." Terry patted him on the back. "But I understand. The things we do for our children."

"True. Thanks for everything, Terry. I know you'll do whatever's needed to ensure their safety. If Coulter doesn't make it before I get a chance to—"

"Hey—" Terry stopped him. "He'll make it, Cole. I know my daughter. She won't stop until she finds a cure and saves his life."

Fighting back emotions, Cole cleared his throat. "So you can kill him yourself?"

Terry smirked. "I considered it. But that would break Marena's heart," he said thoughtfully. "And that's simply something I can't do. Losing her mother and then Coulter was hard. It was enough sorrow to last a lifetime. Regardless of how this turns out, I just want my baby girl happy. She deserves it."

"I feel the same way about my family," Cole said wistfully. "There's been some thawing on Sonia's side, but I won't force her to accept me. It must be her decision—and Coulter's. I'm a patient man. So I'll wait as long as it takes."

"It'll all work out," Terry said with conviction. "Trust me on that, Cole. I'm seldom wrong."

The two friends shared a laugh. Then, leading the way upstairs, Cole led them out the back door to the helicopter waiting on his expansive lawn. The pilot started the engine when he saw them coming.

"Good luck, Terry. Bring my grandson back to me."

"Are you sure you want to do this?"

Coulter turned to Marena and waited for an answer. It was raining outside, so the only sound was the windshield wipers' intermittent noise skidding across the glass.

Marena turned in her seat. "Break into a lab and steal a chemical that we need to create an antidote to save your life? Yep, I sure am," she said firmly.

When they arrived at the Baltimore/Washington International Thurgood Marshall Airport, a Lincoln sedan was waiting for them with the gear they needed to enter the pharmaceutical facility. Coulter maneuvered through congested evening traffic. Eventually, taking US-50 heading west toward Washington, DC, Marena reviewed Alejandro's intel.

"Well, it's closed for repairs from a minor fire, so it's not as bad as it could be, but there are still security guards on-site, so we'll have to be careful," Marena pointed out. "We have the access code and a map of the facility, so the odds of us making it in and out without being detected have improved considerably."

Coulter nodded. "Entering through the basement near the service dock is our best bet on entering undetected."

Biodyne was in Bowie, Maryland, a suburb outside Washington, DC. At the end of an industrial park, it had closed hours ago, so there was no traffic. Coulter parked in an employees-only parking garage and cut the engine.

Marena pointed to the map. "Research and Development will be on the fifth floor. The lab is across the hall."

Coulter studied the blueprint again. "This stairwell will drop us closest to R&D and reduce the possibility of too much company."

Coulter got out and retrieved their bags from the trunk. He handed one to Marena. "You ready?"

Marena slung her backpack on. She took a few deep breaths. "As I'll ever be."

Coulter halted when he reached the building entrance. "How about I go in alone?" he said quietly. "This shouldn't take long, and I'll be back before you've had a chance to miss me."

"No way," she whispered. "We need to stick together, Coulter. Too many things could go wrong."

While they specced out the mission, both agreed on no collateral damage, so Coulter handed Marena a Taser to use if they encountered trouble. Then, with Coulter on point, they entered the access code on the security panel and slipped inside.

Marena's heart was beating wildly in her chest. She tried to control her breathing, but everything started closing in. What if the codes they had didn't work? What if there were surveillance cameras in an area they hadn't accounted for? Sweat formed on the back of her neck. Suddenly, she stopped. Coulter almost ran into her back.

"Marena? What's wrong?"

"Uh, I'm fine," she panted. She grabbed the handrail and leaned over, trying to catch her breath. Closing her eyes, she tried to concentrate on not panicking. "Just need a minute. Is it hot to you?"

He came around in front of her. "Hey, look at me." When she didn't comply, he touched her arm. "Rena, open your eyes and look at me."

It took some effort, but she finally managed it.

Retrieving a penlight from his jacket, Coulter shined it in her face to check her pupils.

"Are you feeling nauseous, light-headed?" He guided her to sit on a step.

"No, I'm okay. But aren't you worried about what happens if it's not there, or we get stopped, or—"

He leaned down and kissed her. The kiss was slow, deliberate, and full of strength. When Coulter ended it moments later, his forehead was still touching hers, and his lips lingered against her mouth. Then, reluctantly, he stood up.

"Marena, we have made it this far, which is miraculous. So, don't worry. We're almost at the finish line, sweetheart. We can do this—you can do this."

"Did you kiss me just to distract me?"

"That depends. Did it work?"

Color seeped into her cheeks. "Yes," she admitted holding out her hand.

He clasped her hand in his firm grip. "Let's go."

After helping her up, he pointed to the stairwell. By the time they reached the fifth floor, both were breathing heavily.

"This is horrible," Coulter complained. "I can't believe I'm winded after that short climb."

Marena turned to him. "Seriously? That is what's occupying your thoughts right now?"

He grinned. "Stick close," he warned and then opened the door.

The hallway was dim, with only running lights strategically placed along the baseboards.

Following behind Coulter, Marena tried to move as silently as he did.

As they rounded the corner, they heard footsteps coming their way, and muffled voices. He took Marena's hand and bolted down the opposite corridor. There were several offices. He had to try three before finding one that was open.

Pulling Marena inside, he shut the door. Not bothering to let her go, they both stood against the entryway. The only sound to be heard was their mingled breaths. As men's laughter and talking grew louder, Marena closed her eyes and tried to remain calm. Being close to Coulter had always caused her pulse to race. That had not changed.

She felt Coulter squeeze her shoulders. Their gazes locked when she opened her eyes, and neither looked away. Despite the danger of discovery, Coulter smiled and kissed the bridge of her nose. Marena wasn't aware that she was holding her breath until he mouthed the word *breathe*.

Chapter 25

Expelling her breath slowly, she nodded. He let her go and moved her aside. Opening the door just a few inches, Coulter checked the corridor.

"It's clear. Let's move."

They didn't run into anyone else on the way to the lab. Once they reached the door, Coulter gave Marena the signal to stop. He motioned for her to stay put while going inside to check things out.

When he returned, he gave Marena a thumbs-up sign before stepping aside so that she could enter. She searched the room with practiced efficiency. First, she looked through several glass cabinets before finding the drug she needed. Taking two vials, Marena placed them in a shockproof case and slipped them into a compartment in her backpack.

When she opened the door and went cautiously out into the hallway, she found Coulter in a fight with a guard. She set her backpack down and was about to go help when another man rushed onto the scene."

"Hold it right there," he told her. "Who are you?"

"I'm not giving my name," she replied.

"Oh, I think you will, little lady." He handed her some handcuffs. "Do you want to put these on, or shall I do the honors?" He grinned at her lustfully.

Her lips curled in distaste. Before she could say anything, he grabbed her hand and tried to put them on.

Marena didn't waste time asking him to let go. She made him.

Winding her arm around, she applied counterpressure to the man's wrist until he yelped in pain and dropped her hand. He recovered and clutched her by the jacket, but Marena placed her hands on either side of his neck and began applying pressure to choke him out.

She tried to see how Coulter was faring with the other man when she noticed a second approaching.

While she was preoccupied, the man broke free and shoved her to the floor. She hit her head upon impact. Dazed, Marena tried to get her bearings when she saw the man looming above.

"This is going to sting a little." The man retrieved a Taser from his tactical duty belt and was about to use it. Marena tried to kick him in the shin but missed. He aimed and was about to pull the trigger when Coulter came up behind him and caught him in a chokehold. The guard tried to fight but passed out.

Coulter knelt by her side. "Are you okay?"

"Yes, I hit my head when I fell. It's not serious."

He took a moment to look it over. "You're right. There isn't any skin broken."

"Told you."

"Then we should go." Coulter retrieved the backpack, took her hand, and rushed to the stairwell.

After making it out safely, Coulter asked again if she was alright.

"I'm fine," she said, catching her breath. "You?"

"Five by five."

Marena drove to the airport while Coulter sent a message to Liam to check his progress on finding out more

about his missing friends. His hand began to shake, but he didn't say anything.

"I think now is a good time to talk about worst-case scenarios. You know, just in case."

She frowned. "I don't want to talk about that right now. We'll be successful, so let's focus our efforts on healing you, not what happens if things go south."

"You know that's not realistic," he pressed.

"Then we're going to suspend reality for as long as possible."

Coulter shook his head. "You always were stubborn."

She smiled. "And you're not?"

At the airport, they left the car where they'd picked it up and headed to the plane. Coulter was walking up the stairs and stopped. A few seconds ticked by, and he was still immobile. Marena called his name. He swayed a moment before collapsing. Luckily, he held on to the railing and didn't fall backward. Marena yelled for help.

The pilot and flight attendant helped get Coulter in a seat while Marena searched for one of the canisters of medicine that Cutty had provided. She found it, injected Coulter with the drug, and waited.

Before the plane took off, she texted Lucas to check their progress.

Please tell me you have it.

Hi to you, too. Met up with Alexa. Not yet, but everything is on track. We leave shortly. Wow, you didn't tell me that she's like an Amazon.

Luke, stay focused.

You know I was always good at multitasking. How's Coulter?

Not good. Our mission went fine, but then he collapsed as we were leaving.

How is he?

I don't know yet. I gave him one of the vials of medicine that Cutty gave me. I hope that improves his symptoms, but I'm getting worried, Luke. He's getting worse.

Marena had to wipe the tears from her eyes that dropped onto the cell phone. She tried to remain calm, but she got more emotional as Coulter's condition deteriorated.

Listen to me, sis. We're so close. This was the last hurdle. I'll be back as soon as possible with the final ingredient, and then you can work on creating this antidote. You will save him. I have faith in your abilities, Marena.

She was crying so hard she started hiccupping.

Thank you, Lucas. I love you.

Love you too. Now get some sleep.

Despite the tears, she smiled.

Will do. Safe travels, and see you soon.

Roger that.

Cole rushed up the steps to the front door. He didn't hesitate as he pressed the doorbell and then banged on the door for good measure. His lips were drawn into a tight line as he impatiently waited.

"Dad?" Sonia was standing behind Alvin when he cau-

tiously opened the door and peered outside, a baseball bat firmly hanging in his left hand. "What's going on? It's two o'clock in the morning." She stopped talking and stared at her father's grim expression.

"Oh no, is it Coulter? Is he—" Without warning, Sonia's legs buckled, and she collapsed on the hardwood floor in a heap.

Alvin threw the bat aside to help his wife.

Letting himself in, Cole rushed over. "No," he said quickly. "He's still alive, Sonia, but we have a problem."

"Sweetheart, let's get you to the couch." Alvin ushered his wife to the family room. He sat next to her while Cole sat in a chair opposite them.

Cole rubbed his stubbled jaw. "There's no easy way to say this. Coulter has been injected with a biological toxin. There's no cure, and it will kill him in days unless one is created."

"No!" Sonia screamed, bolting from the sofa. "Where is he? I need to see him."

Cole got up, too. "It's complicated," he said, holding back the tears. "He was in North Carolina. Turns out he went to Marena so that she could help him. That was a few days ago. Now they're in Sedona, Arizona."

"Marena?" Sonia cried. "I don't understand. They broke up years ago. Why did he go to her and not to a hospital? Why didn't he tell us?"

"This is a specific creation that Marena and her colleagues had prior experience with when she worked at Beecham Pharmaceuticals. If he'd gone anywhere else, they'd have been stumbling around in the dark. The breakthrough serum Marena created helps wounded people heal in a substantially short amount of time. Right now, she's trying to engineer an antidote for Coulter." He glanced at them. "I'm not going to lie. It's a race against time. This toxin is

aggressive. Once injected, the person has six days before they're—dead."

"Where is he?" Alvin replied. "No matter where it is, we need to be there."

"They're at a laboratory that belongs to one of her colleagues. Terry is on his way there now to help. I'll be honest. Some people don't want Coulter alive or this bioweapon stopped. So they will do everything in their power to ensure Marena fails."

Sonia wiped her tears. "He called me the other day. I thought Coulter sounded strange, but I had no idea—" she struggled with the words "—that he was sick. I wish he'd told me what was going on. Why didn't he tell me?"

"Sonia, I'm sure he didn't want us worrying," Alvin replied.

"Our son is dying," she cried. "Why wouldn't we want to know that?" Agitated, she started pacing. "Plus, we're worrying now, so what was the point in keeping us all in the dark?" she said bitterly.

Alvin hugged his wife reassuringly. "I know Marena is doing all she can to save him."

"How do we know that? We don't know anything at this point except that our son has mere days to live."

"Sonia, you know how much Marena cares about Coulter. They were engaged, for goodness' sake. I know she'll move mountains to save him," Alvin replied.

She turned to her father. "Dad, where is he? We need to get there as soon as possible."

"I'll call the pilot and arrange to have you both flown there as soon as the jet returns and is ready to go."

"And you," Sonia corrected.

Cole shook his head. "I don't want to complicate anything by being there. It's better if I just hang back and you two go."

"No," she replied. "We don't know how this is going to turn out. You're Coulter's grandfather. You should be there, too, in case—" Sonia couldn't even complete her sentence.

Cole hesitated.

She went over to him. "I know things haven't been the best between us over the years, and it's mostly my fault."

"No, it's not," he corrected.

"Yes, it is. I'm the one that banned you from coming to see us. I'm the one that fractured this family. So, it's up to me to repair the damage. There have been so many wasted years. We'll never get those back, but we can move forward. Coulter needs to know who you are, Dad. It's time."

Cole stared at his daughter and then at his son-in-law. Alvin nodded.

"Okay." He struggled to keep his voice from breaking under the weight of renewed optimism. "I'll go make some calls."

The blow to Derek's jaw sent him crashing to the floor. Slowly getting to his knees, he spit out the blood in his mouth.

"You had two jobs to do, and you've failed me in both," Javier Palacios said in disgust while he flexed the fingers on the hand he had used to hit Derek. "I ought to kill you now and be done with it."

It took him a few moments to clear his head, but eventually, Derek staggered to his feet.

"You could," he told Javier. "But then you'd have nothing. No Brinkley and no Silent Night." He allowed himself a smile, the blood still on his gums and teeth. "Only I can deliver them to you because I know where Brinkley is heading, and you don't."

"I could just torture it out of you," Javier said matter-of-factly. "At this point, I'm indifferent either way."

"You could, but I doubt that'll yield the results you're looking for. If you kill me, I'll go to my grave before I utter one syllable that'll help you get what you want."

Chapter 26

Javier pondered Derek's words. Then, after what seemed like minutes, he burst out laughing.

"Fine, have it your way. I find your audacity refreshing, Mr. Falconi. Most people don't say whatever they want to me—and live."

"Then I'm honored to be the exception," Falconi stated boldly before spitting blood out of his mouth.

Javier laughed heartily at that. "Fine, I will allow you a chance to redeem yourself, but don't think I plan to make a habit of accepting your failures," he warned. "I don't even accept my family's, so you certainly won't be the exception."

Derek's face was throbbing, but he managed a slight smile. "I appreciate that."

He let himself out of the presidential suite where Palacios resided while in town. Calling the elevator, Falconi strode through the lobby, oblivious to the people gasping and staring at his disheveled and bloody appearance.

"I've had enough of your threats, Palacios," he sneered. "Kill me? I promise you that the first thing I will do when the opportunity presents itself is return the favor."

He surveyed himself in the rearview mirror when he got to his car. After assessing the damage, he opened his glove compartment and retrieved a packet of disposable wipes.

Falconi gingerly wiped the blood off his face before balling up the wipes and tossing them on the passenger-side floor.

He was about to start the car when his cell phone rang. He glanced at the number. Then, closing his eyes and sighing, he finally answered it.

"Where have you been?" Brinkley roared into the phone.

"Tied up," he responded.

"Meet me at the old warehouse in twenty minutes."

"I don't think I'll—"

"Twenty minutes, Derek. And don't be late."

Brinkley hung up before he could reply.

He pondered if the millions of dollars he stood to receive were worth the aggravation.

Decision made, Derek started the car.

"Yes," he finally said aloud. "It definitely is."

Eighteen minutes later, Falconi entered the dark warehouse. He was walking cautiously across the room when he heard a gun cock.

"That's far enough."

He halted and put his arms in the air.

"I'm unarmed."

"I don't believe that for a second," Brinkley snapped. He walked into the faint moonlight and stared at Falconi with distaste.

"Why would I lie?" Derek said impatiently.

"Probably the same reason you set me up—because it suits you," Brinkley accused. His anger fueled the edge in his voice. He kept his gun trained on Falconi.

"And exactly how did I set *you* up?"

"You told Cole where to find me, didn't you? He and his errand boy, Terry Dash, tried to interrogate me about Silent Night and Coulter's whereabouts. I almost got tortured to death by snakes because of your screwups. And you know what? I hate snakes!" he yelled. "It wasn't on my watch that

Cole's grandson got injected with Silent Night, it was yours, yet somehow I'm the one knocked around because of it?"

When Brinkley got closer to Falconi, he noticed his battered appearance. "What happened to you?"

"Me? Oh, I was busy getting interrogated by Javier Palacios. It seems he is still holding a grudge about his weapons being destroyed and Silent Night's auction up in the air. He blamed you and decided to use me to deliver a message. So, you see, I was a little too busy getting the crap beaten out of me to be setting *you* up," he snapped.

Brinkley looked like he was trying to decide whether or not to believe Derek's explanation. Finally, he clicked the safety on and holstered his gun. "If you're feeding me a line, Derek, I swear I'll bury you."

"Yeah, well, it appears to be two-for-one day on torture and death threats, so get in line."

"Need I remind you that if I go down, you go down?"

"Great, another threat."

"It's an observation," Brinkley clarified. "Like it or not, the two of us are tied together, so if you're thinking of double-crossing me, Derek, you'd better rethink that plan because I've got safety measures in place to ensure my longevity."

"For the last time, I'm not trying to play you. I've always been loyal to you and have just as much to lose as you do."

Brinkley looked skeptical.

"When have I ever given you a reason to doubt me?"

"Can you blame me?" Brinkley countered. "This net has gone pretty wide. If it weren't for one of your men injecting Coulter with Silent Night, we wouldn't even be in this predicament. You knew he was off-limits. Everything we set up, all the hard work, connections, and millions of dollars in payouts are at stake."

"Like I want to see everything go up in flames?"

"Well, what are you doing to prevent it? We need those

codes, Derek. He's a dead man walking, and yet for some reason, he's the hardest man in the world to find."

"I told you I'd handle it, and I will."

"Yeah, you've been handling it for days now. At the rate you're going, Coulter will be in a morgue by the time we catch up with him."

"I don't need a recap," Derek snapped. All efforts at civility were gone.

"Oh, you don't?" Brinkley crossed his arms. "Great, group activity leader, so what's your plan?"

Falconi's cell phone beeped before he could answer Brinkley. He checked the screen and quickly connected the call.

"What?" he demanded. "What?…When?…Good job. I'll be in touch."

When he hung up, Brinkley said, "Well? What was all that about?"

"I just received word that a flight plan for the company jet was just recorded."

"So?"

"So," Derek repeated impatiently, "it went to Sedona, Arizona. It will be prepped and refueled for another flight carrying Cole, his daughter, and his son-in-law when it returns to Ghost Town. To the same location."

Brinkley digested that information. "So that means—"

"You got it. They know where Coulter is hiding. We follow them, and they'll lead us straight to McKendrick."

Brinkley smiled broadly but instantly regretted it when the skin was taut across his busted lips. "I'm going with you. McKendrick's time of holding all the cards is finally up."

And so is yours, Falconi thought to himself.

Coulter awakened to complete, unnerving silence. Feeling sweaty, he wanted nothing more than a long, hot shower, but first he checked on Marena. He found her asleep in the lab but sitting on the couch with her head cocked back.

Her glasses were at a weird angle on her face. Quietly, he went over and gently lifted her legs and rotated her body to lie down. Then, kneeling beside the couch, he watched her sleep.

It was one of his favorite things to do. When they were together, he would usually get up earlier than she did for that very reason. Coulter was fascinated by how her nose crinkled when she smiled in her sleep or the low-level snore she never owned up to.

Marena Dash was his whole entire world.

He almost lost his mind from heartbreak when he left the last time. He couldn't envision having to do it again. Still, if Marena didn't want to be with him, he would respect her wishes and leave. No questions asked. He had put them both through hell the last time. He'd rather die than make the same mistake twice.

You are dying anyway, he reasoned. Coulter had been trained to accept that he could die at a moment's notice. He wasn't afraid of it. In truth, he had always envisioned it would be quick and unexpected but in the line of duty. Nothing had prepared him to have it dragged out for days on end. Or the volatile, yo-yo side effects he was enduring from Silent Night. He had an intuitive feeling that his time was almost up. Suddenly, Coulter was overcome with emotion. Tears lurked in his eyes at the thought of leaving the woman he loved. Of having to let her go permanently. Coulter rubbed his chest to ease the physical pain.

Marena rolled over onto her side. Coulter went to grab a nearby throw. When he returned, he placed it over her and kissed her forehead. "Get some rest, my love," he whispered.

Marena murmured something incoherent.

He didn't have much appetite but decided to go warm up some soup to help keep his strength up. He checked his text messages while waiting for it to boil. There was one

from Liam. When he read it, he sighed with relief at the news that his buddy Neil had resurfaced.

That's fantastic news. I'm pleased to hear it, he typed back.

Tex-Mex wanted me to give you a message. He said not to worry about him. He aims to stay off the radar. I told him about what happened to you, and he said, "Remember that guy that gave up? Well, neither does anybody else, so you fight like your life depends on it because it does."

A lump lodged in Coulter's throat. He was overwhelmed with emotion at reading Neil's message. He didn't tell Liam, but part of it was a code for him. A-I-M-S meant that his friend had arrived in Melbourne, Australia, safely.

As for continuing to fight, Coulter was doing his best, but deep down, he knew that he was losing the battle and that Silent Night was winning.

He would continue to fight for Marena's sake and not give up. But each day that brought him closer to death was a struggle for survival.

Coulter heard a firm tapping on the front door and glanced at his wristwatch. It was two-thirty in the morning. He knew that Lucas was due back but was unsure of the time. Careful not to wake Marena, he went to let him in.

When he opened the door, it was Marena's father standing on the other side.

"General Dash," Coulter said in surprise.

Terry came in, bringing two duffel bags with him.

"How are you, Colt?"

"I've been better, sir." They were indoors, which was the only reason why Coulter didn't salute Marena's father.

He set his bags down. There were a few moments of awkward silence before Terry moved in and hugged Coulter. He clapped him on the back a few times.

"I'm sorry to hear about what happened."

"Thank you, sir. I can't imagine what you must think of my being here."

"Nonsense," Terry dismissed. "You did the right thing seeking Marena out. I know she would've wanted you to find her, given the circumstances."

"I won't lie. My chances are extremely slim, sir."

"I didn't come all this way for a funeral, Colt," Terry retorted.

Chapter 27

"Nor did I, but—"

"There are no *but*s. Dashes don't quit. We don't know how. Marena will give it everything she's got to ensure you survive. Don't give up."

"Never," he vowed.

"Speaking of which, where is my daughter?"

"She's sleeping. Would you like me to—"

"No, let her sleep. She must be exhausted. You, too."

"Yes, she is."

Coulter remembered his soup was cooking. He excused himself to retrieve it. He wasn't surprised when he turned back around to find Terry standing in the doorway.

He offered Terry some, but he declined.

Sitting down at the table, Coulter moved the spoon around in the bowl more than he ate.

"Not that good?"

"It's fine. I just don't have much of an appetite."

"I'm sure you have a lot on your mind."

"A lot pales in comparison to everything going through my mind right now."

"I promise you that we'll bring all our resources to bear."

"Thank you. I'm still baffled why I got injected in the first place. I can't imagine why someone would waste Silent Night on me just because we thwarted a weapons deal."

"I had a nice, long, painful conversation with Joe Brinkley at Ghost Town. Well, painful for him," Terry corrected. "He claims not to know what Falconi was up to, but I'm not buying it. Derek doesn't make a move without Brinkley knowing it. Either way, the net we're casting is to get the bigger fish in this scheme. So far, Javier Palacios and several other bidders think they're anonymous and aren't implicating themselves directly. However, we've had our eye on them for a long time. We've followed the money trail from Beecham Pharmaceuticals on down. Brinkley's involvement is just the tip of the iceberg where this bioweapon is concerned."

Coulter's back hurt, so after he cleaned up, they moved into the living room so that he could sit on the sofa. He propped his feet up on the coffee table. Closing his eyes, Coulter took a few deep breaths, but the pain was etched on his face. Terry tried to mask his worried expression.

"Better?"

"Yes, a little," Coulter replied, his voice coming out in a strained whisper.

"What else do you know about Silent Night?" Terry asked, trying to give Coulter something else to focus on besides the pain.

"It's useless without the key unlocking the cipher codes used to activate the sequence," Coulter told him. "It was on the thumb drive we took. I uploaded the data to a secure server before destroying it."

"So someone unlocked the sequence for one vial before you stole the drive?"

"Looks that way."

"Then injecting you with it was part of the plan."

Coulter nodded. "Yes, and we're back to the question of why."

"I'm going to be honest, Colt. I never thought we'd see

you again. Not after the way things ended between you and Marena."

Feeling better, Coulter stood up and cautiously stretched.

"I know," he replied as he moved around the room to stretch his limbs.

Terry's gaze followed him.

"While I can't condone your leaving my daughter three years ago, Coulter, I know how it feels to want to protect the one you love at any cost. But I also know how ripped apart you can feel inside at losing your soul mate. Lily was my entire world, Colt. She was my partner—in all things. And when she died—" Terry struggled to get the words out. "My whole life collapsed in on itself. I was just a shell of a man for so long that I honestly thought I was losing my mind. And to never have caught the cowards that did it. Well, let's just say that I went down a dangerous black hole and didn't think I'd be able to pull myself back out."

"I was scared that what I do every day, the danger I face, could somehow affect Marena," Coulter admitted. "I didn't want her on the receiving end of anything that would cause her harm. I didn't want to lose her—"

"The way I lost Lily," Terry finished for him.

"I'm sorry."

"It's okay. We've never really talked about it, have we?"

"No, but that's my fault, too. I got so freaked out about Mrs. Dash's death that I just went off the deep end. I didn't process what I was feeling and couldn't put into words how it affected me until it was too late."

Coulter returned to the couch. A tortured sigh escaped his lips.

"I never meant to shut Marena out or hurt her the way I did. I thought I was saving her from future heartache, but instead, I caused more by not being open about what I was going through."

"Coulter, I loved you like a son. So now I'm going to

give you some fatherly advice. You've been given a second chance to fix the damage you created, but time is running out. Marena needs to know the truth about what happened, and it's time she heard it from you."

"Actually, she and I discussed it," Coulter confessed.

"And?"

"Marena said she wanted to focus on saving my life before we waded through the swamp that was our past relationship."

Terry arched an eyebrow. A smirk came across Coulter's face.

"My daughter said that?"

"In so many words, yes."

He chuckled. "Marena has always been one to tackle one problem at a time with a laser-like focus and single-minded intensity." Terry looked up. "And now, you're the subject of all her energy and efforts. Who knows when you'll be able to have that talk?"

"If I survive this, it's worth the wait—she's worth the wait, sir."

Terry mulled over Coulter's words.

"You know, my wife used to say, 'Don't be discouraged. It's often the last key in the bunch that opens the lock.' She wasn't the one that created that quote, but each time she used it, it was apropos."

"Sage words, indeed. I miss Mrs. Dash very much."

Terry smiled sadly. "So do I, Colt."

"Dad?"

Both men turned to find Marena staring at them with surprise."

"Hello, my beauty," Terry said, greeting his daughter.

She ran into his arms. "I'm glad you came," she sobbed against his jacket. "I've missed you."

"And I've missed you."

Closing her eyes, Marena breathed in his signature co-

logne. She held on to her father like she was in the middle of a storm, and he was a lifeline.

"I'll give you both some time," Coulter replied before slipping out.

"I'm sorry I couldn't have been here sooner, honey. I know this has been a lot to deal with on your own. Why didn't you tell us what was going on? You know we'd have dropped everything to help."

She released him and sat down on the edge of the coffee table. "I know. Lucas has been fantastic since he's been here. Honestly, I wouldn't be this far without him."

He took a seat. "So, are we going to talk about the elephant in the room?"

Marena snorted. "Which one?"

"The tracking device?"

She stared pensively at her father. "We're absolutely going to talk about it—just not now."

"Fair enough," Terry agreed.

Her father brought her up to speed on his encounter with Brinkley and Falconi. He purposefully left Cole out of the recap.

"The two of you aren't safe, Marena. There's no telling who'll be after you next. We should move you and Colt to a more secure facility."

"Dad, all the equipment I need is here. Luke is in London bringing back the one thing I'm missing. I know you're worried, but Coulter has been through so much. The last thing I want to do is move him again. This place has high-tech security, so we'll be safe."

Terry leaned back in his chair. "If you insist on staying here, I'll review this place's security features and get one of my teams out here to help protect you."

"Dad, that's not necessary."

"Yes, it is, so don't argue. We both know in the end that I'm going to get my way."

* * *

Marena knew there was no trying to convince her dad once he'd made up his mind about something. So, she promptly let it go.

"Suit yourself. I'm going to check on Coulter."

"Sounds like a plan." Her father got up and stretched. "How about pointing me to a bedroom?"

"Down the hall and the last door on the left. You'll be bunking with Lucas, but it has an en suite bathroom."

"You mean Lucas will be bunking with me," her father corrected.

Marena chuckled and left the kitchen.

Terry waited until she was gone before he took out his cell phone and dialed a number.

"It's me," he said when the line connected. "I'm here. You got the address I texted you?"

"Yep, sure did. Thanks," Cole replied.

"Small hiccup. Brinkley's signal has dropped. He must've taken off the Band-Aid because I'm not getting a location for him anymore."

"Meaning we can't track his movements." Cole let out a loud sigh. "Well, now what?"

"I've already dispatched my team here, but they won't arrive until tomorrow night at the earliest."

"I'll see what I can do about getting there sooner."

"Thanks. I have no idea what Brinkley and Falconi will be up to next. Or Palacios, for that matter. We need to be prepared for anything."

"Roger that," Cole replied. "Keep me posted. We're about to head to the airport. I'll check in when we land, then text you the address to the hotel."

"Okay, but I'm staying with Marena and Coulter. Just Lucas being here isn't enough. Heck, neither am I, but we're all they've got for now."

"How's Coulter?"

Terry pondered sugarcoating it, but he finally said, "Not good, Cole."

After a few moments, Cole said, "Thanks for leveling with me. See you soon, my friend."

Ending the call, Terry went to the bedroom to get settled in.

Two men dressed in suits rushed into the room. "You have a phone call, Señor Palacios."

They stopped short at seeing their boss playing a game.

"And? I asked not to be disturbed," Javier replied, not bothering to stop throwing the small missile in his hand.

"But, señor, it's Derek Falconi. He said it's urgent."

The missile hit dead center. Smiling, he picked up another dart and hurled it at the board on the paneled wall.

He snapped his fingers, and the man holding the cell phone rushed over and handed it to him.

"Do we have the location?" he asked, skipping the pleasantries.

"Not yet," Falconi responded. "But we'll find them. There aren't that many labs here that can accommodate the security level needed to create an antidote."

He turned around and motioned toward his assistant to retrieve his darts.

"Perfect. Let the pilot know that we're heading to Sedona as soon as possible. I'm not waiting around. Falconi, I want their location when I land."

"Understood."

"I want to look Brinkley in the eye when I take Silent Night from him—right before I kill him."

Falconi glanced up to see Brinkley heading his way. The last thing he needed was to be caught talking to Palacios.

"I have to go. I'll check back in when we have something."

Brinkley came back from the gas station market and jumped up into the rented Jeep. He retrieved the pack-

age of beef jerky and tore the top open. Taking out a thick piece, he gnawed on it before popping the lid on the can of an energy drink.

"You want some?"

Falconi looked at the hard, dried meat and shook his head. Sliding into the driver's seat, he started the engine and took off down the road. An hour later, they were on a dirt road on the outskirts of town.

"Are you even bothering to follow the GPS directions?"

"Of course I am," Falconi said tersely. "There's nothing out here. We must've made a wrong turn."

Chapter 28

"You're the one driving," Brinkley pointed out. "Any mistake is on you."

"Fine," he sighed loudly. "I'm turning around and heading back to the main road."

"That sounds like a—"

When he didn't finish his sentence, Falconi glanced over. "A what?"

"Why would... Stop the car."

"What?"

"Stop the freaking car!" Brinkley yelled.

Falconi mumbled something before applying the brakes and pulling over.

"What's going on?"

"It's a solar farm."

Falconi stared at him. "So?"

"So, how many solar farms have you seen since we got here? Besides, with all this heat, they're not as efficient. So why would there be a farm sitting here in the middle of nowhere?"

"Beats me."

"For a power source that isn't on the city grid," Brinkley reasoned. "My instincts tell me this is what we've been looking for, Derek. So follow this and see where it goes."

A few minutes later, they came upon the sizable building.

"That's it," Brinkley enthused. "Cut your lights and pull over. We don't want to get any closer and risk tipping them off."

Falconi complied. "Okay, now what?"

"Now we give the team our coordinates and tell them to get here on the double. I want to strike while we still have the element of surprise."

"Makes sense," Falconi replied. Taking out his cell phone, he sent two text messages. One was to their Ghost Town team. The second was to provide Palacios with their coordinates.

"Why'd you send two messages?" Brinkley inquired after he'd finished.

"This is too important to leave anything to chance. If only one person gets it, what happens if it takes them a while to check messages, or overlook it? This way, I can be certain the message is received, and the team is mobilizing."

"We're back in business, Derek," Brinkley said gleefully. "Now, we'll have Silent Night back under our control, and we can resume our auction as planned."

Brinkley leaned back in his chair, a smug look planted on his face. "And no one has to know how close to going off the rails this whole enterprise came, right?"

Derek nodded. "As you said, everything is unfolding just as it should be."

Poking her head into Coulter's bedroom, Marena found him asleep, so she closed the door and headed for the lab.

An hour later, she was sitting at her desk doing some calculations when she got a weird feeling. Right afterward, the lights went out. When they didn't immediately go back on, she felt around on the desk for her cell phone.

"How is this possible? The lab has a separate generator."

Finding the flashlight app on her phone, Marena turned it on. She walked over and flipped the light switch on the

wall off and on. Next, she walked down the hallway and noticed that the lights were on in the rest of the house.

"Great," she muttered. "I must have tripped a circuit breaker or something."

Flustered, she went looking for the circuit breaker box. Unable to get the power restored, Marena headed outside to check out the backup generator.

Not seeing the problem, Marena turned to go back inside when she spotted a man dressed in all black going across the lawn, carrying something over his shoulders. She stared in shock. When she saw the difficulty he was having, followed by movement, she realized it was a body and took off running to intercept them.

Using her body as a weapon, Marena dove onto the man, knocking him off balance. When he fell, she realized Coulter was the one tied up. She quickly yanked the gag off his mouth.

"Marena, run," he yelled.

She smelled the metallic scent of blood. "Coulter, you're bleeding." Marena's gazed traveled over him to figure out the origin. Then, while trying to untie his hands, a man yanked Marena around her waist, lifting her off the ground.

"Get your hands off of her," Coulter roared.

"This doesn't concern you," he said in a muffled voice. "Just let us take him, and we'll let you live."

Marena struggled to free herself. "I don't think so," she responded before kicking him repeatedly in his shin and following up with an elbow to the stomach.

Her assailant dropped her before doubling over in pain. Seizing the opportunity, she spun around and delivered a knee to his solar plexus.

He let out a strangled sound as the wind was knocked out of him before crumpling to the ground.

"Watch out," Coulter warned.

She turned around, but not fast enough to keep from

being hit in the face. The blow made her stagger backward. The aggressor used the opportunity to try and take Marena to the ground. She evaded him, but not his punch to her middle section. Taking a moment, Marena was able to muster up enough strength to deliver a roundhouse kick, but he grabbed hold of her foot and started pulling it away from her body to throw her off balance.

"Rena, flex and clinch," Coulter called out.

Flexing her toes, she countered by pulling him toward her so that she could clinch up and deliver a blow to his head. She followed up with a flurry of elbow strikes until he went down.

Rushing over to Coulter, Marena tried again to free his hands, but they were bound with a zip tie. She was breathing heavily from the exertion.

"Just help me up. I've got these."

Helping him to his feet, she watched him try to break free, but he didn't have the strength.

"Wait, I've got it," she said, trying to assist him with the momentum needed to snap the tie.

Two other men were advancing on their position.

"They're coming," he warned.

Turning around, Marena placed Coulter behind her.

"Rena, I can—"

"You're in no shape to fight," she cut him off. "You're the one they're after, Colt. I need you to try and get back to the house while I distract them."

"I'm not leaving you here to fight them off by yourself." He tried again to break the restraint but failed. He let out a roar of frustration.

Dodging the first attacker, Marena hit the carotid artery in his neck, rendering him unconscious in seconds. He collapsed to the ground in a heap.

When his counterpart lunged for Marena, she placed her arms on the inside of his grasp. Next, she guided his upper

body away from her and then applied a lot of pressure to the weak point between two of his ribs. Howling in pain, he dropped to his knees.

A car pulled up, and several men jumped out and ran toward them.

"No, don't engage them," Coulter called out. "Let's go."

Holding on to Coulter's arm, she ran with him back to the entry door. Before they reached it, Terry rushed past them with a high-powered assault rifle and laid down covering fire. Once they were clear, Terry took out the attackers, but the driver got away.

Terry kept the car in his scope sight until it faded from view.

"Dad, help me!" Marena screamed from inside the house. "It's Coulter."

Terry bolted through the door. "Where are you?" he yelled.

"In the hallway."

He slung the rifle over his shoulder and ran. He found Marena hunched over, taking almost all of Coulter's body weight. He got on the other side and lifted Coulter upright. Working together, the two of them helped Coulter get to the lab.

"You're cut," she said after removing his shirt and assessing his injuries. "You've lost a lot of blood, and this will require stitches."

"What about you? Your lip is swollen.

"I'll live," she replied, keeping her anger in check. Unfortunately, the effort was too great. "What were you thinking risking your life, Coulter? You should've just gone back to the house as I asked."

"If you think I would leave you out there to take on those men while I slinked back to the house with my tail between my legs, you're crazy. I wasn't about to allow them to hurt you or risk you ending up dead."

"The goal was for *you* not to end up dead," she argued. "I had the situation under control, Coulter."

"I don't care how it looked. The odds were not in your favor, Marena—and you know that."

"We agreed before that you would listen to me and not risk your life—"

"*You* are my life, Marena!" he roared. "So don't ever ask me to walk away and not try to protect you from harm. Not as long as I draw breath."

"Okay, you two. Let's calm down," Terry interjected. "You are both safe, and the immediate threat has been eliminated for now. That's all that matters."

"You're right, Dad," Marena concurred. "But they'll be back."

"Then we'd better get ready."

Coulter opened his mouth to speak but then stopped. A weird look crossed his face before he glanced up at Marena.

She leaned in. "Colt? What's wrong?"

Without warning, he slumped over on the examination table. He would have pitched forward onto the floor if Marena hadn't been standing before him with her body keeping his stationary.

"Coulter? Can you hear me?" She laid him down and grabbed a stethoscope to check his heartbeat. "Dad, can you hand me that pressure cuff?"

Terry hurried to get it.

"Would you mind?"

He nodded and wrapped it around Coulter's arm and, using the second hand on his watch, took his blood pressure.

"It's ninety over sixty."

"That's way too low," she replied. "And he's having heart palpitations."

Marena retook his vitals ten minutes later.

"They haven't improved." She retrieved the case Dr. Cutty had given her and took out the last vial.

"What's that?"

"It's the medication Frank gave me," she said while preparing to give Coulter the shot. "It's not a cure, but it will help alleviate some of his symptoms."

After she injected it into his arm, they waited for it to start working.

Terry glanced at his daughter.

"That looks like more than just worry," he noted. "What's wrong, honey?"

"That was the last dose, Dad. If anything happens to him between now and when I'm finished creating the antidote, I won't be able to slow down the poison."

He walked around the table and hugged his daughter. "Have faith, Marena. Just take this one step at a time."

Just then, Lucas flew into the door with his gun drawn. When he spotted his family, he relaxed and holstered his weapon.

"Luke," Marena cried. She rushed over and hugged her brother. "I'm glad to see you."

"Glad to see you, too," he replied, returning the hug. He tilted his head toward the door. "What's with all the dead people littering the front lawn?"

"They tried to take Coulter. We stopped them," Terry said matter-of-factly before coming over and hugging his son. He slapped him on the back. "Probably Brinkley's men."

"Ah." Lucas sat his backpack on the table. He retrieved a canister from one of the zipper pockets and handed it to his sister.

"As promised."

"This couldn't be better timing," she replied. "Coulter isn't doing so great."

"Then you'd better get moving." Lucas squeezed her shoulder.

"We'll be outside clearing away the debris," her father said. "Call us if you need anything or something changes."

"I will," she agreed and got to work.

Lucas tried waking his sister up by calling her name from across the room. When that didn't work, he came over and shook her.

"Marena? Marena, come on, wake up."

Marena turned her face in the opposite direction with a loud groan, her head still lying on her arms.

"Five more minutes."

"Come on, sis. It's Coulter. He needs you. Right now."

The last word relayed a sense of urgency that eventually sliced through the sleep-induced fog in Marena's brain. She opened her eyes and bolted upright. Her head spun from the effort. Marena rubbed her hands over her face before glancing around, trying to get her bearings. "How long have I been out?"

"Beats me. I just popped my head in to check on you a few minutes ago. You were passed out, so I went to see Coulter," her brother replied. "Rena, he's not doing so well."

Marena jumped off her chair so fast she stumbled. Catching herself, she ran to his bedroom. The bed was empty. Before she could look around, she heard Coulter retching in the bathroom. She found him draped over the toilet bowl. Blood was everywhere. "Oh my God, Coulter."

Chapter 29

She pulled two towels from the linen closet and stepped over him. Then, throwing one towel on the floor to sop up the blood, she crouched down and used the other to wipe his face. "Coulter, when did this start?"

"Not sure," he said tiredly. "I was asleep, and the pain woke me up. After that, I felt sick and—"

She cringed when he doubled over again and vomited. His whole body was racked with violent spasms.

"We've got to get him to a hospital," Lucas called from the door.

"He won't go. Silent Night can't become common knowledge, remember?"

"Marena, he's throwing up blood—"

"Help me get him cleaned up and to the bed," she said, cutting him off.

Her brother nodded. "I will, but he needs help, and we may be too late from the looks of it."

"Shut up," she railed at him. "Get in here and help him. I'll be back in a minute. And so help me, Lucas, if you say something like that again—"

Her brother threw his hands up. "I'm sorry, okay? Now go."

She touched Coulter's arm. "I'll be right back."

"Make...make sure you bring a miracle back with you," he joked between spasms.

Marena stepped over him and rushed past her brother. She ran back into the lab and began yanking cabinets open. Her fingers were shakily going over vials and bottles of supplies they had brought with them. Finally, she grabbed one and ran to the crash cart.

"What are you looking for?"

Marena spun around. "Luke, why did you leave him alone?"

"He stopped vomiting. I got him cleaned up, and he's back in bed. What's happening?"

Marena shot past him to retrieve something off the work-table. "We're running out of time, that's what. Bring that." She pointed across the room. "We'll need to monitor his heart rate and blood pressure continually. Luke, hurry," she yelled over her shoulder.

Once in Coulter's bedroom, Marena flicked on the overhead light.

Coulter cringed at the brightness. "Am I dead? I've always heard there was a bright light." His breathing was labored before he was reduced to a fit of coughing.

"Save the jokes for when you're not coughing up a lung," Marena chided while she worked.

"Rena."

She halted, and their gazes locked. Her expression brooked no arguments. "If you say it, I swear I'll stop your heart and then shock it to life again just for the heck of it."

Coulter tried to grin, but it took too much effort. "I wasn't going to."

She sat next to him and placed his arm in her lap. "For the record, you don't lie that well—at least not to me."

Coulter reached out with his other hand. He touched her face lightly before his arm shook and fell back from the

effort. Tears rolled down his cheeks. "We're out of time, sweetheart. It's okay. You did your best."

Tears welled up in her eyes, too. "Soldier, you haven't seen my best. Now stop acting like a quitter and listen to me."

Coulter's eyebrow rose. "Did you…just…call me a quitter?"

Lucas's smile was grim as he hovered on the other side of the bed.

Marena wiped the tears from her eyes. "Coulter, I need you to listen," she told him again in a severe tone. "You're right. We are out of time, but I figured out a way to give us a little more."

Coulter's eyes opened. "How?"

"I'm going to put you in a deep sleep. Hopefully, this will slow the progress of the poison and give me the time I need to finish the antidote."

A worried expression crossed his face. "You're going to put me in a coma?"

"A medically induced one, yes. Don't worry," Marena soothed. "I'm going to use phenobarbital. It works quickly, and it's safe. There aren't any issues with respiratory depression, so we won't have to worry that you'll suddenly stop breathing."

"That's good to know," Coulter shot back. "Because I do enjoy breathing."

Lucas knelt beside the bed. "Sis, are you sure?"

"We'll be monitoring his heart and blood pressure the whole time." She turned back to Coulter. "I'll pull you out if there's any sign of trouble, okay?"

He nodded, but his expression remained pensive. "If you think it'll work."

She rubbed his shoulder. "I do. I wouldn't suggest it otherwise."

Decision made, Coulter's eyes glistened with unshed tears. "Okay, doc," his voice trembled. "Let's get this going."

"Get what going?" Terry called from the door.

Lucas filled him in on what was going on with Coulter. Terry's expression was severe as he said, "This is the best course of action?"

Marena nodded. "It is, Dad."

"Okay, what can I do?"

She lowered Coulter's arm back to the bed and stood. "Dad, can you bring that IV stand over here, please?"

Lucas stepped out of the way while Terry went to get it. He rolled it over to the left side of the bed while Marena secured the IV bag she had brought in and hooked up the line. Coulter watched her as much as he could, but most of the time, his eyes were closed as he struggled to overcome his shaking body.

"Okay, we're all set," she said softly. Then, returning to the seat by Coulter's side, she took his hand and entwined their fingers. "The medicine is going in."

Coulter looked briefly at Lucas. "Keep her safe."

Lucas leaned in and squeezed his arm. "Of course. You just keep fighting, bro."

"Roger that," Coulter whispered.

Terry knelt so that he was at eye level with Coulter. "We will see you soon, son."

After exchanging glances with Marena, Lucas and their father slipped out of the room and shut the door.

A shadow of a wicked grin flittered across Coulter's face. "I thought they'd never leave."

Marena tried to look stern, but his smile was infectious. "Relax." Her hand stroked his face. "You should be feeling the effects of the medicine now."

"Yep," he said slowly. "High as a kite."

She leaned in and rested her forehead on his. She tried to keep her voice even, but it shook when she said, "My face will be the first one you see when you wake up." When she

pulled back, he was staring at her intently as if committing every facet of her to memory.

"Promise?"

Marena linked her fingers through his and squeezed. Coulter faintly returned the pressure. It wasn't strong, but it was enough for her.

She kissed him softly on the lips. Their tears mingled together on their faces.

"I promise. I love you, Coulter Aaron McKendrick—I never stopped."

"And I love you, Marena Lillian Dash." His eyes closed. "More than my life."

When he didn't respond, panic prompted her to nudge him. Marena said, "Hey, you hold on to that life when his eyes opened. Do you hear me, soldier? You fight, Coulter. I need you to fight for your life—for our future."

"I'm trying, my love."

Relieved, Marena let out a slow breath. "That's all I need." She swiped the tears away with the back of her lab coat. Her gaze traveled to the monitor equipment and then back to Coulter.

He looked at her a final time before saying, "I'll see… you… Rena."

Tears flowed unchecked down her face. "You'd better."

Marena watched him drift entirely under. It broke her heart, but there was no other way. She double-checked his vitals before easing the covers up to his chest. It was difficult, but she got up and trudged to the door. Unable to stop herself, Marena turned and looked at him a final time. Her heart constricted at seeing him lying there deathly still. So vulnerable and unlike the man she loved. Marena turned the light off and quietly closed the door.

Lucas was right outside. "He's—"

"Yeah," Marena confirmed with a sigh. "He's under."

Her brother hugged her. Marena was rigid in his arms.

When he released her, he kissed her cold cheek. "I'd say it was time for that miracle."

Unable to get the words out, Marena merely nodded.

Without warning, Marena bolted down the hallway and out the back door. She ran down a gravel path, past the pool and gazebo, and didn't stop until she had run right up to where a trailhead began. She was winded and huffing with exertion. Dropping to her knees, Marena covered her mouth with both hands and began to cry. Her muffled sobs racked her entire body. Finally, doubling over, she succumbed to the pain and fear threatening to overtake her.

This time, another pair of strong arms encircled her and held her close.

"It's okay, baby," Terry murmured into her hair.

"Dad," Marena said in a voice burdened with all the pain and hurt she was feeling.

"I'm here."

"He's in a coma, Dad. I put him in a coma."

"Hey, you're saving his life, Marena. You did what you had to do. This gives you the time you need to save him."

"What if it's not enough?"

"Only time will tell, honey. But I do know that never in your life have you shrunk away from a challenge. This is no different."

Terry continued kneeling there in companionable silence until she said, "Thank you, Dad."

"Listen, I have something to tell you. First, I want to apologize for my methods in trying to protect you over the years—"

"Dad, you don't—"

"No, please hear me out."

Marena nodded.

"I was in such a nonproductive, unhelpful headspace that I couldn't see my way out of it. Then, after your mom died, I saw danger lurking around every corner, waiting,

biding its time until it could strike again. That car explosion weighs heavily on me, Marena—still. I was supposed to protect Lily, and I failed. It should've been me in that car, not her." He struggled to maintain his composure.

"Dad, you can't protect us all twenty-four seven. Nothing is guaranteed. You have to trust that what you've tried to teach us has stuck. I know how to defend myself because of you."

"I did my best. But I never wanted either of you to feel defenseless. You're a fighter, Marena. You always have been. I merely gave you a target."

"Dad, while I understand your motivation, it doesn't excuse any of your, Lucas's, or Coulter's methods of tracking my movements. Can't you see that it was invasive and a violation of trust? Plus, you can't tell me how amazing, wonderful and adept at handling dangerous situations I am in one breath yet justify putting a tracking device in Mom's necklace and monitoring my movements in another."

Terry pondered her words. Finally, he said, "You're right. Marena, it was wrong of me to do so without your knowledge. You have my word that I will never put another tracking device on you again. I will respect your privacy, and try not to hover so much. Notice that I said *try*."

Marena grinned. "Yes, I did."

He hugged her tight. "As for Silent Night, you can do this, my beauty. I don't want you to experience the loss of someone you love dearly—not like this. I know you'll be able to create an antidote, Marena."

"How? How do you know that?"

"Because I have confidence in you. I know it's overwhelming, but adversity is where you excel, sweetheart. Do you remember when Mom used to say that running away from any problem—"

"Only increases the distance from the solution," she finished for him.

He tilted her face up to meet his gaze. "No truer words," he replied. "Coulter is counting on you to save his life— we all are. You have all the tools you need right in here," he told her, pointing a finger at her head. "And here." Terry pointed to her heart.

He stood up, bringing Marena with him. "You're a Dash," he said firmly. "*Defeat* is a foreign language that we never want to learn. So, dust that dirt off your shoulders, and go in there and save the man you love."

Chapter 30

Lucas squeezed Marena's shoulders. "We're here for you, sis. You've got this."

Marena took a deep breath before glancing over at Lucas. "Thanks, big brother." She held up the crystalline substance and peered through the glass test tube. "I'm going to need to use the gas box to finish up."

"Wait," Lucas said, scanning the lab. "That huge, ominous thing over there that looks like some kind of medieval incubator?"

"Yes, that's the inert glove box," Marena replied, not bothering to look up. "It allows us to safely work in a controlled atmosphere. We'll need it to finish the counteragent."

"We?" Lucas's eyebrows flew upward. "Don't even try and suggest I'm much of a help in all of this."

"You are—more than you know, Luke. This wouldn't be possible if it weren't for you and Alexa. We're indebted to you both."

"Nonsense, we're family, Marena. I'd do anything for you—and Coulter."

"Well, when all this is over, I'll have to thank Frank for putting us in contact with his associate. I couldn't have finished without him."

Lucas glanced away.

Noticing the quiet, Marena stopped and looked up. "What is it?"

He sighed loudly. "Alexa received news that Dr. Cutty went missing."

She frowned. "What? How? I thought he was under Alejandro's care?"

"He left. He told Alejandro that he wanted to go home and that nothing would stop him. So, what could he do? He let Frank leave, but he did keep a security detail on him for surveillance."

She smiled. "That sounds like Dro."

"There's more, Rena. His detail reported back that Frank was in a car accident. It was awful, Marena. Unfortunately, he may not make it."

"No," she croaked, backing up. "No, I don't believe that."

"Dr. Cutty was driving home and somehow lost control of his car and slammed into a concrete partition. The car burst into flames. A few motorists stopped and worked to get him out. They saved his life, but he's in critical condition. Guards are posted outside of his hospital room per Alejandro's orders. You know, in case it wasn't an accident."

Marena sat heavily on a nearby chair. She lowered her head into her hands. "Frank."

"I'm sorry. That's all the information I could get for now."

She sat back in her chair, a worried expression on her face. "Thanks for letting me know, but you know as well as I do that this wasn't an accident."

Lucas sighed. "Probably not. That's why I'm not leaving your side. There's no telling what he might've said and to whom before that accident."

"He doesn't know where we are. I never told him my destination."

"Still, if Brinkley were responsible for Cutty's accident, he'd know you'd be relatively close by and that Coulter would be unable to travel long distances."

"It's because of me that Frank is in that hospital bed fighting for his life."

Sliding a chair up, Lucas straddled it to face his sister. "Hey, don't go there. You had nothing to do with Cutty working on that project. You're no more to blame for this than Coulter. He knew it was wrong and could cost who knows how many lives, and he did it anyway. Frank is to blame for his own selfish, vanity-driven ambition. As for Brinkley and Falconi, they betrayed their country and set all this in motion. They deserve what they get. Unfortunately for Cutty, he's collateral damage in a much bigger game."

"Not if I can help it," Marena vowed. "I won't let Frank's contribution be in vain or allow Coulter to suffer for Brinkley's twisted machinations. Their sacrifices won't be for nothing."

With that, she turned her concentration back to the antidote. Marena worked feverishly through the night to finish. Her father often brought in something to eat or sat down and spoke to Lucas in hushed tones.

When Marena trudged over to the couch Lucas was draped across, sleeping, it was almost dawn. When she tapped him on the shoulder, his eyes flew open.

"What's wrong?"

"It's finished."

He bolted upright and followed her over to her workstation.

"The antidote? Wow, it's done," Lucas said, pointing to the solo vial in a test-tube holder.

"Yes, but I don't have time to test it before giving it to him," she lamented. "If it doesn't work—if any calculations are wrong—it could kill him."

"If you don't give it to him, he's dead anyway."

They turned to see Terry standing behind them.

"So, this is it?"

"This is it," she repeated. "Now we give it to Coulter and pray that it works."

Terry and Lucas followed Marena into Coulter's room. They watched as Marena injected him with medication to bring him out of the induced vegetative state. Then, sitting at his bedside, Marena held his hand.

"Now what?"

"Now we wait," she told her brother. "I want his vitals to come up substantially before I give him the antidote."

Turning her attention back to Coulter, she touched his cheek.

"Sis, it's been who knows how long since you've gotten some rest. How about I watch over the patient while you go get some sleep?"

She hesitated. "I don't know, Lucas. I really should stay in case something happens."

"Dad and I are here. Go ahead. I promise you that I'll come to get you the minute there is any change in his condition."

Reluctantly, Marena took her brother's advice. She kissed Coulter's lips before leaving.

"Anything at all, Lucas," she reiterated.

"Go, Dr. Dash. I'm on the clock."

"Thanks," she replied before trying unsuccessfully to stifle a yawn.

Marena was sound asleep when she was awakened by a hand over her mouth. Her eyes flew open, but it was dark, and she couldn't make out a target. She instinctively started to struggle. However, it wasn't long before she found out if it was a friend or foe.

"If you utter a sound, I promise you the last thing you'll see is the smile on my face before I snap your neck."

Marena remained quiet as the hand left her mouth. Her attacker started to introduce himself, but she cut him off.

"Save it. I know who you are, Brinkley. Is Falconi with you, or did you let him off his leash?"

He laughed. "Since you know who we are, you're aware of what we're capable of doing. And Falconi should be looking for Coulter as we speak."

Hearing Coulter could be in danger caused her to struggle.

"If you—"

He yanked Marena up to her feet. "Uh-uh. Save your threats. You know what I did to your ex. Do you think I would hesitate to harm you?"

"I don't put anything past you, Brinkley," she jeered. "How you're still walking around and not in jail for treason and attempted murder is anyone's guess."

He sputtered. His face turned a mottled red, but the lights weren't on for anyone to see it.

Marena stumbled in the dark. When Brinkley's grip loosened for a moment, she contemplated trying to break free. He said, as if reading her thoughts, "Don't try anything. I'm not kidding."

Instantly, she stopped struggling and let Brinkley guide her out of the room and down the hallway. Her eyes scrunched up, trying to avoid the bright light. Fear gripped Marena as she frantically wondered about her father's and brother's whereabouts. She didn't want to do anything to tip Brinkley off that she and Coulter may not be alone.

"Where's Coulter?"

"I'd worry less about your ex-fiancé and more about what will happen to you if you don't give me what I want."

"I don't get why you'd try to kill him anyway if he has information that you need."

"An unforeseen setback for sure, but then again, Coulter has an annoying habit of sticking his nose where it doesn't belong. What can I say? He and his team stumbled into the middle of something they shouldn't have."

"Skip the vagueness. I know all about Silent Night and the access codes and your criminal behavior."

Brinkley yanked her closer. "One hundred million dollars can ensure that I never see the inside of a courthouse or do one day of prison time."

"You seem to be forgetting the United States' stance on bioweapons."

"There are loopholes for everything, Dr. Dash. If there weren't, Silent Night would never have been created, and you and I wouldn't be standing here now, having this lovely chat."

When they walked out into the main living space, Marena tried to look around casually. Nothing was out of place, yet she knew her family must be around somewhere.

Even Brinkley noticed the eerie quiet.

"Where is Falconi?" he said with annoyance. He pressed a pistol to her side. "Get moving. I need those codes."

Marena reluctantly guided Brinkley to Coulter's bedroom. Spotting Coulter still asleep, she let out a sigh of relief that he was unharmed.

He shoved Marena forward. "Wake him up."

"That could be dangerous. I haven't finished the antidote yet, so Coulter is in a horrible state. I have him in an induced coma so that—"

"I don't care," Brinkley stormed. "Either you wake him up, or this bullet will," he said, waving his gun. "The choice is yours."

As far as Marena was concerned, there was no choice. She snatched her arm away from Brinkley and headed back to her lab. When she returned, she had two vials and a hypodermic needle.

She turned back to Brinkley. "How do I know that you won't harm us once Coulter gives you what you want?"

"You don't," he laughed. "There will be a major explosion at the lab. It's unfortunate, but there is always a

risk involved in working with dangerous chemicals. But, of course, you two won't survive. That's the nature of the beast sometimes, isn't that right, Dr. Dash?"

"If you think Coulter will give you those codes just so you can turn around and kill us, you're mistaken."

Brinkley got comfortable on a stool and tilted the gun in Coulter's direction.

"No, we both know Coulter would gladly die for his country. But I'm betting he'd move heaven and earth to save you."

"Not if it meant you were getting your hands on Silent Night and selling it to the highest bidder," Marena shot back.

Brinkley shrugged. "I'm willing to test my theory."

Chapter 31

Javier secured his bulletproof jacket and grabbed a rifle from one of his men.

"Has Falconi checked in?"

"Yes, Señor Palacios. It's just Colonel McKendrick, the woman, and Brinkley."

"Good, let's move in. I don't want Brinkley making it out with Silent Night, am I clear?"

"Yes, sir."

Javier's men proceeded up the path to the house.

"Dad, are you sure Marena and Coulter are okay?" Lucas asked.

"Right now, they're the safest of all of us. Brinkley won't do anything to harm either one until he gets those activation codes. So, they're fine, but we don't know for how long, so we need to take out as many targets as we can."

"Roger that."

Lucas got into position and set up his semiautomatic sniper rifle. When he was ready, he said, "On target."

Terry was spotting for him, so he used his spotter's scope and established his position. Then, when he had his wind calls ready, he said, "Spotter ready."

Lucas made a final adjustment based on his father's last wind call. "Shooter ready."

They worked as a team to take out Palacios's men. Terry adjusted where necessary. The suppressor on Lucas's rifle reduced the sound and muzzle flash of the shots, making Lucas less visible to his targets. The night-vision scope on his rifle allowed him to see his marks and take them out in succession before Palacios's men knew what hit them and from which direction.

"Where is that shooter?" Palacios yelled over the noise of his men returning fire. "I want him found."

"We need to fall back," one of his men replied. "We're taking too many casualties."

"No, set up a flanking maneuver. They can't get all of you."

Palacios and his men set out, approaching the house on both sides.

"They're flanking," Terry warned.

"I see it," Lucas called back. "Gonna need you."

Terry grabbed his rifle and positioned himself a short distance from Lucas. They worked together to take out the rest of Palacios's team.

Inside, Marena prepped Coulter and was ready to administer the medication.

"Why do you need two serums?" Brinkley asked.

"Both are needed to bring him out of the coma," she explained.

But in truth, only one of the vials was the antidote.

Shots sounded outside. Surprised, Brinkley turned to Marena.

"Hurry up."

"We can't rush this process," she snapped. "We don't know what it will do to Coulter."

"I don't care. I want McKendrick awake right now. So,

either you do it, or I will. And I guarantee my way will be bloody."

Brinkley released the safety and dropped a bullet into the chamber.

"Okay," Marena said quickly. She set both vials on the table and set up an IV drip of epinephrine for Coulter.

"How long will this take?"

"This delivery method allows the medication to go directly into his bloodstream. If all goes well, it should take about five minutes."

"Lucky for you."

Just then, Falconi came in. He anxiously scanned the room before coming to Brinkley's side. "Shots have been fired outside. We're out of time," he said impatiently.

"Shots from who? Coulter's men?"

"Unknown, but did you get the key?"

"We'll have it in a few minutes. The doc has been nice enough to wake McKendrick up for us. After that, we'll get what we need."

"We may not have a few minutes," Falconi countered.

Brinkley frowned. "Then you need to go out there and buy us more time. He's no good to us dead."

Falconi glared at him before he grabbed his rifle and stomped off.

Turning away from them, Marena focused her attention on Coulter. She stroked his face while she waited for him to regain consciousness. It took some time for him to come to, but eventually, he opened his eyes.

"Rena?" His voice sounded like a car driving over gravel.

"I'm here," she soothed. "You're going to be okay, Coulter. Just take it easy."

"Am I...cured?"

"I don't know yet," she said honestly. "I have to run some tests. But we're in trouble. Brinkley and Falconi are here. They want Silent Night's activation codes."

"Yes, or I'll be forced to put a bullet in your girlfriend's head—and then yours," Brinkley called out from over her shoulder.

Marena turned to glare at Brinkley. "Back off. We need to give him a few minutes. He could have an adverse reaction, go into cardiac arrest, or have other issues. Then you'd get nothing."

Brinkley was thoughtful for a moment. "No tricks," he replied grudgingly.

When Coulter was more lucid, Marena helped him sit up. He was still weak, but he wasn't showing any of the previous symptoms before she put him into the medically induced coma. That made her hopeful.

"We need to hurry," Falconi said, glancing toward the door. "Palacios is here."

"What?" Brinkley bellowed. "How is that possible?"

"I don't know," Falconi replied. "But we need to get those codes and get out of here."

Brinkley spun around to Coulter. "Time's up. I need those codes."

"You're not getting them, Brinkley," Coulter said tiredly. "I'm not about to provide you with the key that you need to activate Silent Night and possibly cause a global incident."

"I'm not really asking. Give me what I want—" Brinkley reached over and yanked Marena to his side "—or the love of your miserable life gets a bullet while you watch."

Coulter tried to get up off the bed.

"No," Marena cried out. "You're not strong enough yet. Don't set yourself back fooling around with Brinkley. He's not worth it."

"Let her go," Coulter warned.

"Or you'll what? Lean on me to death? Look at you. You're barely standing," he laughed. "There's no way you're a threat to me. Now, I'm going to ask you one last time.

Give me those codes, or you'll be wearing little pieces of your girlfriend."

"Okay," Coulter sighed. "I'll give you the codes, but Marena walks away unharmed."

"No, Coulter. Don't believe him. He will kill us both when he gets what he wants."

"I'm not giving you anything until Marena is gone."

"I'm not leaving you," she countered.

"Rena, it's okay." Coulter managed a smile.

"Deal," Brinkley agreed. "Where are they?"

"I need my laptop."

"Where is it?" Falconi replied.

"It's in the lab."

"Let's go," Brinkley announced. He tried to yank Marena behind him, but she went over to help Coulter walk.

Coulter pointed to his laptop when they reached the lab while Marena helped him sit down. Falconi retrieved it and handed it over.

Marena contemplated breaking free, but she caught Coulter's gaze. He shook his head, which was barely noticeable, but she saw it.

Sitting at the table, Coulter logged into his computer. "I need a thumb drive," he stated.

"Done." Brinkley nodded to Falconi, who retrieved one from his jacket pocket.

Coulter downloaded the codes and removed the portable drive from his computer. He handed it back to Falconi. "Here. Now keep your promise. Let her go."

Brinkley shoved Marena away from him, and she ran straight to Coulter. They embraced.

Kneeling in front of him, Marena placed a shaky hand on the side of his face. "Are you okay?"

Coulter's hand covered hers. He was slowly trying to stand, so she helped him up.

His voice was strained when he said, "Not really, but at least I don't feel like I'm going to die any second."

When Falconi reached his side, Brinkley held his hand out for the thumb drive.

Instead of handing it to him, Falconi placed it in his pocket.

"What's going on? Give me that drive."

Falconi backed up to put some distance between them. "I don't think so."

Brinkley looked shocked. He shook his head as if he hadn't heard correctly. "What did you say?"

"I said no."

Brinkley was shaking with barely controlled anger. "This is no time for jokes, Derek," he said sternly.

Falconi raised the gun up in the air. "I'm not laughing. Well, at least not yet."

Coulter turned so that Marena would be behind him and backed them away from Brinkley and Falconi. "Looks like you got double-crossed, Brinkley."

Brinkley's mouth curled up into a snarl. His head snapped toward the direction of Falconi.

"What's the meaning of this?" he demanded.

"I'd have thought it was obvious by now, Joe. It's time to get rid of you," Falconi replied with the gun still raised.

"How dare you try to usurp me," Brinkley bellowed, his hands flexing at his sides. "I'm the one who put this all together. Not you, me. I'm the one who used my contacts over the years to ensure that Ghost Town thrived. You were just a worker bee that dreamed of grandeur while I made things happen."

"You did help me," Falconi agreed, "but I've found someone else who can help me more."

Falconi glanced past Brinkley to find Palacios standing there.

"Hello, Joe."

Brinkley spun around. "Palacios." He turned and fixed Falconi with a mutinous glare. "You're a fool if you think you're safe. I taught you better than this, Derek. He'll betray you the first chance he gets."

"Maybe so, but I'll have one hundred million all to myself—and Ghost Town. So the way I see it, it's a win-win."

"What?"

"You always did underestimate me, Joe. Ghost Town has been my goal the entire time. The money from all the bidding deposits for Silent Night was a bonus. And one that will set me up for life after you and Cole Everett die, of course."

"Are you truly this stupid, or are you faking?" Brinkley said with disdain. "Either way, you'll pay for it with your life. You won't last five minutes partnering with Palacios, much less long enough to withdraw any of that money he's pretending to give you."

Falconi's face turned red. "Shut up." He turned to Javier. "Now, if you'd be so kind as to transfer the rest of my money, I'll give you the codes."

Javier smiled. He retrieved a cell phone from his vest pocket and dialed a number.

When the line picked up, he switched to Spanish. Coulter glanced toward Javier and then over to Falconi.

Coulter gripped her hand firmly. "Get ready to run," he whispered to Marena.

"What? Why?"

"This deal is about to go south," he replied confidently. "Brinkley was right. Falconi is a bigger fool than we thought. He doesn't realize he's getting played."

Javier hung up the phone. "Done."

Falconi retrieved his cell phone and used it to check his bank account. After verifying the money was there, he glanced up at Javier and smiled.

"It's a pleasure doing business with you, Palacios. As

for the money you thought you'd steal back from me, it's now safely in another account. One that you won't be able to find." He added the last part in Spanish.

The smug look on Palacios's face slid off like an avalanche of snow sliding down a mountain.

Before he could say a word, Falconi shot him in the chest. Coulter and Marena hit the floor, and Brinkley ducked as Javier gasped and dropped. Then, without warning, Falconi's chest lit up with the red dots of laser scopes. Before he could blink, Palacios's men opened fire. The sound of glass shattering was deafening as Falconi got riddled with bullets.

He sank to the ground next to Brinkley. A startled look was still on his face as the life ebbed out of him. Brinkley watched him struggle to say something before he gurgled and his eyes closed a final time.

Closing his eyes, Brinkley shook his head. "It didn't have to be this way, Derek."

Diving his hand into Falconi's pocket, he retrieved his thumb drive and cell phone. He glanced down at his dead partner. "I said you were too stupid to survive, and I was right." He jumped up and tried to make a run for it.

Faster than Coulter, Marena rushed over to Brinkley and attempted to stop him by clutching his arm. Using her momentum against her, he maneuvered her into a headlock.

"Marena," Coulter yelled.

"You're not walking out of here, you traitor," Lucas taunted from across the room, his gun trained on Brinkley. "Let my sister go."

Unfazed, he tightened his grip on Marena. "Oh, I think I am. I'll wager neither of you wants Marena to die—do you?" He backed up a bit, holding her in front of him like a shield. "And you can call me whatever you want. Thanks to that dimwit's betrayal I can buy myself a whole new life in another country, if need be, with the money I'll have. With

my connections, I'll disappear and now I have the launch codes for Silent Night, too."

His hold on Marena tightened. "This lovely lady will be my ticket out of here." He glanced between Lucas and Coulter. "Let's call her my insurance policy because neither one of you would do anything to risk her life."

As if to prove his point, Brinkley bent down to retrieve Falconi's gun.

"Not another move, Brinkley. You'll have to get through me if you want to take her."

"Not a problem." Brinkley aimed and shot Lucas.

Marena screamed as her brother went down. Then, shifting her weight, she headbutted Brinkley, throwing them off balance. As they crashed to the floor, Marena scrambled to get up. Brinkley grabbed her foot and tried to yank her toward him.

"Marena," Coulter called out as he tried to get to her.

"No," she called out. "Stay there."

Winded, a strange look crossed Coulter's face before he dropped to his knees.

"Coulter?" Marena kicked free from Brinkley. Then, in a conundrum over who to check on first, she decided on Lucas and rushed to his side. "Colt, I'll be right there."

Brinkley grabbed her before she could make a move.

Chapter 32

Marena broke free and delivered a blow to his jaw. He counterpunched, knocking her to the floor. Before she could recover, Coulter jumped on Brinkley and tried to wrest the gun from him. They grappled for a few moments before Coulter delivered a solid blow to his middle. Remaining on his feet, Brinkley struck Coulter on the head with the butt of his gun and laughed when he dropped.

"Stop right there." Brinkley raised his gun when Coulter recovered and tried to advance. He trained it on Marena, aiming at her head. "We both know that I'll use this if I have to."

Coulter stopped. Suddenly, a perplexed look crossed Brinkley's face, and his eyebrows furrowed in concentration.

"You know, I just thought of something." Using his gun, Brinkley motioned Marena over to Coulter's laptop. Taking the thumb drive out of his pocket, he dropped it into her hand.

"Put it in. We're going to check the codes that your loverboy gave me."

Marena's hands remained at her side. "No."

"Don't test me, Marena. I told you before that I would kill everyone here to get what I want. That hasn't changed. Now log in."

Fingers trembling, she opened Coulter's laptop and inserted the thumb drive.

Looking at the screen, Marena turned to Brinkley. "It's encrypted. I'll need a password."

He stared at Coulter with an arched eyebrow.

"Marena," Coulter stated. "The password is Marena."

Surprised, Marena's gaze traveled to Coulter. They shared a look before he winked.

Marena entered the code and extracted the files from the thumb drive.

"You don't have Silent Night here. So how will you even know if these codes won't work?" she pointed out.

"It's easy. I bet my life these codes are fake. Coulter wouldn't just hand over the codes without a fight. I want the real ones." He turned and faced Coulter.

"That's not happening," he said with a smile.

Brinkley fired a round into the ceiling and pointed it at Marena, who was trembling.

"I will fire until this gun is empty."

Coulter held up his hands in surrender. "Okay." He gave Brinkley the next passcode.

"Now, was that so hard?" Brinkley asked while waiting for Marena to log in to Coulter's server.

"Your time's up, Brinkley."

"Don't be stupid, McKendrick." He waved his arm in an arc. "I'm the one holding all the cards. I've got the money, the codes, and the girl—what do you have?"

Coulter stared over Brinkley's shoulder and smiled triumphantly.

"I've got backup. By all means, take him out, General."

Brinkley laughed at the not-so-clever ruse. "You're bluffing."

"No, he's not."

Upon hearing a menacing voice behind him, Brinkley whipped around to see Marena's father pointing a gun.

The gloating expression on his face fell like a landslide. Roaring in frustration, Brinkley instinctively raised his gun to defend himself, but it was too late. He was outnumbered.

General Dash's men rushed in, but Brinkley fired several shots into the room anyway and used the diversion to run.

He flew down the hallway toward the back of the house. Brinkley threw anything he could find behind him to slow down anyone who would be following.

"Dad, Lucas is down," Marena frantically told her father once the shooting ended. "Please check on him," she called over her shoulder while she rushed to Coulter's side and immediately scanned for injuries. "Are you okay?"

He hugged her with as much energy as he could muster. "As long as you are, I'm fine."

Marena sagged against him with relief. She took a few moments to calm herself before she could help Coulter up.

Cole rushed through the door with his gun drawn, followed by teams of men working for him and General Dash. He took a moment to assess the situation. He was about to check on Javier when Terry called over his shoulder, "Go after Brinkley."

Cole nodded and ran down the hallway.

"Dad, I'm fine," Lucas replied as his father hovered over him while the medical team put down their equipment. "The bullet went straight through."

"You're not fine," Terry insisted, trying to inspect the wound. "So quit giving me grief and let the medical team do their job."

Seeing that Lucas would make it flooded Marena with relief. Helping Coulter back onto the table, she staunched the bleeding above his eye and bandaged him up.

Sonia and Alvin rushed in, followed by another group of medics.

"Coulter," Sonia cried out, rushing to her son's side. She leaned over and hugged him.

"Easy," Alvin warned. "He still looks to be in rough shape."

"He is," Marena replied protectively.

"Thank God we made it in time," Sonia cried. "I was so worried it would be too late." She touched his cheek before pulling up a chair.

Coulter stared at his parents. "Mom? Dad? What are you doing here? How'd you know I was sick?"

"It's a long story, sweetie. One that's best left to when you're feeling better," his mother decided.

Another doctor tried to examine Coulter, but he declined. "I'm in excellent hands," he concluded, but being military medical staff, they insisted.

Cole caught up to Brinkley as he tried to get out of a tall window. He had hoisted a chair over and was about to hop up.

"Stop," Cole warned as he trained a gun on Brinkley's back.

Brinkley put his hands up. "Don't shoot."

"Slowly. I know you have a gun, so drop it, Joe—it's over."

Brinkley did as his partner instructed. He got off the chair and slowly faced him. "I admit that I'm surprised to see you here, Cole."

"I don't know how you could be. You came for me, my company, and my family. You had to know that I'd retaliate."

Brinkley shrugged. "Yeah, I guess I did, but it's still a surprise. But, honestly, I didn't think you'd get your hands dirty."

Overcome with emotion, Cole said, "I don't understand this, Joe—any of it. We've been in business together for over thirty-five years. We were the best of friends. We broke bread together, we worked and played together, talked about our dreams for the future."

"Your point?"

"You were at Sonia's wedding and my grandson's christening. You knew that I named Ghost Town after that beautiful vacation with Sonia and her family in Calico and that it was the last time that I saw my grandson in person."

"Things change, Cole," Brinkley replied.

Anger caused Cole to lash out. He rushed over to Brinkley before he had time to react and hauled him up by the lapels of his jacket.

"You injected my grandson with Silent Night. You tried to kill him. *My* flesh and blood." Cole punched Brinkley in the jaw. "And for what, Joe? Because you wanted money and a company that wasn't yours to run? I'll tear it down brick by brick before letting you have it."

Brinkley shoved Cole away. His face contorted with rage. "Don't I know it? You've made it perfectly clear that your precious grandson is inheriting it. Out of nowhere, you just randomly decided that you were leaving Ghost Town to him? He doesn't even know you, Cole," Brinkley argued. "But I've been the one with you all these years. In the trenches, right by your side, sweating and scraping to build this company and help make it prosper. And not once did you ever consider my taking over as CEO when you stepped down. We were partners, Cole, yet I got swept out with the trash because you don't have a relationship with Coulter, and you want to make amends? That's nothing but your guilty conscience talking."

"That's not true. You were going to be taken care of, Joe. You would've still been a vice president at Ghost Town. That didn't have to change. But *you* changed. Your over-inflated ego became seduced by power, and greed. You betrayed me, your family, your country—and all for money. I didn't trust you, Joe. I haven't for some time now. And it breaks my heart to see that my apprehension was warranted. But I've got proof."

Brinkley snorted. "Proof of what?"

"Proof of your deception, proof of the lies, the weapons you were selling, the black market deals you were making. I know everything now, thanks to Coulter and his team. All your dirty deals are in black and white, and you're going to jail. You'd get the maximum sentence for your crimes if it were up to me. And in case there's any doubt, you're fired. I don't ever want to see you again."

A sound of pure rage rushed out of Brinkley's mouth in a torrent. He charged Cole, knocking him into a table. It broke from the weight of the two men, and they crashed to the floor. Brinkley was the first to get to his feet. He kicked Cole in the stomach and sprinted to the window.

"Stop."

Brinkley didn't until he heard the safety disengage on Cole's pistol.

"Put your hands up."

He still hadn't turned around. "You don't want to do this, Cole."

"You're right, Joe. I don't want to. But I will. Now turn around."

Brinkley leaned over for a moment as if catching his breath, but then spun around with a knife in his hand. Before he could throw it, a gunshot rang out. The bullet struck Brinkley in the leg. He dropped and howled.

Startled, Cole turned to find Coulter holding a pistol. Dual expressions of shock and disbelief on his face.

"Is it true?"

Cole hesitated.

"Is what Brinkley said about me true?" Coulter yelled in an angry tone.

"Coulter, I can—" was all Cole got to say before his grandson collapsed in his arms.

Chapter 33

"Will he be alright?" Sonia asked for the third time that day. She paced the empty waiting room like a protective lioness defending her cub.

"Yes, the antidote was a success," Marena replied in a patient voice. She lowered the magazine she wasn't really reading and set it down on the table across from her chair. "It will take some time, but Coulter will make a full recovery.

Sonia rushed to her side. "Because of you." Fighting back the tears, she grasped Marena's hands. "I can't thank you enough for saving my son, Marena. I admit I was a bit surprised when I found out that he'd come to you, but I'm so glad that he did. You saved his life."

"Colt would've done the same for me had the situation been reversed."

"I know he would have," Sonia said, her voice losing some of its upbeat tone.

"Mrs. McKendrick, is there something the matter?"

"I haven't been able to see him. They've been running tests on him, and when I come in, he's sleeping."

"Why don't we try now? The nurse that was drawing his blood should be done."

Sonia rushed to her chair to retrieve her purse. "That would be wonderful."

The two continued to chat as they walked down the corridor to Coulter's room. He smiled when Marena walked in, and she returned the gesture, but when he spotted his mother, the smile disappeared.

Seeing the abrupt change, his mother clutched her purse tightly and sat down next to his bedside.

"Hi, son—"

"Mom, I can't imagine there's much we need to talk about."

"Coulter," Marena said in shock. He had never taken that tone with his mother before.

Sonia blanched. "Yes, there is."

Marena glanced between mother and son. "I, uh, think I'll leave you two alone to chat. I'm going to check on Lucas."

Coulter held out a hand to stop her and pulled her to his side. "Rena, you don't have to go," he said firmly.

"Yes, I do," she said softly, tilting her head toward Sonia. "The two of you need to talk."

Coulter's jaw clenched. "No, we don't."

Touching his arm, Marena squeezed his firm biceps. "Yes, you do, but I'll be back," she promised before brushing her lips against his cheek.

"You're a tad bit off target," he teased.

Marena playfully ignored him and left.

When she was gone, Coulter's light, easy smile disappeared and was replaced by a look of frustration.

Sonia got up and moved to sit on the edge of his bed. Coulter moved his leg a fraction of an inch, but it was enough for her to bristle.

"Honey, are we ever going to talk about it?"

"What's to talk about?" he said tiredly. "You purposefully kept my grandfather from me for over twenty-eight years. I'll never get that time back. Heck, I was even named after Cole, though I have no recollection of him as a child."

Sonia absentmindedly twisted the straps on her purse. "There were extenuating circumstances, Coulter."

His eyebrows shot upward. "What was extenuating about it, Mom? You felt he failed you as a father. You weren't happy with the army life and moving around a lot. I get it. But, as I got older, I should've been given a chance to get to know my grandfather—to decide for myself if I wanted him in my life, especially since we have so little family as it is. Instead, you made it seem like he was always too busy, like he didn't want to be bothered, but that wasn't true."

"He was always working," she hedged. "Remember when we were in Calico, California, at that ghost town? He was there with us."

"I sort of remember that. I recall having a lot of fun, and a man being there with us, but I can't even remember his face." Coulter's voice had a brittle edginess to it.

"We were having a wonderful time, and I wanted our renewed closeness to work. But then he cut the vacation short and left to handle a business deal. That's when I realized that nothing had changed—that's the way it would always be."

"I'm sorry that I made you feel like you didn't matter, Sonia. Nothing could've been further from the truth."

They both looked up to see Cole standing in the doorway. He walked in and sat down in the chair on the opposite side of the bed, the care package he had for Coulter at his feet.

Clasping his hands together, Cole leaned forward. His casual attire of jeans and a short-sleeve polo shirt looked out of place compared to the stiff severity of his expression.

"Honestly, I've made a lot of mistakes in my life. And I regret not being there when you needed me. So, Sonia, I'm asking for a chance to wipe the slate clean between us. To start again—if you're willing."

Glancing between her father and son, Sonia hesitated but

eventually nodded. "I'd like that. And you're not the only one. I shouldn't have shut you out like that."

Sonia dove her hand into her purse to retrieve a few tissues. She dabbed furiously at her eyes before scrunching it up in her hand. "For Coulter's sake, I should've made more effort. If his illness has taught me nothing else, it's that time is promised to no one. We need to mend fences with our loved ones before it's too late."

Cole nodded. He looked relieved and hopeful. That expression wavered when Coulter remained quiet, and an awkward silence descended on the room like a bird swooping in for its evening meal.

"I think I'll go see what your father is up to and give you two time to chat."

Standing, she leaned over and kissed Coulter on the cheek. When he didn't turn away, Sonia relaxed and squeezed his hand.

"So," Coulter replied when they were alone. "I guess we have quite a bit of catching up to do."

"Yeah, we do—if you're okay with that."

Coulter nodded. "So, when you hired me, it was to keep tabs on me?"

"No, not like that." Cole shifted in his chair. "There comes a time in a man's life when he wants to know how the story ends. I wanted to know about you and what you were doing. I've followed your career your whole life, Coulter. I knew that I couldn't be directly involved, so I resigned myself to take whatever I could get."

"But why didn't you just tell me who you were when I agreed to take the assignments at Ghost Town?" Coulter reasoned. "Why all the secrecy?"

"I didn't want to upset your mother," he answered truthfully. Cole glanced away as he recounted his side of events. "I'd resigned myself to the realization that I'd need to re-

spect her wishes and do as she'd asked of me. So, I stayed away."

"But I missed having a grandfather in my life."

"As I missed having a daughter and grandson in mine."

Coulter frowned. "Just a heap of wasted years, and for what? Because mom didn't like military life?"

"Don't be hard on her, Coulter. You mean the world to her. I know she was just worried about you joining the army and getting hurt or killed. It's any mother's worse nightmare. Give her some grace, Colt. She's been through a lot."

Coulter was introspective and seemed lost in his thoughts. Eventually, Cole spoke up.

"Can I ask you a question?"

"Sure."

"How are things between you and Marena?"

"We're on better footing than when I arrived."

Cole smiled. "Good. Everything's settled between you?"

"Nope, not yet."

"My advice is don't delay too long. Not clearing the air doesn't get better with time."

Two weeks later, Marena returned to Beaufort with Coulter so that he could recuperate under her watchful eye. However, he was experiencing residual fatigue, so she warned him to take things slow.

Coulter had attempted to broach the subject of their relationship, but Marena would say she needed more time.

Assuring her that he would be patient, Coulter didn't press it. But, to him, they were glorified friends. He still slept in the guest room, they weren't intimate, and on any occasion when things turned romantic, Marena pulled away first. He didn't know how to move their relationship along. But the longer things remained unsettled between them, the antsier he became.

One day, Marena was working at the Sea Lily, and Coul-

ter had remained home to do a videoconference call with Liam, Neil, and the rest of his employees.

He admitted that he wasn't ready to resume his duties at his company. However, he was determined not to cause any reductions in capacity, so he announced that Liam would be taking over as interim chief executive officer. Ghost Town Security would provide additional personnel if needed to ensure the company continued meeting its workload.

Satisfied with the outcome, Coulter hung up and went into the kitchen. He decided to make a romantic dinner for Marena. However, still aware of his limitations, he opted for an Italian feast of spaghetti with meat sauce, a garden salad with Marena's favorite toppings, garlic bread, and dessert. He was about to get started when the doorbell rang.

Coulter opened the door to find Burt standing on the other side.

"Hello, Mr. Templeton. If you're looking for Marena, she's at work."

"I'm looking for you, Colonel McKendrick."

Surprise registered on Coulter's face before he said, "Sure." He stepped aside to let him come in. He'd mentioned to Burt about as many times as Marena had that he could call him Coulter or Colt, but he never did.

"Is the living room fine? Or did you want to go out on the patio?"

"Outside. It's a beautiful day today."

Burt followed Coulter through the house and out the back door, the cane at his side making a rhythmic tap with each step. They both sat at the table. Coulter waited for the older man to proceed.

"I always speak my mind," Burt said, jumping right in. "I'm not one for pussyfooting around."

"I can appreciate that."

Burt grunted. "Sir, I think what you did to my Marigold

was deplorable. You broke her heart, and it ain't mended yet."

Coulter was familiar with his nickname for Marena. He thought it fit her well.

"I understand your concerns, Mr. Templeton. I agree with your assessment. I acknowledge my part in hurting Marena and the wreckage our relationship became. I've been trying to make amends and repair the damage I've done since my arrival. I know that it will be a slow process. But I also know that anything in life worth having is worth sticking your neck out to fight for."

"Humph seems you missed the mark the first time around."

"I honestly thought I was protecting her," Coulter countered, shifting on the wooden bench. "That she would be safer without me. Look, I'm under no illusion that Marena trusting me again will be an uphill battle, but it's a mountain I'm willing to scale. I love Marena. I always have, and I want to spend my entire life being worthy of the privilege of a second chance at making her happy."

Burt leaned in and peered into Coulter's eyes. "You'd better be telling the truth, McKendrick."

"I never lie, sir."

Grunting again, Burt sat back in his chair and crossed his arms over his chest. Burt's belly was stout, so it took more than one try to get himself comfortable.

"Well, it isn't just me you have to convince, is it?"

"No, it's not."

"So, what's your plan?"

"Plan?"

"Of course. You've messed up, and now you have to set things right again." Burt shook his head. "I can't believe I have to tell you how to win back your own woman."

Coulter's eyebrows shot up to his hairline, but his expression managed to remain neutral.

"I've had several discussions with Marena on the subject. She wanted to take things slow and figure out what she envisions for the future."

Burt began fake snoring. "You're going to put her to sleep waiting for you to kick things into high gear."

Coulter looked confused. "She asked for time, and I'm giving her what she needs."

"Don't be waiting around. You are the one that broke trust. Now you gotta fix it."

"I'm all for doing that," Coulter explained. "I just don't know what more I can do to provide Marena with enough assurance to let her guard down."

Burt's mouth dropped open. "Pshaw. How you made it this far is a blooming miracle. Son, you gotta be straight with her. Tell her your vision for your future. Women want to know you have a plan and you've thought things through."

"I get it," Coulter said with a grin. He truly liked Burt and was glad that Marena had such a good friend looking out for her well-being. "And I will do everything that you suggest."

Burt relaxed and nodded his approval. "That's good." Eventually, Burt extended his hand. "Now, you may call me Burt."

"Thank you, Burt," Coulter said solemnly, shaking his hand. "And please, call me Coulter."

"I'll call you Coulter when you've taken my advice with positive results. So don't screw around, Colonel McKendrick. Because second chances don't grow on trees."

Chapter 34

Marena sat the glass of iced tea she was drinking down and shook her head in disgust, the black-and-blue steak salad in front of her only half-eaten.

"A ten-thousand-dollar fine and twenty years in prison is all Brinkley gets?"

Marena grimaced. "He got off light if you ask me. He tried to kill Coulter, Dad."

General Dash attacked his seafood salad sandwich with gusto. "His legal team argued that he wasn't the one that injected Coulter. That was Derek, and he's dead. So, there's no proof implicating Brinkley for that, but there are more crimes he'll need to answer to," her father pointed out. "He won't be getting out of prison any time soon."

"He deserves to rot under the jail for all the damage he's done."

"He'll get what's coming to him, don't worry. We'll see to that."

"Has Javier Palacios been found yet?"

"No. In all the commotion that night, he slipped past everyone. He was probably wearing a bulletproof vest. Who knows where he is now. But I'm sure he'll turn up like bad pennies always do. Enough about the bad guys. You have a decision to make, sweetheart."

"I know, Dad. It's a big one. What if I make the wrong one?"

"That's your defense mechanism talking. You need to talk to Coulter about this, honey. Your decision affects him, too."

"I will," Marena replied. "Tonight."

"Good."

"How's Lucas?"

"He's on assignment doing some consulting for Ghost Town. Cole said he's planning to make Lucas his VP."

Marena glanced up in surprise. "Is Lucas interested?"

Her father shrugged. "Beats me. Your brother loves being in the field. He's not much for desk work, but I know Cole. He could entice the spots off a leopard."

"Can you image Cole and Lucas running a company together?"

"Oddly, yes. They make a great team. Who knows? There could be a lot of changes in store for the future."

Marena sighed. "That's true. Starting with a big one tonight. I have to go, Dad."

"Okay, but you call me tomorrow and tell me how it went."

"I will. How long will you be in town? Not that I'm trying to get rid of you," she said with a grin.

Terry chuckled. "I didn't think that at all. Probably just till the weekend. I have a meeting in Washington on Monday."

"Okay. I'm glad you came. You should visit more often."

"Don't worry, I plan to. No more staying away too long. Family should be more of a priority for us."

"Agreed. Thanks, Dad. I love you."

"Love you too, sweetheart."

Marena decided to leave early. She'd hired an interim manager while she was gone, and he was working out well. Even Burt had given his seal of approval.

She thought about Burt's progress. Finally, he and De-lores were officially dating. Marena had been thrilled to hear the delightful news.

As she was getting into the ride-sharing car she had or-dered, Vivica called.

"Did you tell him yet?"

Marena sighed. "No, I haven't."

"Why are you waiting? Worried how he might take it?"

"Vivica."

"What? I'm just asking."

"I wish everyone would stop asking me questions—this is my decision."

"Okay, okay. But I'm calling tomorrow to see how it went."

"Vivi, everything will be fine, you'll see."

"Are you trying to convince me of that, or you?"

A few minutes later, Marena arrived home. She paid her driver and headed up the walkway to the house. Then, tak-ing a deep breath, she opened the door and stepped inside.

Astonished by the vision in front of her, Marena's mouth dropped open.

Flowers and candles were everywhere, and soft music drifted around the room like a mist in the forest at dawn.

The beautiful scene was enhanced tenfold by Coulter standing in the kitchen wearing an apron. It looked like a flour bomb had exploded, and he had used his body to ab-sorb the blast.

When he saw her, he looked flustered.

Marena made a beeline for the kitchen. "Coulter, what's all this?"

"Hey, Rena. You're home early." He kissed her.

"Yeah, I decided to leave early today since I had some things on my mind."

"Really? What's going on?" He took off the apron and

tried to clear the flour from the counter next to the half-filled bowl of cookie dough ingredients.

Marena tried to jump in to help, but he batted her away. Instead, she became overly occupied with the drawstring belt on her khaki utility shorts.

Taking a deep breath, she said, "Well, that's what I wanted to speak with you about."

"I have something to say to you, too. But, ladies first."

"No," Marena blurted out, seizing the opportunity to stall a little longer like a kitten about to pounce on a ball of yarn. "What's your news?" The high-pitched tone of her voice caused Coulter to look up in alarm.

He studied her for a moment before turning the music down. Then, grabbing a dish towel, he wiped the flour from his hands and set it back on the counter.

"Marena, I need you to know that I have no intention of pressuring you to do anything."

Marena appeared baffled. "What are you talking about?"

"I think you know."

"Honestly, I don't have a clue, so I'll need you to tell me."

He blew out a breath in frustration. "Tell you what? That this isn't working?"

She stilled. "What's not working?"

"You and me. Like this," he said, waving his arm between them. "I know you want to take things slow, and I agreed, but truthfully, I don't know how."

"I don't understand."

"I can't be your friend, Rena. We were never *just* friends—and we'll never be." Coulter's expression was grim like he had just given the worst news of his life.

She stared at him.

Her quietness propelled him forward. He reached out and took both her hands.

"I've made so many mistakes where you're concerned, Marena. I wanted to earn your trust back."

"You have earned it. We're in a much better place now than when you first arrived."

He continued as if her words didn't register. "Leaving you for your good, well, that backfired. I promised myself that it was a maneuver I'd never repeat, but I will if that's what you want."

Her hands twitched in his grasp. "You think I want you gone?"

"Well, don't you?"

Hearing the words aloud made Marena antsy. She moved into the living room. When she turned around, he was standing in the same spot as if he were a statue.

"No, of course not. I don't want you to leave, Coulter. I never did."

"Then why are you keeping me at arm's length?"

Marena looked uncomfortable.

"I admit that's what I wanted at first, but it was more for self-preservation than anything else. After that, I couldn't let my guard down again, because I had to protect my heart and keep it safe. And not wanting you? Are you kidding? Do you know how many times I've longed to throw myself into your arms and let whatever happened happen?"

"No, I didn't know."

"I admit I've needed to tell you something, but I didn't know how you'd react."

Coulter stood ramrod straight. "Rena, just say it."

"I've been offered a position to go back to research and development for a start-up pharmaceutical company that's won a few government contracts," she said in practically one breath. "I need to give them an answer soon and wanted your thoughts."

He blinked. "That's what you've wanted to tell me?"

"Yes. What did you think it was?"

"That we were over."

Marena's mouth dropped open. "What? Of course not.

I've been trying to sort things out, but it was always with the understanding that you'd be here—in my life—with me."

Coulter strode into the living room. "Marena, I guess I'm still in awe that you'd give me a second chance. That I'm deserving of one after what I put you through—us through."

"Coulter, I forgave you when you showed up on my doorstep with days to live. I realized it wasn't so that I could try and save your life. It was because time was short and you wanted to be with me. I knew then that you still loved me as much as I loved you."

Coulter gazed at Marena with an intensity that made her breath hitch.

"Of course I do—I never stopped. When I woke up, and you told me the antidote worked and that I would live, I began thinking about the future. Marena, there isn't one aspect of it that didn't include you. I love you, and only you, Rena. You're my best friend, my confidant, and you bring out the best in me. I want to wake up by your side every day. I want to love you, fight with you, have babies with you, and build a family. I want you to be mine in every way imaginable—for life."

Coulter retrieved a velvet ring box from his pocket, knelt, and opened it. Gasping, Marena backed up so much she would have fallen over the coffee table if he hadn't steadied her.

She stared at the two-carat oval-shaped diamond surrounded by two round diamonds with additional diamonds on either side for so long that her eyes blurred. When she finally blinked to clear them, she started crying.

"My ring. You kept it."

He nodded. "It never should have left your hand, my love. Marena Lillian Dash, would you please do me the honor of becoming my wife?"

Marena was nodding before the words tumbled out. "Yes, Coulter Aaron McKendrick. I will marry you."

Coulter slid the engagement ring back on Marena's left ring finger and kissed it before his grin went borderline supernova.

Marena glanced at the ring on her finger a few seconds before launching herself into the arms of her fiancé. They toppled onto the floor in a heap.

"I'm never letting you go," Coulter whispered into her ear.

"Forever?"

"Forever," he vowed.

"Well done," a familiar voice called from behind them, followed by loud cheering and clapping.

Marena glanced past Coulter. "Dad?"

She nudged Coulter, and he pulled her up with him. He smoothed her shirt back down before kissing her lightly on the lips. The newly engaged couple turned to find their family and friends piled into Marena's living room. Lucas had recorded the moment on his cell phone while Coulter's mother and Vivica poured glasses of champagne and sparkling cider for the guests.

Shocked to see everyone there, Marena turned to Coulter. Her gaze was still bright with unshed tears of happiness.

"How'd you arrange all this?"

"Your father whipped us all into shape," he joked. "I thought we'd have a bit more time, though. I didn't expect you home this soon, so we had to scrap the plans for more decorating."

Marena shook her head. "This was perfect."

He turned to the group. "I hope you've brought food, because I didn't cook enough for everyone."

"I've had your cooking, bro. Don't worry, we've come

prepared," Lucas joked. "And that was the most roundabout proposal I've ever heard."

"Shut up. It was wonderful," Marena gushed.

Everyone took turns coming up to congratulate the happy couple. Cole embraced his new granddaughter before hugging Coulter and slapping him soundly on the back.

"Thank you," he said solemnly. "This is one of the best days of my life. I never thought I'd get to celebrate with you like this. I wish you every happiness, Coulter. Marena is one in a million."

"Thanks, Cole." Coulter stopped. "I think the name *Grandfather* is long overdue, don't you?"

"I'd like that." Cole's voice trembled, but his smile was steady.

Coulter's parents came up behind Cole. They hugged everyone.

"Another woman in the family is long overdue—that and grandchildren."

"Mom, can we get married first?" Coulter laughed. "I promise we'll devote ourselves with laser-like focus to providing grandbabies for you to spoil rotten."

Marena lovingly elbowed Coulter in the ribs. "Not too soon, though," he amended. "I want my bride all to myself for a while before expanding our family."

When it was Burt and Delores's turn, Burt leaned in to speak to Coulter while Delores hugged Marena.

"I wouldn't part with my Marigold for anyone who wasn't worthy of being by her side. Well done, Coulter. I'm pleased to see that you've redeemed yourself."

Coulter grinned at hearing Burt finally use his first name.

He shook Burt's hand firmly before being engulfed in a bear hug.

"Thank you, Burt."

Marena's dad was the last to come up and congratulate them.

"Your mother would be so proud and happy for you both."

Marena hugged him tightly. "I know she's here."

He picked up her mother's locket at her neck and held it. "Yes, she is."

"Are you happy, sweetheart?"

"Ecstatic, Dad."

"Thank you for giving me your blessing, General," Coulter replied, shaking Terry's hand.

"Now that you're going to become a member of our family, officially, I think it's high time you started calling me General Dad."

Coulter laughed. "Roger that."

"Guard my Marena with your life, Coulter," Terry said seriously. "She's my most valuable treasure."

"I will, sir. Because she's mine as well."

Later that night, they were outside in the backyard, sharing a hammock. The sun drifted lazily below the horizon in brilliant hues of purple and orange.

"Are you happy, soon-to-be Mrs. McKendrick?"

"So much so that I keep thinking this is a dream that I'll wake up from at any moment."

Coulter pulled her closer to his side. "So, when do you want to marry me?"

A dazzling smile plastered itself onto Marena's face.

"I guess we need to set a date, don't we? Any thoughts?"

"I think that depends."

She glanced up. "On what?"

"On if you're going to accept that new job offer."

"That's right, we didn't finish discussing it, did we?"

"Well, it was kind of hectic, getting engaged and all," he teased.

Marena laughed. "Honestly, I don't know. But, if I do,

that'll mean relocating to London. Is that something you'd be willing to consider?"

"Sweetheart, wherever you are is home to me. I will support you no matter where we are or what you decide to do for your career. So, whether we live in Beaufort and you continue to run the Sea Lily, or we relocate to London, and you work in a lab, I'm all in."

Marena leaned up to kiss Coulter. "Thank you. I love you."

"I love you, too, my beautiful, amazing, and sexy shop-owning scientist."

Epilogue

Marena and Coulter were married one month later on the beach in Beaufort. It was a picturesque October day celebrating with family and friends. They decided to spend a few days of their honeymoon at Crystal's family retreat in Morehead City before flying to visit Liam in the Bahamas and then seeing the Turks and Caicos Islands.

After dinner, they walked down to the water's edge and watched the sunset.

"How are you this evening, Mrs. McKendrick?"

Marena beamed at her new moniker. "Very well, my gorgeous, amazing husband."

Coulter leaned down and kissed her soundly. "You know, I'm glad you decided to keep the Sea Lily. I love North Carolina. I can see why you moved here."

"I'm glad I did, too. I agree that staying was a wonderful choice. It's great having our family just a few hours away."

"Yes, indeed. Close, but not too close," he laughed. Coulter touched her cheek before leaning in to kiss her again. "Have I thanked you lately for saving my life?"

She wrapped her arms around his waist. "Every chance you get."

"That's because I'm so grateful to you. You've saved me, Marena. In every sense of the word."

"We've always been better together than apart."

He entwined their fingers. "North and south poles of a magnet."

She laughed. "Mom was on to something with that one."

They stood there in companionable silence a few minutes before Coulter said, "I forgot to ask, what did you name the antidote that saved my life?"

Marena gazed at her husband and said, "Its name is M.A.R.E.N.A."

"Seriously?" he said in amazement. "What's it stand for?"

"Molecular. Antigen. Reversal. Enzymatic. Nerve. Agent."

Coulter grabbed both sides of her face and kissed her passionately.

"I knew that you would always be in my heart the moment we met. And now you'll always be running through my veins."

"You're very poetic tonight. You'll have my heart racing if you keep this up."

"There's much more in store for you tonight than just poetry, my love."

"Then I suggest you lead the way, soldier," she said seductively.

Marena gasped when Coulter swept her up into his arms and double-timed it back to the house.

* * * * *

#2207 TO TRUST A COLTON COWBOY
The Coltons of Colorado • by Dana Nussio

Jasper Colton could never act on his crush—not only is Kayla St. James his employee, but his father's corruption sent her dad to prison. And yet he can't help but step in when she's dealing with a stalker. As the threats escalate, the two of them find their attraction hard to resist.

#2208 IN THE ARMS OF THE LAW
To Serve and Seduce • by Deborah Fletcher Mello

Attorney Ellington Black will sacrifice everything for his family. But when his brother is charged with murder, Special Agent Angela Stanfield puts his loyalty to the test. As her investigation puts her in danger—and points to a different killer than his brother—Ellington finds himself in the role of protector...and desire turns to love!

#2209 HOTSHOT HEROES UNDER THREAT
Hotshot Heroes • by Lisa Childs

Hotshot firefighter Patrick McRooney goes undercover to find the saboteur on his brother-in-law's elite Hotshot team, but as his investigation gets closer to the truth—and he gets closer to Henrietta Rowlins—threats are made. And Patrick isn't the only one they're targeting....

#2210 TEXAS LAW: UNDERCOVER JUSTICE
Texas Law • by Jennifer D. Bokal

Clare Chambers is a woman on the run and Isaac Patton is undercover, trying to find a hit man. When a body is found in the small town of Mercy, Texas, the two have to work together to catch a killer before Clare becomes the next victim.

The whole desperate plan began simply as a last-ditch attempt to save his life. He never intended for anyone to get hurt. That day, not long after Thanksgiving, he walked into the bank full of hope. It was the first time he'd ever asked for a loan. It was also the first time he'd ever seen executive loan officer Carla Richmond.

When he tapped at her open doorway, she looked up from that big desk of hers. He thought she was too young and pretty with her big blue eyes and all that curly chestnut-brown hair to make the decision as to whether he lived or died.

She had a great smile as she got to her feet to offer him a seat.

He felt so out of place in her plush office that he stood in the doorway nervously kneading the brim of his worn baseball cap for a moment before stepping in. As he did, her blue-eyed gaze took in his ill-fitting clothing hanging on his rangy body, his bad haircut, his large, weathered hands.

He told himself that she'd already made up her mind before he even sat down. She didn't give men like him a second look—let alone money. Like his father always said, bankers never gave dough to poor people who actually needed it. They just helped their rich friends.

Right away Carla Richmond made him feel small with her questions about his employment record, what he had for collateral, why he needed the money and how he planned to repay it. He'd recently lost one crappy job and was in the process of starting another temporary one, and all he had to show for the years he'd worked hard labor since high school was an old pickup and a pile of bills.

He took the forms she handed him and thanked her, knowing he wasn't going to bother filling them in. On the way out of her office, he balled them up and dropped them in the trash. All the way to his pickup, he mentally kicked himself for being such a fool. What had he expected?

HIEXP0922

Recycling programs for this product may not exist in your area.

ISBN-13: 978-1-335-73813-4

Six Days to Live

Copyright © 2022 by Lisa Dodson

For questions and comments about the quality of this book, please contact us at CustomerService@Harlequin.com.

Harlequin Enterprises ULC
22 Adelaide St. West, 41st Floor
Toronto, Ontario M5H 4E3, Canada
www.Harlequin.com

Printed in U.S.A.

SIX DAYS TO LIVE

———

Lisa Dodson

HARLEQUIN

ROMANTIC
SUSPENSE